Get **more** out of libraries

Please return or renew this item by the last date shown.

You can renew online at www.hants.gov.uk/library

Or by phoning 0845 603 5631

Hampshire
County Council

MOTHER'S MILK

Recent Titles by Charles Atkins

THE CADAVER'S BALL
THE PORTRAIT
RISK FACTOR
ASHES ASHES *
MOTHER'S MILK *

* *available from Severn House*

MOTHER'S MILK

Charles Atkins

This first world edition published 2009
in Great Britain and in the USA by
SEVERN HOUSE PUBLISHERS LTD of
9–15 High Street, Sutton, Surrey, England, SM1 1DF.

British Library Cataloguing in Publication Data

Atkins, Charles.
  Mother's Milk.
  1. Conyors, Barrett (Fictitious character)–Fiction.
  2. Forensic psychiatrists–Fiction. 3. Drug abusers–Death–
  Fiction. 4. Schizophrenics–Fiction. 5. Suspense fiction.
  I. Title
  813.5'4-dc22

ISBN-13: 978-0-7278-6795-7   (cased)

All Severn House titles are printed on acid-free paper.

Typeset by Palimpsest Book Production Ltd.,
Grangemouth, Stirlingshire, Scotland.
Printed and bound in Great Britain by
MPG Books Ltd., Bodmin, Cornwall.

To:
Lynn Zinno
Carol Genova
Marie Johnston
Mary Frigiani
For all of your skill, grace, humor, compassion and hope in the face of inestimable suffering.

ACKNOWLEDGEMENTS

I'd like to thank the following for all of their help, guidance and honest criticism. My agent Al Zuckerman, friend and freelance editor Elizabeth Fitzgerald and Gary S. Jayson, who always gets the first read. I'm indebted to Stacey Asip and daughter Nika Kneitschel, for helping me dress Barrett, and Doreen Elnitsky for steering me straight on the ins and outs of breast feeding. I'd also like to thank all those at Severn House, who helped polish this book into its final form – Edwin Buckhalter, Rachel Simpson Hutchens and Nick Blake. And of course my parents – Cynthia and Harvey Atkins for their unconditional and unwavering support.

Finally, and perhaps most importantly, to my patients, who over the years have taught me so much.

ONE

Barrett gagged at the stench of death – a mix of escaped gases and something slightly sweet, even though the two teens, a boy and a girl, hadn't been that way long. To the tall, darkly beautiful, thirty-three-year-old forensic psychiatrist they looked asleep, slumped on a pile of decorative pillows like the fussy ones you get at discount stores with purple, hot pink, and wine-colored silk with exotic tassels and bits of gold and silver embroidery. Someone had tried to make this top-floor Alphabet City tenement apartment a home. Barrett struggled to push past the shock, the sheer waste of two young lives. She had to get her bearings and figure out what she'd stumbled into – the room had a purpose; mattresses heaped with pillows lined three walls, each separated from the next by an artistically stenciled and painted table – a twenty-first-century opium den with a do-it-yourself makeover.

As her nose, more acute since the birth of Max four months ago, took in the smells – Indian patchouli, a trace of pot, and that unmistakable reek, sweet, not yet rot – she touched the girl first, praying she was wrong. *So young, please let there be a pulse.* Two long fingers of her right hand homed in on the carotid, pushing in, the flesh still warm, her hair, streaked with honey highlights, soft and scented with a fruity conditioner . . . no pulse. The girl's eyes were open, the whites starting to dry, staring at the ceiling with its layers of flaked paint over zinc tiles. The boy was handsome, still with a bit of baby fat to his cheeks, dark curly hair, his brown-eyed gaze fixed on his arm where a spot of fresh dried blood showed his last injection site. The needle and the small alcohol burner they'd used to cook their dope lay on the floor between them. Barrett eyed the Ziploc bags on the table, some still filled with dirty white heroin – an overdose with dope to spare. She muttered and caught the panic-stricken expression of Lydia, the crisis outreach social worker from the forensic center and mother of four she'd dragged along after the call from Jerod. *And where the hell are you?* she thought, picturing the young man who'd been so frantic on the phone.

'I'll call the cops,' Lydia said, pulling out her cell, her thick frame plastered against the far wall of the room.

Barrett crouched by the bodies and half-listened as Lydia phoned the crisis team and told them to send the police. Tears welled; these were just kids . . . so young . . . somebody's children.

She froze at the sound of footsteps in the hallway. She called out, 'Jerod, is that you? It's Dr. Conyors . . . Show yourself.' She glanced toward the open door and saw movement in the shadows and a disturbance in the dust that glittered in the light. She wiped back a tear as fear throbbed and awful thoughts barreled into her brain, like if something should happen to her, who'd care for her baby? And shouldn't she have thought of that before coming on this outreach? *What am I doing here?*

The footsteps stopped. Barrett slowed her breath, everything about this felt wrong; a set-up, but now was not the time to try and figure out why Jerod, a twenty-two-year-old homeless schizo-phrenic with a drug problem, would do this to her, one of the few people in his sad life who actually gave a damn. The fingers of her right hand snaked inside her shoulder bag and into the leather holster where she kept a small 9mm Kahr polymer handgun – a gift from Detective Ed Hobbs. She motioned for a wide-eyed Lydia to keep back as she pulled the slide on the pistol and edged flat-footed toward the door. She made no sound as she listened for whoever was outside. If it were Jerod, he'd make noise – almost couldn't stop himself, with his jangled energy and the voices inside his head that ordered him about whenever he stopped his medication, which was most of the time.

Her gut twisted at the hard-metal click of a safety not more than a few yards away on the other side of the door. She pictured her baby – Max – safe with her mother. She had a split-second recognition that once again she'd placed herself in mortal danger and could imagine what Hobbs would say, how she was supposed to be a 'goddamn shrink and not Rambo'. A siren wailed from down the avenue, grew louder. Barrett held her position, the footsteps started again. She raised the pistol, aiming at the door frame. They were getting closer, moving faster, and then stopped. The siren pulsed louder; it was joined by a second.

She stood frozen, her gun raised, body tense, and then she both felt and heard footsteps running away. Carefully, she peered around the door. She spotted a man in jeans, sneakers, a leather coat, and short spiky blond hair running toward the stairwell – she couldn't see his face. 'Jerod!' She sprinted after him, her heart pounding. It didn't look like him, unless he'd lopped off his trademark dreadlocks, and this man was shorter.

'Barrett!' Lydia shrieked, her voice an octave higher than usual. 'Where are you going? Don't leave me!'

Barrett stopped and looked back at Lydia, her chunky body in jeans and a green button-down blouse, one hand clutching the door and the other gripping her cell phone. Her dark eyes bore into Barrett's. 'What are you doing?' she asked, her tone accusatory, angry and close to tears. 'You're not a cop.' Lydia fixed on the gun. 'Why are you carrying that? Please don't leave me. I'm so frightened.'

Barrett said nothing as they heard the commotion of heavy feet running up the stairs. A woman's voice called out, 'Dr. Conyors, are you there?'

'We're up here . . . top floor,' Barrett called, putting the safety back on the Kahr and slipping it into its holster. A female officer entered, followed a few steps later by her uniformed male counterpart. They looked at the dead teenagers, and the woman, looking to Barrett, commented, 'They drop like flies . . . overdose?'

'Seems like,' but something was off, she was finding it hard to think. 'Problem is we came here to pick up one of our regulars at the forensic center. He said he needed to go into the hospital.'

'Jerod hates the hospital,' Lydia said, talking fast. 'We should have known something was wrong. He was different on the phone, not his usual. Scared . . . And you can't trust a thing out of a junkie's mouth. We should have brought an escort. I told you that. Oh my God. We could have been killed.'

'Who's this Jerod?' the female cop asked, as her partner called for the crime-scene team.

'Jerod Blank,' Barrett said, feeling bad for Lydia, who was shaking. 'Twenty-two, raised mostly by the Department of Family and Youth Services and now pretty much living on the streets with occasional trips to psych hospitals . . . or jail, where he gets put on meds for his schizophrenia. But he never stays on them.'

'So where is he? And why did he want you here?' the cop asked.

'Good questions.' Barrett walked over to a boarded-up window and peered through a crack. She saw a bunch of kids shooting hoops in the pocket park between this building and the next. 'There was someone else up here,' she said, 'ran off when you all came.'

'Your Jerod guy?'

'I don't think so.' Barrett pictured Jerod – rail-thin, tall, weird tattoos on his arms, pale blue eyes, and a mass of dirty-blond dreads – and her last interaction with him a couple months back. He'd been arrested for shoplifting a cell phone and the judge had looked at his record of bouncing in and out of psychiatric hospitals, stabilizing, stopping his meds, doing drugs and petty crimes. He'd wanted to send the youth to prison for a few months to teach him a lesson. Jerod had been desperate, begging Barrett to help him. Frightened witless, he'd started to talk about killing himself, better to be dead than go to prison; he knew he wouldn't survive there. Barrett, who genuinely liked Jerod and saw in him a good heart, a twisted wit, and potential that might never get tapped because of his shitty birth family and all the bad things that had happened to him growing up as a ward of the state, had gone to bat with the judge, putting together yet another in-patient stay with the promise of a group home once he got out – problem was after two weeks in the hospital he'd been released and gone AWOL from his group home.

Now she looked across at Lydia. 'It wasn't him. Someone else wanted a look at these two.'

'Maybe they had a stash and some of their friends wanted the leftovers,' the male officer remarked, as he snapped digital photos of the youths.

'Maybe.' Barrett, unconvinced, thought up a list of questions and bits of information that didn't lie flat, starting with the two dead kids who didn't look like street junkies, well dressed, good haircuts, clean . . . somebody's kids, probably eighteen or nineteen . . . maybe younger. Plus, even down-at-the-heel apartments in the East Village weren't cheap. 'You need us here?' she asked, feeling a desperate need to get out of that place and to see her baby.

'Nah,' the female officer said, 'we'll just get the basic information from you. I don't think the ME is going to have a lot to say about these two; probably just run the toxicology. We get at least half a dozen of these a week, the life expectancy of a New York City junkie is not a long one.' She shook her head. 'The thing that kills me is they seem to keep getting younger.'

TWO

Outside the apartment, Barrett put on dark glasses and tried to steady her breath. Her pulse raced, the beats pounding in her ears. 'Lydia,' she said, trying to keep the tremor from her voice, 'why don't you take the state car and go back to the office without me. I've got some business to take care of.'

'I have to fill out an adverse-incident report,' Lydia said, her expression unreadable, as she fished out the keys.

'Of course,' Barrett said, wishing there was something she could say to make this long-time state employee feel less freaked out. 'You did well in there, Lydia. You kept your cool.'

'I'm shaking . . . I can't stop thinking about what might have just happened. There was someone else there. I heard it. I kept thinking about my kids . . .' She looked around nervously. 'He could still be here.'

Barrett scanned the block, noting how the building they'd been in, and the ones on either side, seemed to be the only holdouts in this neighborhood of recently rehabbed and pricey apartments. 'I know, but we're out of there; it's OK. The cops will take care of it.'

Lydia looked at her. 'Why would Jerod do that? He could have gotten us killed.'

'I don't know,' Barrett said. 'But I intend to find out.'

'We should have had a police escort.'

Barrett sensed a veiled accusation – *You're supposed to be the boss, why would you put us . . . me . . . in this kind of jeopardy?* 'Are you going to be OK? If you wanted to take the rest of the day that would be fine.'

'Seriously?'

'Of course, just let your supervisor know that I approved it.'

'But I have to fill out the adverse-incident form first, if you don't do it within twenty-four hours it's considered delinquent, and they write you up.'

'Right,' Barrett said, and felt a moment's concern over how Lydia might interpret the morning's events. But she'd just have to deal with that; right now her internal clock was racing a mile a minute, she desperately wanted out of there, all she could think about was seeing Max and the growing urgency in her chest. 'I got to run, Lydia, fill out the form and leave it with my secretary – I'll do my section when I get back. Then go home.'

Without looking back, and realizing she should have done more of a debriefing with Lydia, she nearly ran toward Avenue A, her eyes trained on the northbound lane looking for a cab. She flagged one down and as she got in, glanced at the digital clock on the small TV screen on the back of the driver's seat. 11:15 and she had to be back at the office no later than 12:30, and God help her if she missed her one o'clock with Janice Fleet, the Commissioner of the Department of Mental Health. She gave the driver her address. 'Please hurry.' Twelve minutes later he pulled up to her condo, in a somewhat drab-fronted red-brick building on West 27th.

She keyed in through the security door and sprinted up the three flights to the one-bedroom condo she'd bought with her husband Ralph – the first anniversary of his murder just past. She unlocked and caught the first saliva-stirring whiff of just-out-of-the-oven cheese biscuits. Her mother Ruth was in the galley kitchen, her thick auburn hair tied back in a blue kerchief, gold hoops in her ears and dressed in jeans and a form-hugging black T-shirt with the logo for the Night Shade, a gay bar in the East Village where she'd worked as a bartender for over fifteen years.

'Hey, Mom,' Barrett said, dropping her briefcase by the door, slipping off her blazer, and unbuttoning her blouse; she made a beeline for Max in his mesh-walled playpen. He had just gotten to the stage where he could raise his head on his own, and he attempted to pull himself up by his chubby arms, nearly making it, almost crawling. His crystal-blue eyes looked up at her as she knelt down and scooped him up. She settled back in the massive oak rocker her sister had bought for her at the 26th Street flea market, and which her mother had embellished with vibrant needlework pillows. She held Max close and breathed deep the intoxicating mix of baby shampoo and that other indescribable scent that was . . . well . . . Max. His mouth searched out her nipple while his tiny fingers kneaded the flesh of her breast.

A word passed through her mind – *sanctuary*. Followed by a surge of panic as she thought back to where she'd just been.

'Have you eaten?' Ruth asked, as she peeled overripe bananas and threw them into the bright red enamel mixer that Barrett had received as a wedding present, and which up until her mom had come to help with Max had been in its box buried at the back of a cabinet.

'No time,' she said. 'I've got a meeting from hell in –' she glanced at the clock – 'a little over an hour and a stack of paperwork I need to get through before then.'

'You can't keep this up,' Ruth said, her voice rich with the slow open vowels of rural Georgia. 'Do you have any dark rum?' she asked as she proceeded to throw ingredients into the mixer without benefit of measuring cups or spoons – butter, vanilla, egg yolks, flour, baking soda, salt, chopped walnuts, raisins.

'Not likely,' Barrett said, as she cradled Max, marveling at his silky hair . . . and not wanting to think about how he was probably too blond for people to think that he was the child of her and her half-Cuban husband.

'What about nutmeg?'

'Sorry. I'd have thought you'd know by now, if you don't buy it, I probably don't have it.'

'Shameful. I know I taught you how to cook. Cinnamon?' Ruth persisted.

'Maybe, I think I made eggnog a couple years back, check in the cupboard over the silverware.'

Barrett repositioned her chair so she could watch her mom as she fussed in the kitchen. She gently rocked and let herself enjoy the moments of peaceful nursing, a blissful island in the too-fast chaos of her life. Since returning to work two months back it had felt as though she was on some hellish treadmill and that no matter how fast she ran, she was constantly falling behind. The fact that Max was born a month premature, her water breaking in the middle of a case conference she was chairing at Croton Forensic Hospital, was almost a symbol of how everything happened just too fast.

She rocked and marveled at the efficiency of her mother in the kitchen, like a dancer, trained by years of raising two children and dealing nightly with a bar-room full of thirsty patrons. At nearly fifty, Ruth looked like a woman in her thirties, even though

Barrett knew her dark auburn hair now came from a bottle. 'So what have you and Max been up to?' she asked.

Ruth leveled her gaze at her daughter. 'Well, considering I didn't get off work till four A.M., we took a nap until ten. I thought this afternoon we could take a walk through the park and do a bit of shopping. You in the mood for a pork roast? Or how about a spiral ham, sweet potatoes, and collard greens with bacon?'

'You're trying to kill me, aren't you? Fried chicken last night, you've used my bread-maker more in the past few months than —'

'Dear, it was still in the box, as was this gorgeous mixer. Which, if you're wondering what to get me for my birthday . . .'

'Duly noted,' Barrett said.

'You need to eat,' Ruth said, 'if not for yourself, for my little prince.'

'So that's what this is all about, fatten me up for Max.'

'Do you know how many calories you lose through breast milk? And you were saying you were worrying that you didn't have enough.'

'Point taken, but I'm not sure the Paula Dean diet is the way to go.'

'You watch what you say about Paula. I love her, in fact this banana-bread recipe is off her website.'

'The woman would deep-fry water,' Barrett said, 'it can't be good for you.'

'Moderation,' Ruth shot back, 'all things in moderation,' and then, lowering her voice, 'Not that you'd know a thing about that.'

'I heard that.'

'Good.'

'Mom, please don't start.'

'I didn't say a word . . . but if I did it would be to say that you're working too many hours and too many days, and with a new baby and no husband you're not going to be able to keep this up. Trust me, I know.'

Barrett shook her head, as she looked at Max, who seemed to have had his fill. She reached for one of the many blue terry-cloth nappies Ruth had whipped up out of old towels and laid it over her shoulder. She draped him over it, and ran her hand over his soft smooth back, rubbing, patting, and waiting for her reward of a juicy belch. 'We do what we have to do. And what I have to do is work and make money to keep a roof over our heads. And don't tell me you don't know what that's like.'

'Of course I know what that's like,' Ruth said, pulling a brown-paper bag from out of a drawer. 'I just didn't want you to repeat my mistakes.'

Barrett looked at the milky wet spot on the nappy and gave Max an extra few pats to see if anything more needed to come up. A random thought zipped through her head. *Mission accomplished*. She'd made it home, nursed; a quick glance at the clock showed she'd probably just make it back in time. 'Mom,' Barrett said, 'I don't think you really made mistakes. You married too young because you got pregnant and that's what girls in Williamson, Georgia, were supposed to do. You had no choice, and getting me and Justine away from that place and our father was the bravest thing anyone could have done. I don't remember a lot about him, but I know that he beat you, and that I'd hide under my bed, and I still get nightmares about that night he came and tried to take us back.' Her eyes misted. 'Those weren't mistakes, if I can be even half as brave.'

'Hush,' Ruth said, wrapping biscuits in tinfoil and throwing them into the paper bag along with a bottle of iced tea, a sandwich, and something else covered in foil. 'I was out of my mind. I don't think I was brave, more scared than anything, and too young and stupid to realize the risks I took. I knew if I stayed with your daddy it was only going to get worse.'

Barrett felt torn, desperate to get back to the office, but hungry for these scraps about her early childhood and the family her mother had left when she was only twenty, and which she rarely spoke of. 'Don't you ever miss them?' she asked, having seen her mom weep over Christmas cards that arrived each year from her mother – a grandmother Barrett couldn't even picture.

'Only my mother,' Ruth said, 'but just like I don't want you to repeat my mistakes – and yes, I made my choices and some were just plain stupid – I won't repeat hers. I remember something she used to say about my father after he'd yelled at her, or called her stupid, or embarrassed her in front of company, she'd tell me, "I pick my battles." Problem is, I don't think she ever won any. And wouldn't you know, the first time I fall in love, it's with a man just like my daddy only better-looking and meaner. That night we left Georgia, I truly believed he was going to kill me. I can't even remember what set him off. All I could think with him pounding away at me,' she continued, now pouring batter into just-purchased loaf pans, 'was, *I'll be dead and who's going to take care of my girls?* When he finally passed out, I just grabbed you and Justine, got in the car, and drove. I remember thinking, *Please God, just let me win this one battle.*'

'I remember some of it,' Barrett said. 'Your face was horrible, by the end of the ride you had huge black eyes.'

'I was a mess, twenty years old, two babies, and a Chevy station wagon that blew its transmission on the Bowery.'

Barrett glanced again at the clock; 12:15, her paperwork was not going to get done, but she loved the next part of the story. 'And that's when you met Sophie and Max,' she said, reluctantly standing, as loving memories of the elderly Polish couple – Holocaust survivors who had taken them in – flooded her. She rubbed her nose against her baby's and put him back down in the pen. He looked at her wide-eyed, his arms reached toward her, and he tumbled forward.

'I love that you named the baby after him,' Ruth said, heading toward the door as Barrett buttoned up.

'If he'd been a girl I would have called her Sophia . . . I miss them both so much.'

'Me too,' Ruth said, while trying to stuff the too-full paper bag into the gaping side pocket of Barrett's briefcase.

Barrett was about to protest – she had no time for lunch – when her eye caught the blinking light on her phone. 'Who called?'

'Someone from the hospital, some kind of review board or something.'

Barrett's island of calm evaporated, replaced by a dull dread. She pressed play and heard a secretary's practiced lines. 'Dr. Conyors, this is to inform you that the six-month review for James Cyrus Martin IV is scheduled for July 15th. If you wish to give testimony at the hearing please respond to the office of the Release Board no later than June 30th.' She left the number and the machine clicked off. She looked at her mother. 'Why didn't you tell me?'

'I figured you'd hear it later. Will you go?'

'I don't know . . . I have to get back to the office, love you, Mom,' she said, making a fast exit, running down the stairs, needing to get out of there and away from Ruth's searching eyes. The mere mention of Jimmy Martin filled Barrett with a fear that seemed endless. And the secrets that she'd kept from her mother, who knew only that James Martin and his twin Ellen had kidnapped Barrett and her sister, and killed a number of people, including Barrett's husband, Ralph. Barrett had killed Ellen Martin in the process of breaking free and Jimmy had been imprisoned in the forensic hospital, from which he should never have been released. And what Ruth Conyors most crucially didn't know, and what Barrett would never tell her, was that Jimmy Martin had raped her, albeit through artificial insemination, and that he – not Ralph – was Max's biological father.

THREE

With minutes to spare, Barrett made it back to her ninth-floor office with the bagged lunch her mother had stuffed into her briefcase. It was an odd mix of Barrett's usual super-healthy regimen and Ruth's comfort foods – a turkey and Swiss on homemade multigrain, honey-mustard oil-free dressing, lettuce, tomato, with an unsweetened bottle of iced tea, also four cheese biscuits, still warm wrapped inside the foil, and two pieces of cold fried chicken left over from yesterday. She was starving and quickly popped one of the buttery biscuits into her mouth. She could hear her mother's voice as she savored the first bite – *You're losing the weight too fast, it's no wonder your milk is drying up*. 'God, this is good,' she said aloud, as she picked at the crispy skin on a chicken breast. She settled back into her chair, cracked open the iced tea, and sank her teeth into the chicken as the intercom buzzed and one of the lights lit. Her secretary and front-door watchdog, Marla, told her, 'Dr. Houssman on line two.'

With her mouth full of deliciously juicy chicken, she picked up. 'Hi, George.'

'I got your message,' her eighty-something-year-old mentor started. 'Thought I wasn't going to call you back, didn't you?'

'One can hope,' she said, trying to swallow and take a swig of iced tea.

'Are you feeling any better?' he asked, honing into the heart of the talk they'd been having, even before the birth of Max.

'Well, some yes and some no, it rips me apart every morning
when I have to leave. He follows me with his eyes, and he can
keep his head up now. He starts to cry the second I'm out the
door; it's heartbreaking. But I have to work, I have to make
money. I try not to think about how everything hangs by this
tiny little thread. If I don't bring home a paycheck, it's like a
house of cards that starts to collapse . . . my house, Mom's health
insurance, Justine's apartment.'

'How often are you getting attacks?'

Barrett felt the pounding in her chest, and a lightheaded feel
from starting to hyperventilate. 'Mostly I can control it. Exercise
helps, and at least when I'm back in the kung-fu studio or out
running I can shut my mind down, but it never stops. It's like
when people used to talk about having nervous breakdowns,
maybe there's this edge and I feel like it's not so far off. Problem
is, I can't afford to have a breakdown; it's not in my schedule.'

'I hate to bring this up . . . there are meds for this.'

'I can't,' she said firmly. 'Even when they claim they don't
get in the breast milk,' she said, feeling fullness in her breasts
even having just nursed, 'you know there's some; I refuse to do
that. He's got enough going against him genetically, and I swear
to God I'm not going to do anything to make it worse. And
speaking of which . . . there was a message on my machine saying
Jimmy's six-month review is coming up next month.'

George sighed. 'It would have been so much better if he'd
gone to trial.'

'Top lawyers and a ton of money,' she commented. 'And he
is one of the most psychically damaged people I've ever known.'

'Are you getting any sleep?'

'Some, not much. Thank God Max sleeps through the night.
So I can't blame this on him, if anything just watching him helps.
Some nights I'll just stare at him, wondering how something so
beautiful could have come out of me. But I still wake up every
couple hours and my thoughts go a mile a minute . . . and my
dreams. In the morning I feel like I've been running laps, like
I'm about to jump out of my skin. Although . . .'

'What?'

She took a sip of iced tea. 'I went on an outreach this morning
with one of the social workers.'

'Really? You're the director now; you could have sent someone
else.'

'It was one of my regulars, a young man with schizophrenia, whom I've known for years. Seems he picked up a dope habit. Anyway, he called in a panic and begged me to come out. Said he wanted to get back on meds and go to a hospital. I should have known something was up.'

'Because?'

'I really like Jerod, one of these guys that under all of the badness he's been through, and his low-level crimes, mostly to get food or drugs, you know he's a good person. I mean half the time whatever he steals he gives away. But here's the thing, he hates being on meds and he hates being locked up; it makes him nuts. So he wants us to meet him down in the Lower East Side, says he's too scared to bring himself to an emergency room.'

'I don't like where this is going,' George said.

In spite of her funk, Barrett cracked a smile. 'So we go down there, and we pull up to one of those buildings that if a building inspector ever showed up would be condemned. No working security door, broken steps, graffiti in the hallways . . .'

'For the love of God, Barrett. Are you about to tell me you dragged some poor social worker into a crack house without a police escort?'

'When you say it like that . . . what am I doing in this job, George?'

Houssman chortled. 'Stop fishing . . . no one else wanted it, or at least no one competent. So did you find your schizophrenic junkie with the heart of gold?'

'His name's Jerod,' she said, feeling a twinge of annoyance, and not liking the way George so easily put labels on people. 'Not then, what we did find was two suburban-looking dead teenagers, and there was someone else in that building, someone who didn't want us there.'

'So what you're telling me is that you nearly got yourself and some poor crisis worker killed this morning, is that about right?'

'The funny thing is, here I'm swimming in jitters, always feeling like I'm on the verge of a panic attack, but not when I was in that building. It's like all of that had evaporated, and for a few minutes I started to feel like myself again.'

'Oh, good,' George said dryly, 'mortal danger as a cure for panic disorder. You should be on meds. You breast-fed for four months, switching to formula is not going to make a hill of beans difference.'

'No.'

'Then therapy at least.'

'Yeah, right. With my crappy cash flow I'm going to shell out a couple hundred bucks a week for therapy? I don't think so. Besides, I've got you.' She pictured George, sitting in the living room of his sun-drenched apartment in a dated brown suit, his eyes big behind Coke-bottle lenses, his gray hair uncombed and sticking up at odd angles.

'This isn't therapy, and you know it.'

'Whatever it is, George, and I don't tell you enough, but it helps. Ever since I became the director and not just another staff psychiatrist, everything changed here. People watch what they say around me. It's just different.'

'It has to be,' he said. 'That's the downside of being the boss – lonely at the top.'

'Yeah, and what's quickly become my least favorite part of this is that all the yearly evaluations are due at the end of the month.'

'Horrible stuff,' George agreed.

'It's worse than just that, George. I've got three "hostile work-place" grievances filed against me with the union, all because some of the docs that my predecessor hired are unhappy with their evaluations. I think it's a record. The craziest part is that none of the evaluations are bad; I just didn't give them the very top score – they don't deserve it. Which reminds me,' Barrett said, 'going through my rendition of "These are a few of my least-favorite things," I've got a bullshit meeting with two commissioners in a few minutes.'

'Is Janice one of them?'

'Of course.'

'Be careful,' George said.

'I know,' Barrett said, 'she's made it very clear that I was not her first choice for this job.'

'True, she was gunning for Hugh Osborn. She'd brought him over from DFYS, I'm pretty sure she promised him rapid advance-ment. I thought he was completely unqualified and made that clear to the selection committee; she wasn't at all happy. The politics of that place can drive you crazy. It's this constant tension because of the dual reporting structure, where it's both part of a state agency and attached to the medical school as a training site. Both want control and so whenever it's time to pick a director there's this huge pissing match over which candidate gets selected, someone from the university or someone from the state system.'

'OK, but based on that you'd think I'd have been her choice; I've always turned down faculty positions, not because I have anything against the medical school, but they pay crap.'

'It's not that, Barrett. You're too high profile for someone like Janice, who just wants to keep her agency out of the headlines. You write books, have articles published, and occasionally . . . how do I put it?'

'Get abducted by sociopaths who want to end civilization as we know it.'

'Pretty much. When you chased down Richard Glash last year,' he said, referring to an escaped convict who had nearly introduced a lethal plague into the Manhattan water supply, 'you and the forensic center were front-page. Janice has survived three governors and been commissioner of two agencies. And like all political appointees she lives in constant fear. At any point she can be terminated, which often happens after something bad hits the papers. You make her nervous. And while I don't want to add to your worries, I've heard rumblings.'

'Give me the details,' she said, feeling a knot tighten in her belly. She needed this job, too many people depended on her and even with Ralph's life-insurance settlement there wasn't much of a cushion.

'The deal with the two months you were on maternity leave when she had Osborn fill in as the acting.'

'Hey, he wasn't my pick. In fact, I'd never have hired him in the first place. He's not the brightest bulb in the box, and if you don't keep on him his reports don't get done on time. I've had to field angry calls from half a dozen AGs, needing psychiatric evaluations.'

'So he's broken the cardinal rule of medicine,' George said dryly.

'Which is?'

He chuckled. 'You can be stupid or you can be lazy, but you can't be both.'

'Thanks,' she said. 'And by the by, he's one of the three filing a grievance against me. I couldn't justify giving him all fives, which apparently is what he's always received. It's also very clear he wants my job, and there've been a few occasions – nothing I can prove definitively – where he's gone around my directives on cases.'

'Well, according to Janice he's "solid and dependable." More importantly, he's not the type who'll go running into abandoned crack houses.'

'It wasn't abandoned. And yes, I do have the sense that Janice is waiting for me to fuck up.'

'Sounds like she's not the only one. So be careful, Barrett. I'll call you later, and I still think you should see somebody.'

'Yeah, but you know what they say about doctors . . .'

'Uh-huh, we make the worst patients.'

She hung up, and looked down at her half-eaten chicken and still-wrapped sandwich. She was about to taken another bite when the intercom buzzed.

'Dr. Conyors,' Marla said, 'Commissioners Fleet and Martinez have arrived.'

'Thanks, Marla,' and felt like adding – *and stop calling me doctor; use my first name* – 'send them in.' She stood as Marla, rail-thin, wearing a blue dress with her face shadowed by her long dark bangs, ushered in the two officials. Janice Fleet, Barrett's boss, an aging blond in a form-fitting burnt-red wool suit, the top two buttons of a cream silk blouse open revealing freckled skin and cleavage of surgically enhanced breasts, greeted her coolly.

Barrett watched as Janice looked over her new furniture, an early sore point. Janice had complained fiercely about the budget overrun. Barrett also feared what Janice might make of today's escapade, which if Lydia were to file a grievance could turn into a union nightmare.

Behind Janice came Carlos Martinez, a grandfatherly and slightly rotund PhD in a bulging navy suit, the current Commissioner of Family and Youth Services, an agency now under intense scrutiny for several recent deaths in the foster-care system.

Barrett motioned for the two to take seats around the teak conference table, when Marla buzzed in. 'Dr. Conyors, Dr. Osborn is here.'

Barrett was in no mood to see Hugh, who'd probably come to complain again about his evaluation. 'Tell him I'm busy and have him make an appointment.'

'Dr. Conyors,' Janice interjected, while examining her French-tipped pink-and-white nails, 'I asked Hugh to join us, I was certain you wouldn't mind. I thought with all his experience at the DFYS, he'd be invaluable for this.'

Barrett's anger surged; clearly Hugh and Janice had been having conversations behind her back. 'Marla,' she said into the intercom, 'send Dr. Osborn in.' She fumed as Hugh entered, a broad smile on his politician's face, his short dark hair perfectly coiffed, his navy suit, white shirt, and burgundy tie like a Brooks Brothers ad.'Commissioner Fleet,' he said, 'you look absolutely stunning,' and he planted a kiss on Janice's cheek.

She smiled. 'Such flattery.'

'Nothing but the truth,' he said, his grin broadening. He turned from her, his short compact frame reminding Barrett of a wind-up toy, and focused on Commissioner Martinez, 'Commissioner.' The two men shook hands. Finally, as though observing some unspoken protocol, he turned to Barrett, and nodded his head, 'Dr. Conyors.'

'Dr. Osborn,' Barrett responded, having given up first-name basis with him in the wake of his grievance.

They all sat with Barrett at one end of the table and Janice at the other. 'Dr. Conyors,' Carlos Martinez began, 'thank you for meeting with us on such short notice.' He sniffed the air. 'What is that delicious smell?'

'Please call me Barrett and I have to admit that I was just trying to wolf down a little lunch. What you smell are probably my mother's cheese biscuits.'

'Heavenly,' he said.

Not certain of the protocol, Barrett offered, 'Would you like one? She packed way too many.'

The commissioner's eyes lit. 'If I wouldn't be depriving you of your lunch, I've been in meetings all day and haven't had a bite.'

Barrett went back to her desk and retrieved the foil packet from the bottom drawer. The brown-paper bag next to it reminded her of all the lunches she and Justine used to carry to school, and the frequent lunchroom swaps that would result. The foil was still warm and she had a moment's pause. *What if Janice knows you've been sneaking out a couple times a day to run home and nurse?* She glanced across at Marla, still standing in the doorway.

'Will you want anything else?' her secretary asked from behind her curtain-like bangs.

Barrett felt Janice's gaze on her, and remembered a recent memo about restricting catering budgets for meetings and conferences. Still, it wasn't every day she received a pair of commissioners and her mother had stressed the importance of always offering guests something to eat, and of course there was the article she'd written on violence and hunger – her conclusion being, if people are fed they're less likely to kill you. 'Maybe some coffee and Danish.'

'A bagel?' Carlos asked, perking visibly.

'No problem,' Marla said, giving the older commissioner a shy smile.

'Well,' Janice said abruptly, looking first at Barrett and then at Carlos and finally letting her gaze rest on Hugh, 'we should get straight to the point. We've got a large problem that's getting bigger and we need to put some plans in place fast to turn this around.'

Barrett put the biscuits in front of the commissioner, took her seat, and braced herself, still not clear why these two were so eager to have this meeting. But she sensed they were going to ask her for something and it was going to be big.

Carlos took a bite of biscuit. 'Delicious.' He then leaned forward and smiled at Barrett. 'How much have you been following the foster-care issue?'

'Some,' she said, 'but mostly just what's in the papers, and of course what we see here. That story about the five-year-old who was killed by his foster mother's boyfriend was heart-breaking.'

Carlos shook his head. 'It's a terrible thing, and people can never comprehend the job we're supposed to do, that the State of New York is the legal guardian for tens of thousands of children. When something bad happens to one of those little ones, it's just . . .' He shrugged his shoulders. 'But today it's the older kids we need to talk about. Let me give you the quick background and where we are. Twelve months ago our department was put under a judicial order that stemmed from allegations regarding kids in the foster-care system, especially as they age out. We knew it was coming.' He looked meaningfully at Janice.

'Yes,' she said, 'not to leave this room, but it had a great deal to do with the Governor's decision to have me leave my position at DFYS three years ago and become Commissioner of Mental Health, he foresaw there was going to be a major restructuring of the two agencies.'

'There were damning articles,' Carlos added, 'and that whole black-plastic-bag thing, case workers just dumping all the kids' belongings into a garbage bag when they hit eighteen and telling them that they were on their own now.'

'That happens,' Barrett said. 'Occasionally we get them in here for evaluations, after they've committed some crime, been put in lockup, and told the guards they feel like killing themselves . . . or actually tried to do it. When they get here, they've still got their bag.'

'I just saw one like that,' Hugh interjected, his expression oozing compassion, 'no family, no supports; it breaks your heart.'

'Yes,' Carlos continued, 'it's not a practice we condone. Anyway, the judge appointed a consulting firm to track all the kids in the foster system and report back. That report, based on anonymous interviews with all the kids they could get their hands on, is about to be made public . . . It's not good. The Governor saw an advance copy and is extremely concerned. He wants assurances that we'll address this problem in an "aggressive and timely fashion."'

'Not to be dense,' Barrett said, knowing a shoe was about to drop, likely onto to her, 'what's in this report and how does it relate to the forensic center?'

Carlos sighed as he finished the last crumbs of his first biscuit and looked longingly at the two remaining on their bed of foil. 'All the evils that can be visited on a child. For those of us in the field, it's what we've known all along, but seeing it tallied up is horrific, and John Q. Public is going to wonder where the hell his tax dollars are going. Over fifty percent of the kids report having suffered some kind of abuse in foster care, thirty-five percent are involved with the criminal-justice system, sixty percent are actively using drugs and or alcohol, thirty percent have been sexually victimized, and eight percent have themselves been either accused or convicted of sexually predatory behavior.'

Janice looked at Carlos and then at Barrett. 'This is where things intersect with mental health . . . and forensics. The report makes a big deal of how many of the foster children have serious and persistent mental-health problems. They're putting it at fifty to seventy percent, but the part that's going to blow up in the papers has to do with how many of these kids are known sex offenders. Most have been in residential placements for years, but when they turn eighteen . . .'

'They get released,' Barrett said, having evaluated many such young adults, almost all victims of sexual abuse who as they matured took on the same behaviors as those who had molested and raped them.

'Pretty much, unless there are active charges. But where so many of them have been locked away, we have no legal right to hold them. And we're talking about over a hundred a year. So that's big problem number one, and then we get to biggie number two . . . dead kids.'

'Dead from what?' Barrett asked, the image of the two teens from that morning seared into her brain.

'Mostly drugs, some bad outcomes in the sex trade, a few suicides, ten homicides . . . but mostly overdoses, supposedly accidental,' Janice said.

A knock at the door, and Marla wheeled in the food cart. Barrett watched as Janice scanned the modest offering of coffee, bagels, and a couple small pastries from the deli on the corner – probably tallying up the cost. She'd undoubtedly make mention of it at their next monthly supervision, but considering everything else that had gone on that morning, it was the least of her worries.

Barrett waited for Marla to leave. This meeting she now knew for sure was leading to something big and bad. She watched as Carlos got his bagel, and Janice, looking peeved, poured herself a cup of coffee. Hugh took nothing.

Her thoughts raced, as she grasped the enormity of the problems being put on the table, and the different ways they could get thrown in her lap. As the state's leading forensic psychiatrist, anything that lay at the intersection of mental health and criminal justice could be batted into her court: sex offenders, drug addicts, as well as all the kids with major mental illnesses who'd also committed crimes – the number was staggering.

'Not to overwhelm you,' Janice said, slitting open three sugar packets and pouring them into her coffee, 'we're seeing a major role for the forensic center in whatever plans get put together. Fortunately, we'd already planned an inter-agency conference for this, which in view of this study has been reconfigured as an emergency planning session that's scheduled . . .'

Her next words were swallowed in the blaring of the overhead alarm system, 'Code Blue, ninth floor. Code Blue, ninth floor.'

Barrett shot out of her chair. 'What the—?' as her door flew open and a young white man with shoulder-length dirty blond dreads, wiry arms covered with tattoos, and a wild-eyed expression barreled in with a gun in his hand. His braids whipped around as he looked behind at an advancing phalanx of security guards. He raised the gun in shaky hands to hold them back. 'Dr. Conyors,' he shrieked, 'you got to help me! They're going to kill me! Please God, you got to help me! Help me help me help me!'

FOUR

'Jerod,' Barrett shouted, struggling to be heard over the blaring intercom and his pleas.

'Help me! Help me! Help me!'

'What the hell are you doing?' she shouted, needing to break through to him. The intercom didn't stop. 'Code Blue, ninth floor. Code Blue, ninth floor'

Jerod's pale, lean face was streaked with tears, his blue eyes wide. He looked behind him at the armed and uniformed security force, his gun raised. 'Help me! Help me!' He was hyperventilating. 'They're going to kill me. Help me! Help me!'

With ten feet separating them, Barrett lowered her voice. 'No one,' she said, keeping her voice steady and making eye contact with the nearest of the security guards, 'is getting shot in my office.' She inched toward Jerod, as the intercom finally went quiet. Behind her she heard Janice whisper to Hugh, 'Call the cops, now!'

'They're going to kill me. They're going to kill me.'

'Jerod!' she shouted. *God, why would this normally passive young man pick up a firearm and break in here? Is this paranoia? Drugs? Some other delusion?* 'I will help you, but you've got to put down the gun.'

'I don't know,' he cried incoherently. 'I don't know.' His face was twisted as he blinked back tears, and he shifted from foot to foot, looking at her, and then at the guards. 'They're dead.'

'I know,' Barrett said, trying to make eye contact. 'I was there. I saw.'

'Why? Why would someone do that? They didn't have to do that. They were only kids. They were my friends. I want to die. I want to die.'

Barrett gauged the distance between them, trying to keep him talking while slowly bridging the gap. He had a couple inches on her at just over six feet, but if she could only get close enough . . . She crept closer, feeling his grief; he was a wreck, the blues of his eyes nearly obliterated, the pupils way too big, and he was shivering, gooseflesh popping on his tattooed forearms, even though her office was warm. 'Jerod, let me help you. I'm so sorry about your friends, but you've got to let me help you.' She wanted to scream as she heard Janice behind her whispering on her cell, 'We have a hostage situation at the Forensic Evaluation Center . . .' She tuned out the rest, needing to keep focused. 'Look at me!' she said. 'And the rest of you, move back.'

With his free hand he batted away the tears. He tried to look at her, his head nodded back and forth. The gun, a cheap Korean 9mm, was still raised, not pointed at her but in the air, hovering.

Barrett heard the first siren; it wouldn't take long for the cops to make it up here. This needed to end fast.

From behind her Janice urged, 'Dr. Conyors, let the police handle this. You need to step away.'

She ignored her. 'Jerod, I can help you, but you've got to put the gun down before anyone gets hurt. I know you, you don't want to hurt anyone, you never have. I'm begging you, let me help you.'

He looked so young and frightened. He glanced back at the guards, who'd followed her orders and moved back to the periphery. 'I don't know what to do. They're going to kill me. They killed Bobby and Ashley. Why did they have to do that?'

There was now less than six feet between them, she could smell the acid of his sweat. She tried to make sense of his too-clean clothes, a blue-and-yellow-striped polo shirt, trendy low-riser jeans, bright red Converse sneakers – where the hell did he get those? – and a new black knapsack. The Jerod she knew favored ripped Bob Marley T-shirts and jeans that hadn't seen the inside of a washing machine for months. She heard the bell for the elevators in the corridor outside her suite, knew in a matter of seconds armed police would swarm in. 'Jerod, put down the gun. I promise, I'll keep you safe.'

He looked at her. 'They're going to kill me,' he said softly. 'I shouldn't have come here.' He appeared distracted, as though listening to something or someone no one else could hear. And as though having reached a decision he raised the gun and pointed it at his head.

Once before, Barrett had had a patient commit suicide in front of her. The image, the sound, the smell of burned hair, flesh, and bone were branded into her. That man had been guilty of horrible crimes, and had killed himself instead of facing life in prison – or possibly execution. Jerod was more victim than criminal, and now, as cops swarmed into her waiting room, her options were gone. She heard the click of holsters, 'Hell, no!' and with her years of martial-arts training she closed the remaining few feet between them with a seamless glide. She trapped his gun hand in a double overhand block. She felt his thin body tense as she clamped down hard on his wrist. The gun fell to the floor, she felt a sliver of fear that it would discharge on impact, but not stopping she surged forward, pulling him off balance, and using her body as a fulcrum she controlled his fall so that his head wouldn't hit. She lay on top of him, holding him close, as the security and armed officers closed in. It was strangely intimate as she felt his body shake beneath hers. He was sobbing and shivering, even as sweat drenched his clothes. And then she got it, he was dope sick.

An officer picked up the gun, and reached around the back of his belt for one of the white plastic restraining ties that had mostly replaced handcuffs.

'No,' Barrett said forcefully, realizing that they intended to arrest Jerod and bring him to a precinct lockup or even worse to the Tombs – the large downtown jail that housed nearly a thousand criminals as they awaited sentencing. 'This is Jerod Blank. He has schizophrenia and is suicidal . . . you just saw that. We'll keep him here; we have a locked observation unit on the fourth floor; it's the right place for him. As soon as things settle I'll petition the court to have him go to a forensic hospital. Now everyone needs to clear out of here except for two security guards and a nurse, because I'm going to need to get some medication.'

'And you are?' the officer asked.

'Dr. Barrett Conyors,' she said. 'I'm a psychiatrist and the Director of the Forensic Evaluation Center; Jerod is my patient. This is the right place for him.'

'You're certain about that? Wait a minute, I know you, you're the lady doc who helped track that weirdo who wanted to poison the city water. That's you, isn't it?'

'Yes,' she said, having now repositioned herself, still holding Jerod, but now with the two of them sitting up on the floor, her arms wrapped around the boy's back. He was sweating buckets, his striped shirt dark with sweat around the neck and down his sides, and he reeked.

'Well, I disagree entirely!' Janice Fleet stood from the table. 'Dr. Conyors, this man is a dangerous criminal who just threatened all of our lives. You need to let the officers do their job and take him to jail.'

The officer looked at Janice and then at the other two suited men at the conference table. He sighed. 'You are?'

'I am Dr. Janice Fleet, the Commissioner for the Department of Mental Health.'

'You outrank her?' he asked.

'I do.'

'Not in this case,' Barrett said, realizing she was about to step from only ankle-deep shit into a mess that could drown her. 'I am an MD psychiatrist with the legal authority to commit and confine Jerod, as being an imminent danger to himself or others. She is not. Dr. Fleet is a psychologist who does not have that statutory authority.'

The officer looked at Barrett, still holding tight to the crazed-looking man with his wild hair and wide eyes. He then looked back at Janice. 'I'm sorry,' he said, 'she's right.' And then to Barrett, 'If you even start to think about releasing him, don't,' he warned, 'there's going to be charges, so consider him on a police hold.'

'Fair enough,' Barrett said, sensing Janice's frustration and anger. 'If it looks like he's getting released we'll call.'

Seemingly satisfied, the officer nodded and started to back away.

Barrett whispered to Jerod, 'How much dope have you been doing?'

'They gave it to me,' he sobbed. 'Why would they be dead?

They know how to shoot dope. They told me how to do it. They were always careful.'

'Jerod, how many bags a day have you been doing?'

'A bundle, sometimes a bundle and a half.'

Barrett looked around, nodded toward the two remaining security guards. 'Let's get him downstairs.' She looked over at Hugh and the two commissioners. Janice was flushed, the heavyset DFYS commissioner seemed dazed, and Hugh kept glancing at Janice, as though looking for guidance as to how he was supposed to behave.

She imagined how bizarre this must look – almost comical. She was on the floor, her arms and legs wrapped around a patient who'd just had an armed standoff. She wondered how Janice would spin the episode. This boss had made it abundantly clear that she thought Barrett took unnecessary risks with both her own safety and that of her staff. At one point she'd even accused Barrett of vigilantism – 'We're administrators, not cops. You need to remember that. Your heroism may be appreciated by some, but it's not in your job description, and it's not in the agency's best interest.'

'Jerod,' she said, keeping her arms firmly around his shoulders, to offer comfort and to keep him from trying anything, 'I need you to stay calm and not do any more crazy shit. Can you do that?'

'You should have let me do it,' he said, starting to rock against her arms.

She knew she wouldn't get any rational answers out of him. He was sick and desperate and until that was taken care of she'd get nowhere. 'Jerod, we're going to stand up now, and I'm going to take you to your room. Can you do that?'

He nodded.

Awkwardly she let go of him and stood. 'Come on.' She extended a hand and helped him up.

He stood and then doubled over in pain.

'Jerod, I know you're dope sick and I'll get you some medication as quick as I can, just try to keep it together.' And without waiting for an answer she motioned for the guards and they headed toward the elevators and down to the fourth floor.

Once buzzed into the small eight-bed locked unit, which typically housed prisoner/patients who'd been court mandated for psychiatric evaluations to see if they were competent to stand trial, she spotted Maggie, a diminutive near-retirement nurse who was not easily flustered, and was kind. 'Maggie,' Barrett said, relieved to see a friendly face, 'how long would it take to get the pharmacy to deliver some Suboxone?' she asked, referring to a medication used to handle opiate withdrawal.

The short, sandy-haired woman said with a voice cured by twenty years of two packs a day, 'You write the script, I'll walk it over myself.'

'Thank you. Come on, Jerod.' She led him over to the nearest unoccupied patient room, and left him with the male guard.

'Dr. Conyors,' the female security officer approached, 'do you want anything special done with his belongings?' She was holding his black knapsack while the male officer stayed in Jerod's room, and had him strip off his street clothes. He searched him then handed him a pair of faded blue hospital pajamas and rubber-soled sock slippers.

'My office,' she said, allowing herself a moment's relief that what could have been disastrous was largely over. She glanced at the belts on the two security guards, neither with firearms, although both carried pepper spray and Tasers.

Maggie reappeared from the med room with a triplicate prescription pad and handed it to Barrett with a pen that had the logo for a drug company that marketed a popular antidepressant. Barrett had a moment's hesitation as she looked at Jerod. He had used soft drugs before – mostly pot – but never heroin. Would the medication handle it? A bundle a day could be a lot or a little depending on the strength of the dope. She quickly scribbled out the prescription using the special DEA certification number she'd had to obtain to prescribe a medication specifically used to cover opiate withdrawal and hoped it would be strong enough. She looked up at the dozen or so overhead monitors that gave a clear view of each patient room, the small common living and dining areas, and the unit door.

The unit clerk, a youngish man in a plaid shirt and khakis, pulled an empty plastic binder from off a shelf. He looked at Barrett. 'Who's doing the admission paperwork and orders? And is he medically stable? He looks pretty sick. Maybe he should go to the hospital?'

'Heroin withdrawal,' she said, 'it won't kill him . . . just try to get some fluids into him, and I'll write the orders.'

The buzzer to the outer door sounded. The clerk looked at the monitor. 'Oh my God, it's the Commissioner.' He buzzed the door open.

'Dr. Conyors –' Janice was pissed – 'we were in the middle of a meeting. Were you intending to come back? What should I tell Commissioner Martinez?'

Barrett felt a rush of heat in her cheeks. She wanted to shout, *I'm a little busy right now, having just stopped someone from shooting himself, or someone else . . . or you!* But she needed to stay focused and get Jerod settled and treated, and then try to figure out what this whole day was about, why he'd called her downtown to find a couple dead kids, and why he was so frightened that suicide seemed like a better option. 'Sorry, but it's going to be another forty-five easily,' she said, turning to meet Janice's tight-lipped expression.

'I see,' Janice responded, brushing back a strand of straw-dry hair. 'This is your priority right now?'

'Yes,' Barrett said, her gaze steady, knowing that no amount of explanation would appease her. She felt her chest constrict and wondered if this was the moment when she'd be fired.

'Your choice,' Janice replied, and she turned and walked off the unit.

'Crap,' Barrett muttered, as she looked at the shivering and miserable Jerod and then at the clerk. 'Have somebody sit with him till the meds get here. Give me the paperwork.' She felt a pull to go after Janice, but how do you explain to someone who's not a medical doctor that the patient always comes first? That if the orders for medication aren't written and all of the hundred and one little boxes checked off on the right forms, treatment can't get started? She looked at the monitor trained on the unit's front door and watched Janice storm away. She saw Hugh on the other side, and the two of them talking as they vanished from view. He was probably telling her how Barrett was hounding him, how she was making his life miserable, how she'd not given him the perfect evaluations that he'd always received. How she actually insisted that his reports be finished on time, and how she'd had the gall to make him edit and revise reports she deemed too low on hard facts and filled with half-baked conjecture and supposition and not fit for a courtroom.

She cleared off a stretch of counter in the central nurses' station, while keeping an eye on Jerod through the large expanses of shatterproof glass. He looked like a caged animal pacing in his tiny locked room. She glanced at the screen and then took a quick overview of the other patients, all of whom she knew either from having done the evaluations herself or from having reviewed the cases with her staff. Moving as fast as she could she whipped through the paperwork. As she signed off on the various forms, her eye caught on his black knapsack and beside it a sealed plastic patient-belongings bag. Apparently, his stuff never made it to her office.

She walked over, and knowing she probably shouldn't, she dumped the contents of the knapsack on the counter and broke the seal on the bag. The first thing that struck her was the similarity of Jerod's clothes to those worn by the dead kids. New jeans and a striped polo shirt with the Abercrombie and Fitch logo, and his sneakers were the hottest new high-top Chucks – a hundred bucks easily. He didn't have a wallet, but in a sealed plastic bag there was a wad of bills, a New York State identification card, and a Medicaid card. There were also two cell phones. Which, for starters, was odd. She'd known Jerod for five years; he didn't carry a cell . . . and why two? On the inventory sheet it said there was nearly three hundred in cash. The obvious answer was that Jerod had gotten involved in dealing dope. She picked up the first of the cells and tried to see if she could get into the call history. Apparently it had been left on and all she could get was a signal for low battery. The second too was on its last drop of juice, and showed a single number that didn't have enough digits for a phone number on the caller ID history and that was it. As she flipped through the menu options she saw the number 1 in the video option screen. She pressed play, and saw a few seconds of a pretty brunette, who couldn't have been more than eighteen. She was naked and draped on a burgundy bedspread. She appeared asleep, or drugged. The phone flashed a message about going into sleep mode and then went dead. She shuddered, the way the camera moved slowly around the girl, like she was on display. Her first thought was of the dead girl she'd found earlier, but it wasn't her. And what was Jerod doing with something like this? Had she completely misjudged him? Underneath his craziness, heavy pot smoking, and petty crimes, she'd always found something gentle and sweet about him, more a victim than a perp. But it wouldn't be the first time she'd been fooled by someone trying to avoid prison.

She looked up as Maggie returned. The diminutive nurse held

a brown bag from the pharmacy. She opened it and held up the bottle filled with tiny white pills. 'How much do you want me to give him?'

'Start with two, and as long as he doesn't start puking, keep giving him another two every hour times four. Tell him he has to hold them under his tongue until they dissolve, that if he swallows them they won't work.'

'You got it,' Maggie said, counting the pills, putting two into a small paper cup, and then entering this information onto the narcotic log sheet.

Barrett watched the monitor as Maggie entered Jerod's room. He was face down on the bed, his body curled tight. She turned up the sound and listened as Maggie coaxed him to sit up and take the medication. She'd know within half an hour if she'd picked the right one. She also knew that she wouldn't leave until she'd made good on her promise. She was going to get him through this, and then she was going to figure out what the hell was going on. What had him so desperate that suicide seemed his best option, and what did he know about those dead kids, or that girl in the video? She looked over the inch-thick mound of paperwork she'd just completed, and got it arranged so she could dictate. As she dialed onto the transcription service, something popped into her head, something she'd not wanted to think about. The man who'd run off before getting whatever it was he was after. She could still hear the click of the safety. She looked at Jerod on the screen – *money, dope, cell phones*, and *two dead teenagers* all gave credibility to his ramblings about danger. That piece made some sense. He'd called; he'd been frantic and scared. He wanted to get off the street and into a hospital, not for treatment, but because he wanted safety, someone was after him.

She finished her dictation and walked over to his room as Maggie gave him the second two pills. He was still sweating and in obvious pain, but he seemed less frantic, whether from the medication or from Maggie's husky voice soothing him, 'That's right, just try and relax, everything is going to be all right.'

'Thanks, Maggie, you need me for anything else?' Barrett asked.

'No, and Dr. Conyors, in case no one mentions it, what you did for this boy should get you a medal. Most psychiatrists just stand in the background when bad stuff happens. I sure appreciate what you did. He could have gotten himself killed, or someone else.'

'Thanks, Maggie,' Barrett said, not wanting to think about how close they'd come to a tragedy.

'Don't mention it,' the nurse said. 'I just wish others would take notice. There's not many that would step in like you did.'

Barrett returned to the nurses' station and retrieved Jerod's belongings. She piled them back into the plastic bag and thought through the day's events. It felt messy as hell and standing there holding – and contaminating – what might turn out to be evidence in a double homicide, she needed help. That was yet another problem, she knew the help she wanted: Hobbs . . . Detective Ed Hobbs. So as she often did when faced with tough calls, Barrett forced herself to act. She made toward the exit, punched in her code, and waited for the elevator, all the while thinking of what she'd say to Ed. She'd avoided him since Max's birth. It had become too awkward; Ed had fallen for her, and told her so. She couldn't return it. She'd hurt him, after all he'd done for her, she'd really hurt him and it killed her. Of course she loved him, but not in that way. Although . . . there had been that kiss, the tickle of his moustache, the feel of his strong hands on her face, in her hair. 'Damn,' she said aloud as the elevator came to the ninth floor. She got out, glanced at the clock, surprised to see it was only three. 'Marla,' she said, as she passed her secretary's desk, 'hold my calls.' She closed the door, went into her small private bath, undressed, pumped, put the milk in the fridge, and no longer feeling like her breasts were going to explode, dialed Ed's cell.

He picked up on the second ring.

'Ed, it's Barrett.' She held her breath.

'Barrett who?' he said with uncharacteristic sarcasm.

'Ed, I'm so sorry. It's just between the baby and going back to work and—'

'Please stop. We've known each other way too long for bull-shit. I'm glad you called. What's up?'

'Thank you,' she said. 'You got some time?'

'Yeah, I'm just plugging through some reports. I can't believe how fast they pile up. What gives?'

She started to lay out the events of the day.

Barely into it, Hobbs blurted, 'What the hell were you doing going into that building without a police escort?'

Barrett was struck by something in his voice, something she'd missed, his concern, his wit, his humor. 'It's me, Ed. It was broad daylight, I wasn't alone.'

'For the love of God, Barrett, why do you put yourself in these situations? Don't you think you're getting a little old?'

'Can I finish?'

'Yes, please continue. I can't wait for the part where you single-handedly fight off a drug lord and his minions.'

She laughed. 'How did you know? But that's coming . . .'

At several points in the telling he asked for further details, about the dead kids, and about Jerod's near suicide-by-cop.

'This is where it gets creepy,' she said, and she told him about the cells and the video of the naked girl. 'I mean Jerod I've known for years. He has chronic schizophrenia, hears voices, and lives hand-to-mouth more often than not just staying at the shelter. The first time I met him he was eighteen and smoking a huge amount of pot because the voice of Bob Marley was telling him he was going to be a Rasta messiah. What's he doing with all that cash? The cell phones?'

'Does anyone know you have those phones?'

'Just some guards, and a couple nurses.'

'That's probably what he was looking for.'

'Who?'

'The man you saw running away, the one you thought had a gun. From everything you've said it sounds like your sweet boy Jerod – who, let's be clear, set you up – is dealing dope. It's also unlikely he's far up in any kind of organization. This feels bad, Barrett. Something dangerous has just been dropped at your door. If you're not frightened I suggest you start. I need to see those phones and that video. Don't touch them or do anything else with them. I'll swing by within the hour. I'll also give the ME a call to see what's happening with the autopsies and if they've got positive ID. Because maybe this is just a freaky double overdose, but it stinks like homicide . . . No wonder your kid is scared, he's either seen something or knows something. How good is your security there?'

'Fair. You think I should send him to Croton?' she asked, refer- ring to the high-security forensic hospital near the Connecticut border.

'It's a thought. I mean this could turn out to be small pota- toes, but with two dead, someone pulling a gun, and someone else trying to get himself shot, someone's worried and playing high stakes.'

'Good point,' she said, hearing the concern in his voice. 'And, Ed . . .'

'Yes?'

'Thanks.'

'I'll be by in the hour. And for God's sake, please watch out. If you can't do it for you, think about your kid.'

'Fine,' she said, trying to use humor to battle her mounting fear. 'I'll stay in my office and hide under my desk.' But her every thought triggered fresh waves of jitters. She'd put herself in harm's way, albeit for the best of reasons, Jerod could have gotten shot . . . or someone else, and she had a baby to take care of, and she'd pissed off Janice more than she'd ever done, and it was clear that snaky Hugh was lobbying for her job, and at the rate she was going he'd probably get it too.

'Good, then I'll know where to find you.'

FIVE

At twenty-five, Chase Strand, a Department of Family and Youth Services social worker, could have been a model in the magazines to which he was addicted. Sitting in his small corner office that smelled of citrus zest, he glared at the cover of *Men's Vogue*. Normally, he'd spend an enjoyable half-hour flipping pages while comparing his looks to those of the men in the glossy ads for Prada, Hugo Boss, Calvin Klein, Abercrombie's, and all the rest, commenting aloud, 'He's pretty good looking,' 'I'm better looking than him,' 'I'm much better looking than him,' 'How does that guy even get work?' And then he'd think through the possible surgical solutions that might improve the model's looks, a rhinoplasty, perhaps a chin implant. He'd evaluate the bodies of the underwear models and compare their features to his perfect abs, chest, shoulders, and legs, toned by daily workouts in his state-of-the-art home gym. He'd peer intently at each page as though his gaze could melt through the airbrushing, trying to see who'd had calf or pec implants.

But not now. As he waited for his next pathetic excuse for a human being client, he was worried; his thoughts were dark; and he was furious, shit was coming undone, and he hated this feeling of things being out of his control. Making certain his door was locked, he reached into his Gucci briefcase and pulled out a prepaid and untraceable cell phone. He dialed Marky, and as soon as the phone picked up, laid in to him. 'Where is he?'

'He was running,' Marky said, sounding winded. 'He knew I was looking for him.'

'Why would he think that?' Chase pushed. 'Why was he even with those two? You should have made sure they were alone.'

'Chase, I don't know what Jerod was doing there. He's been hanging around them, doing stuff for them . . . I think he was into that girl Carly. He was spouting some sort of bullshit about her being kidnapped. It didn't make any sense.'

Chase felt rage. 'Don't fuck with me, Marky! Where is he?'

'I don't know, I've been looking everywhere for him. I swear I'll find him.'

'You better, and take care of him.'

Chase wanted to hit something, or someone. Every word from Marky reeked of carelessness and stupidity, but he had to pull it back. 'OK, Marky, I know Bobby had one of the regular cells, and I know you didn't retrieve it. It's either with the body or somehow that nutcase got his hands on it. There's also one missing from my loft; it's not meant to go with the family kids, it's for something else. Do you know anything about it? There were half a dozen on the living-room table next to the leather sofa. When I looked there were only five. Did you take one?'

'Oh shit! I thought that was one of the ones I could take. I thought you'd gotten new phones, and I needed one . . .'

'So you have it?'

'No, oh shit.'

'Who has it?'

'I'm so sorry, Chase, please don't be mad . . . I gave it to Bobby; he said his wasn't working. It was right before . . . I didn't want him to be suspicious.'

Chase looked down at his perfectly manicured nails and his long fingers. He pictured them around Marky's throat. He'd watch as the fair-haired man's face turned bright red. He'd see the fear in his eyes, desire, longing. 'I need those cells, Marky. Find Jerod and get them. Do you understand?'

'Yes, Chase . . . If . . . when I get them, will you see me?'

'Get them and we'll talk.' *At least he's motivated*, Chase mused, knowing that Marky would do anything, absolutely anything, he asked.

'I swear I'll get them back.'

Chase hung up, and stared at the handsome man on the maga- zine cover, knowing that could easily have been him. On numerous occasions, since he'd been a teen, he'd been approached by talent agents and modeling executives. They'd tell him he had *the look*, that he could do both commercial and lucrative editorial and high-fashion work. He'd smile, flash perfect white teeth, let them linger on his blemish-free skin, full lips, high cheekbones that gave his face a slightly feline quality, and his thick head of near-black hair that he currently wore a bit longer than usual so that its natural wave could flop casually across his forehead and curl at the base of his neck. But it was his large golden-brown eyes framed by long lashes that were his best feature. They'd offer him contracts and set him up with import- ant photographers to get a book put together – all on them. He'd enjoyed the photo shoots, and more importantly the hard, cold, photographic evidence of his beauty. But his face, his body . . . his cock were not on the market, at least not to be used by anyone other than Chase; they gave him power and control. Being a male model, or some pretty boy actor, was not the future he envisioned. He was going to have true power, respect, authority, and money; he was going to be a plastic surgeon, and to achieve this he would do whatever it took, which currently included dealing dope to wealthy college kids and the occasional sale of young white girls to foreign brothels or to men with wealth and a taste for something pretty, young, and disposable. Medical school wasn't cheap, and even with scholarships he was looking at 40K a year for tuition alone, not to mention the taxes and fees on his condo – nearly five grand a month – and his need for high-end clothing. He couldn't possibly get by on less than two hundred a year and even that was tight.

His phone rang; it was the receptionist. 'Hi, Chase,' her voice slightly breathless, 'I've got your grandma's aide on the phone. Do you want me to take a message?'

'No,' he said, bracing for the worst, 'put her through'.

The line clicked. 'Mr. Strand, this is Dorothy, I hope you don't mind me calling you at work.'

'Of course not,' he said, wondering what this was about to cost.

'I just thought you should know I'm starting to see skin break-down on Grace's lower back, I don't think second shift have been turning her as often as they're supposed to.'

'How bad is it?' He pictured his grandmother, with her angel-white hair and wrinkle-free face.

'I think I caught it in time, but she needs an inflatable mattress cover, preferably one with adjustable temperature . . . Medicaid won't pay for that.'

'How much?' he asked, knowing he'd pay. Grace Strand was the only person in the world who'd ever given him a taste of that most elusive drug – unconditional love.

'The best one's about fifteen hundred dollars.' She was about to say more when he interrupted.

'Just do it, I'll pay you this weekend, and pick up some more of those microwavable bed-bath packs.'

'Sure, and Mr. Strand . . .'

'Dorothy, after all these years you can call me Chase.'

'Chase, I really appreciate how you take care of her, you'd be amazed how few do.'

'She's a great woman,' he said, flashing on an ancient memory of playing by his grandmother's side as she picked tomatoes and basil from the garden behind her three-story home in Park Slope. As he hung up, he knew that in addition to the $1500 for the inflatable mattress cover – probably an inflated price – he'd also slip Dorothy an extra couple hundred. On Saturday, he'd take the subway to Flatbush, as he did every week, to the hellhole of a nursing home that had warehoused his grandmother for twenty-one years, ever since she suffered a catastrophic stroke, with what the doctors called locked-in syndrome. He'd sit with her and hold her hand, feeling the crêpe-paper fragility of her skin. He'd talk to her about his ambitions, that he was going to be a doctor, that his aunts – her daughters – Kelly and Donna with their fat husbands and ugly children would regret the way they'd treated him, and treated her. Grace had taken Chase in after his parents had died within a year of each other. His nearly famous fashion-model mother OD'd on heroin. Ten months later his cracked-out nightclub-promoting father blew his heart out at the end of a glass pipe – Chase was four. Yet strangely, the following months living with his grandmother were the happiest of his life. Then Grace had her stroke. He found her on the kitchen floor, her eyes open, unable to move, spittle dribbling from the corner of her mouth. The brightest light in his life had just gone out. His aunts Kelly and Donna, both with their own families, refused to take him in. Years later he'd understand why, too jealous of his beautiful mother to give a shit about him, and furious that any money Grace had, as well as the big house in Park Slope, was sucked up by the state to pay for her nursing home. At the age of five Chase became a ward of the state, and like the kids he now worked with, his life was a series of foster homes and group homes. When he was still very young there was always the hope of full adoption, and likely couples dangled the prospect of a stable home, security . . . love. But each time something got in the way, and he'd find himself, battered suitcase in hand, moving toward the next.

The worst came when he was thirteen, just removed from the foster family he'd been with for three years after he'd attacked his foster father, who'd tried to rape him. His foster mother had called him a liar; it wasn't the first time. Given the chance, he would have killed them both and felt no remorse, but now, sitting in his small office, with its single window, he realized that if it hadn't been for that horrible twist of fate he'd never have met Janice. And one of the many ironies in their relationship was that while he regretted not bashing in the skull of his foster father, it was with Janice and her cheating husband that he got his first heady rush of what it feels like to take another's life.

His intercom buzzed again. 'Chase, your three o'clock is here.'

'Send her down.'

Moments later, a knock at his door.

'Yes.' He looked up as someone tried to turn the handle; of course it was locked. Chase couldn't stand being intruded on. He got up, as a girl called through the door.

'It's Morgan. I'm here for my appointment.'

He smoothed back a bang and opened the door onto a fifteen-year-old dressed in a midriff-baring jersey top, low-rider jeans with faux stone-washed stripes that ran up the front of her thighs and down her back from ass to ankle, and bright pink flip-flops with red beads on the straps. Her hair was a mess of home-dyed blonde, streaked with near-white highlights. Her blue eyes, lined in black with mascara that had clumped, looked up at her six-foot-two gorgeous hunk of a counselor. 'Hi, Chase.'

'Hey, Morgan, come on in.' He met her gaze, enjoying the

effect he had on her. 'How's your month been?' he asked, motioning her toward a chair on the other side of his desk.

'You have no idea,' she said dramatically as she flopped down, her left leg hooked over the seat's padded arm, her midriff exposed. 'Everything sucks! My life sucks! I wish I were dead. I can't believe I have to stay at that place for three years. You got to get me out of there.'

'OK,' he said, 'let's get the details. I take it that you're not loving the new group home.'

'Yeah, right, that place is for retards, Chase. They don't let me do anything; it's like being a prisoner. The food sucks, there's a nine o'clock curfew, they don't have TVs in the bedrooms, and they won't let us have cell phones; they don't even have Internet! My roommate's on medication and I don't mean to be a total bitch, but she stinks, like shit, the whole place stinks.'

'How long have you been in there?' he asked, not caring, but finding that the words just came.

'Two weeks. I can't take it. Please get me back into a foster family.'

Chase looked at the top folder on his desk; they were all thick and Morgan's was no exception. She'd been a ward of the system since she was two. Failed out of a dozen foster homes, and was now in her fourth or fifth group-home placement. 'OK,' he said, looking at the little piece of trash as she slathered on a fresh layer of pink lipgloss, 'I think your last foster family was the final nail in that particular coffin.'

'What are you saying?' she asked, not liking it when he criticized her. 'It wasn't my fault. He's the one who came on to me. Aren't you supposed to keep shit like that from happening? Don't you even screen those creeps?'

'Of course we do,' he said, having had to handle a few horny creeps of his own as a child and teenager. Though his tactics had been different from Morgan's, who viewed herself as a victim of everything and everyone. The first time he'd been molested was when he was nine, by his foster mother's boyfriend. It didn't go far, but the man begged Chase to tell no one, and promised it would never happen again. Chase could still see the raw fear in Jack Harrigan's eyes and smell the whiskey on his breath. More importantly, he knew that Jack's fear gave him power. He'd stayed in that placement for another year, when he'd left, it was with fifteen hundred dollars in cash and a gold pocket watch that had belonged to Jack's father. 'But human nature,' Chase said, looking at Morgan, 'stuff happens. You're a pretty girl, Morgan. I don't think we'll be able to get you back into a foster family. They want them younger, so you're left with either a group home or one of the bigger facilities. Which if you think it feels like a prison now, those places have ten times more rules. And frankly, we're running out of group homes. This is your fourth?'

'Fifth,' she said. 'Chase, you've got to help me. I'm not kidding. I can't stay there. I'll do something crazy. You know I will. You've got to get me out of there. I spoke to my mom . . . she said I could stay there.'

Chase looked at her. He had more important things to do now, but he was struck by her monumental stupidity, that despite all the horrible things her crack-addicted prostitute of a mother had done to her, she still wanted to go back to her. 'Morgan, first there's no way the department would ever let you return to your mother while you're a minor; she has no parental rights, they were terminated when you were eight. Second, the five or six times that reunification was tried ended up with either you running away or the department having to pick you up after Cathy overdosed or got arrested. It's not an option.'

'It's not fair,' she repeated, pulling at a lock of her frizzed-out hair. Her lower lip pouted as she looked at Chase. 'I don't know why I have to stay there.'

'It's stable, you can walk to school. It's the best we've got.'

'What do I need high school for? It's not like anyone cares about that, and I'm going to be an actress. I don't think they check diplomas in Hollywood . . . Is that a new watch?' Her eyes caught on Chase's gold Movado with its sleek black onyx face and absence of numbers.

'Nice, isn't it?' he said, letting her view the recent purchase. 'This is why you need to finish high school. You can't get nice things unless you have a way to make money. I don't want to destroy any dreams you have, but Hollywood is a long shot. Thinking you can just go out there and hit it big lands people in trouble. Suddenly you're in California, no friends, no connections. You start making some bad choices, hook up with the wrong people. It doesn't go well.'

'I don't care,' she said, digging in. 'The first chance I get I'm out of here.'

Chase sighed. 'You thinking of running away . . . again?'

'What else can I do?' she intoned. Her eyes started to tear, further smudging her thick mascara. 'You're not helping me. None of you ever do. It's just, "Here's another group home, Morgan," and then all the things I can't do. I want to see my mother. I want to stay with her. Why can't I?'

He leaned back, watching as this train wreck of a human being collapsed. Her runny makeup was rapidly transforming her into a puffy blond raccoon, but underneath the bad dye job, and the amateurish attempts with cheap cosmetics, she wasn't bad looking. Unlike many of the girls who insisted on midriff-baring clothes, Morgan's belly was flat and toned. With a little work, he thought, she'd be a respectable piece of merchandise. She was also at that critical age – fifteen – when if a kid ran from a group home, not much was done to get them back. A missing person's report would be filed, and that's about it. There were too many others, and it was the younger kids that got prefer- ence. 'Look, Morgan,' he said, pushing a box of tissues toward the weeping girl, 'you know I care about you.' His voice was soft as a kiss. 'I'd worry if you ran away, bad things happen out there.'

'I don't care,' she sobbed and pulled a hunk of tissues from the box. 'I can't stay in that place.'

'I hear you,' he said, shaping his words and the way he said them carefully. 'If you're really serious, I might be able to help.'

She looked up. 'How?'

He leaned back, looked at her meaningfully, paused, and then reached into his desk. He pulled out a blank piece of paper and wrote a number on it. 'Memorize this,' he said, giving her ample time to do so, watching the corners of her mouth move. 'This is for a friend of mine, who's connected in showbiz. She's gotten a lot of kids their first jobs.'

'Like an agent?' Morgan asked.

'Exactly,' he said, spinning the story like a length of fishing line, 'but don't think Hollywood . . . at least not yet. It's more bread-and-butter stuff, cruise ships, convention work, traveling productions of some of the Broadway shows, catalog modeling, that kind of thing.' He tore the paper with the number on it into tiny pieces. He had a moment's pause, there was huge risk with minors, but also the possibility of a big payday, and keeping up the flow of money was everything. 'Of course, I never said any of this, and if you can stick it out in that group home and finish high school, it would be better for you.'

She pulled more tissues from the box, 'You don't know what it's like in that place,' she said.

While Chase would never share this with a girl like Morgan, he knew exactly what those places were like. Unlike her, he'd figured out how to work the system, just like now. 'You have to be careful,' he said. 'I'd hate to see anything bad happen to you, Morgan.'

Her eyes lingered on his, and then his cell phone rang, the dial tone set to a simple ring on low volume.

'Our time's up, make an appointment with the secretary and I'll see you in a month.'

Morgan got herself out of the chair. She moved slowly and stared back into Chase's beautiful amber-flecked eyes. She seemed confused, the phone number he showed her, the way her gorgeous counselor was breaking rules for her, looking at her. She wished there was a mirror, as she knew her makeup had smeared, and she'd spent over an hour primping for her monthly meeting with him. Her legs felt weak and rubbery. 'I might not be here in a month,' she said, wondering if maybe he was interested in her. Because if he was, she'd do anything for him . . . absolutely anything.

There was a second and then third ring. 'I've got to take this call, Morgan . . . goodbye,' and he closed the door behind her.

He pressed the on button and heard Janice Fleet's voice. 'Are you alone?'

'I am now,' he said, looking out his single dirt-smeared window, which afforded a dreary view of the adjacent municipal garage.

'Did you get the cell back? Just tell me you did, because I'm having one hell of a day.'

'No, and you better sit down because it's about to get worse,' he said, wondering how she'd handle the news. 'It isn't just one of the regular phones that's missing. I think Bobby had one of the others.'

'What are you talking about?'

'The videophones . . . the ones we use with the girls.' He waited, while catching his reflection in the window, appreciating the way the three-hundred-dollar sweater showed off the V-shape of his torso. His exercise and diet regimen was a meticulously crafted balance of protein shakes, supplements, yoga, weights, and aerobics, giving him just the right amount of lean, defined muscle but not that bullish steroid look.

'How did that happen?'

'It happened,' he said, not wanting to deal with Janice's tirades and finger-pointing, while getting a sadistic thrill at the fear in her voice. 'Worst-case scenario, someone looks at a video of a naked girl, they won't know who she is and there's no audio.' He filled her in on the specifics, how Marky went to retrieve the phones only to find a couple of female social-worker types in the apartment. How one of them called out the name Jerod.

'Jerod who?'

'Crazy Jerod. A nut job who's been hanging around some of the kids in the family.'

'What does he look like?' she asked, her tone urgent.

Her questions took him off guard. Janice rarely wanted details about the disposable kids that Chase carefully culled as they aged out of the foster system. Young adults with no family, nowhere to go, just ripe for a caring adult to show them some attention, give them a safe place to live, money, clothes, and a job . . . of sorts. Marky, as his lieutenant, showed them how easy it was to blend in with the undergraduates in the big dormitories, setting them up with the right look and fake IDs. He'd teach them how to reel in the children of middle- and upper-class families, starting with a few free tastes, showing them how to snort dope and eventually shoot it, and in a matter of a few short weeks turning an experiment with drugs into an insatiable habit that could last – or destroy – a lifetime. 'Just some crazy kid who's been hanging out with the family, I saw him once or twice when he was still in the system.'

'What does he look like?' she repeated. 'White Rasta? Dirty blond?'

'Yes, thin, might be good looking if he ever got near a bar of soap.'

'What's his last name?' she asked.

'I think it's Blank,' he said, hearing the click of a keyboard over the phone.

'This is very bad.'

'What are you talking about?' he asked.

'Just listen, Chase,' she said, 'he barged into a meeting I was at this afternoon. He had a gun. Apparently the current head of the Forensic Evaluation Center – a Dr. Conyors, who's a royal pain in the ass, but too smart to mess with – is his shrink. I'd also be willing to bet she was one of the two women sniffing around those dead kids. He was rambling about people trying to kill him. We've got a major problem . . .' There was a pause. 'And possibly an opportunity. At least we know where he is, and I'm willing to bet he had those cell phones on him. There's no love lost between Dr. Conyors and me . . . If she's trying to set me up, which I wouldn't put past her, I swear she won't live to regret it.'

'How do we get them back?'

'We don't,' she said, 'you do, and do it tonight. You'll need a key card to get in . . . I know where I can get you one. And while you're at it, make sure that crazy Jerod never makes it to his next appointment. And if he's told that shrink anything at all, take care of her.'

SIX

B arrett ran her key card over her office door's electronic pad. She didn't hear the usual click and realized it was not latched. Her pulse quickened; something was wrong. She resisted the first rush of adrenalin as she turned the handle that should have been locked . . . had been locked, and now wasn't. She opened the door thinking of all the reasons. *Maybe the cleaning crew, maybe Marla came in early, maybe* . . . She stood unmoving in the open door. 'This can't be.' In shock, she surveyed her corner office, the early morning light leaving no doubt why the door was unlocked; someone had broken in and ransacked it. She stepped over the threshold, her senses like radar, was the perp still here? She listened intently, the hum of the air conditioner, the ding of the elevator and the doors opening from out in the hall and a buzzing from a poorly seated fluorescent bulb, but that was all. Moving silently, she swept through the space, her feet flat on the floor, her eyes taking in the busted locks on her filing cabinets and desk. Papers, reports, articles, and journals that had all been filed, shelved, or piled in tidy stacks by Marla were now spilled onto the floor. She flung open the door to the small closet and saw her just-in-case wardrobe of a go-to-court navy suit and workout clothes for kung-fu or a quick run tossed to the floor. Her heart skipped as she saw one of her sports bras plainly visible on top of the heap. She swallowed, not wanting to think about the hands that had touched it. What did they want? What were they looking for? Her eyes flew to the computer monitor; it was on. She always shut it down at the end of the day. She resisted the urge to check the history, realizing that maybe the perp had left prints. She circled behind her desk and into the tiny bathroom that was one of the perks of being the center's director. Her breast pump still sat on the metal shelf over the sink, but the medicine cabinet was open and the contents, all the personal things she didn't want in the open, from aspirin to tampons, had been spilled on the floor and into the sink. Back in the main office, her eye caught on the open door of the dorm-size refrigerator she kept under her desk. A white plastic bottle of breast milk that she'd forgotten to take home lay on the floor. She struggled to stay detached, this was a crime scene, and she knew the best course was to get out of there, call security . . . call Hobbs, but the thought of others going through her things, it felt dirty and frightening.

She startled at the sound of Marla coming into the outer office. She caught her secretary's expression – fear. 'Call security,' she said, 'tell them there's been a break-in.'

Marla nodded and backed away, her face trained on Barrett as she picked up the phone and dialed.

From behind her desk, Barrett tried to make sense of the avalanche of papers. She tried to push away the feelings of violation and of being watched. This was no random break-in. Marla's office hadn't been touched, there'd been no call in the night from security saying the Center had been broken into. Someone had deliberately come to her office and trashed it. *Why? What were they looking for?* Her gut twisted at a horrible thought. Not caring about contaminating potential evidence, she pulled open her smashed top right-hand drawer. Her hands flew inside. *I'd left it on top.* 'Where is it?'

'What?' Marla asked, standing on the other side of the door, looking in, her eyes wide beneath her dark bangs. Barrett sensed her fear, knowing it mirrored her own.

She dug through the drawer spilling papers and clips, her fingers desperate for the familiar feel of the framed photomontage her mother had made of Max. It included the recovery-room picture of her holding him, surrounded by a snapshot a week for his first eight weeks of life. Her mom had given it to her the morning she'd had to return to work from her maternity leave. She left it in the drawer, and would look at it countless times, of course it had been on top. And now . . . it was gone.

'What's missing?' Marla repeated. 'What did they take?'

Barrett flung open every drawer, a sick feel in her gut. 'It's got to be here.' She looked at Marla. 'They took Max's pictures. Why?' She stepped back, feeling lightheaded and numb. 'And why such a mess?' Clearly whoever did this was looking for something, and they wanted her to know they'd been there, been through her things, and knew she had a baby. She tried to piece it together, how someone could have gotten into her office; the only locks that hadn't been broken were the ones on her door and Marla's outer door. They'd gotten into Marla's office – assumed there was nothing there they wanted – and then into hers without any force – someone with either a key card or master key – but that was a short list.

A phone rang. Barrett startled and then searched over the chaos on her desk to find the buried phone. She picked up; it was Hobbs. His deep voice just what she needed.

'We still on for Croton?' he asked.

'Ed, someone broke into my office.'

'When?' his tone serious.

'Sometime overnight, they've torn it up pretty good; it had to have been an inside job. They must have had a passkey or a key card.'

'What's missing?'

'I can't tell. I'm freaking . . . the only thing I know is gone is Max's picture.'

'Are you sure?'

'Ed, I don't put out any personal photos in my office, but I've had his in my desk drawer . . . it's like . . . I just need to look at it.' She looked at Marla still in the door. 'Marla, this is Detective Hobbs, would you mind . . .'

'Of course not,' and she left, closing the door behind.

'Ed, what if this is Jimmy's doing? What if he knows about Max?'

'Don't go there, Barrett. Jimmy's locked away. There's no way he could know.'

'Yeah, but with his kind of money he's had people do his dirty work enough times before.'

'I'm not ruling it out, but step back and tell me what else is gone or disturbed in any way.'

'They've been on my computer. My files are password-protected, but . . .'

'I'm on my way. Try not to touch anything else.' And then he added, 'This could have to do with the kid?'

She first thought of Max, but then realized, 'Jerod? It's possible, I don't know.'

'It could be, but if it's an inside job, it's someone who didn't know you had him moved to Croton last night.'

'Right,' and holding the phone she looked up as her door banged open. She expected Marla, but it was Hugh Osborn in a dark suit. 'I got to go, Ed.'

'Dr. Conyors,' Hugh said, not acknowledging the wreck of her office. He held a Manila folder in one hand and a document that Barrett immediately recognized as his year-end evaluation in the other. 'This is unacceptable.' He waved the disputed report in the air. His fingers crumpled the pages. 'I will not let you put this in my file.'

'Hugh,' Barrett said, not about to get sucked in, 'I gave you ample warning about what was going in there. I told you the areas you needed to improve . . .'

'Unacceptable! I've worked for the State of New York for over fifteen years, and I have always received the highest marks on my evaluations. If you think you can slander my reputation this way, you've got another thing coming; this is libel! I am not going to stand by and let you do this.'

'That's fine, Hugh,' Barrett said, picturing what it would feel like to land a roundhouse kick on his perfectly combed head; if only he put half the time in his work that he did in being so immaculately groomed. 'You're a member of the union; bring it up with your delegate. There's a process for that. Other than that, what I put in there is accurate and stands. Now, I've got more important matters to deal with,' she said, opening her arms.

He blinked and finally took in the wreckage of her office. 'What happened?'

'Don't know yet,' she said, realizing that high up on her list of insiders who might have a grudge against her would be Hugh. 'Intend to find out . . . what time did you leave yesterday?'

'You think I had something to do with this?' his tone incredulous.

'Of course not, but maybe you saw something.'

His dark eyes scanned her office. 'I left the regular time, didn't see a thing.'

Barrett detected a rapid shift in his expression, it was hard to pin down, but he was worried. Stepping toward him and the open door. 'Looks like someone came after something, someone who knew where my office was, someone who had access to the building.'

As she advanced he stepped back. 'You certain you didn't see anyone,' she asked, 'or know anything?'

'Of course not.' He broke from her gaze. 'I have reports I need to finish.'

You lying, sneaky bastard, she thought, *you know something.* But then again, *He seems genuinely surprised by the break-in . . .* 'Yes,' she said, 'you sure do, and that's why you got the evaluation you did. You have a lot of overdue reports. And if you decide to push the grievance with the union – which is entirely your right – I have all the data I need to back up your evaluation. I could have made it much worse.'

'I'm not surprised someone did this,' he said maliciously, 'you can't treat people this way, and I know my rights; I am not going to let this go into my file. I refuse to sign it.'

'Fine.' She noted the flare of his nostrils and the clenching of his jaw. 'I'll make a notation that you refused to acknowledge receiving your evaluation. Some might call that insubordination. You can leave now,' she said, feeling a hair's breath from losing her cool, which was not an option and would only add fuel for whatever new grievance he'd bring. To try and get him out of there she walked past him, his fury palpable. In another setting she was certain he'd try to hit her. She went over to Marla. 'Did you get Jim?' she asked, referring to the Center's head of security. Her anger was boiling, and with her back turned, she heard Hugh storm out, almost slamming Marla's door in the process. She finally let out her breath.

'He's a piece of work,' Marla commented.

'That's for sure,' Barrett said, and then realized that in among the mess in her office were all the employee files, including Hugh's. *What if he'd come looking for it?*

'I don't trust him,' Marla said, as one by one she opened her desk drawers.

'Why?' Barrett asked, having learned over the years to pay attention to her normally mouse-quiet secretary.

'When you were on maternity leave,' Marla said, 'he wanted to use your office. Said he was the acting director and it would be the right thing to do. He got mad when you told me to tell him no, and that he could just use his own office.'

'What did he do?' Barrett asked.

'Kind of like now, yelled at me, told me I was incompetent, and that if he were director, he'd have to get a different assistant.' She looked up at Barrett.

'I'm sorry,' Barrett said, 'I wish you'd told me he'd been such an ass.'

'I've been through worse,' Marla said, with a shy smile. 'But there was other stuff, like he was doing an evaluation on a patient you'd seen before and he wanted me to cut entire pages from one of your reports and paste them into his. I told him I'd have to check with you first; he didn't like that, told me I was insubordinate. Or when he'd send out letters, he'd want me to use director under his name. I told him that was inaccurate, that he was the acting director. It was lots of little stuff like that; he doesn't like to be told no.'

'Why didn't you tell me any of this before?' Barrett asked.

'I should have,' Marla admitted, 'but men like that scare the hell out of me. He even looks a little bit like my ex. He sure acts like him.'

Barrett didn't press, Marla's past history was a painful one, and few other than she and George Houssman knew the details, that over twenty years ago Marla, in the midst of a psychotic depression, had set her home on fire intending to end both her life and that of her brutally sadistic husband. She'd survived; he hadn't. She'd ended up being sent to a forensic hospital, and through a release program had come to work as George Houssman's secretary at the Center over a decade ago. 'If he does anything in the future to upset you,' Barrett said, 'let me know right away.'

'I will,' Marla said.

'Good, because between me and you, I don't trust him.'

'Do you think he had something to do with the break-in?'

At which point Jim Cray – the ex-marine head of security – popped his shaved head in the open door. 'What happened?' he asked, and then looked past the two women into Barrett's office. 'You have got to be kidding!'

SEVEN

Jerod stared out the window of his locked cell-like room at a sweeping expanse of green lawns and fruit trees shedding the last of their vivid pink and white flowers. Further in the distance he caught the sparkle of the Hudson as it snaked its way through the landscape. The room was sparse, a platform bed and thin mattress, a brown metal chair bolted to the floor and a wood dresser carved with layers of graffiti from past residents – mostly names and dates, etched with teeth and fingernails. In the back, behind a floor-to-ceiling oak partition, was an uncovered toilet and small sink with no mirror. There were no hooks or knobs on the dresser and no closet. Even the sink had squat rounded handles and a retracted faucet, just in case anyone was looking for a place to attach a noose, or do some other mischief.

Early last night he was told he was being transferred to Croton Forensic. The nurse had given him more of the pills to put under his tongue, and the cramping and shakes and waves of sweats and chills had receded. Physically, he was better, but the pictures in his head and the ache in his chest were unbearable. He saw Bobby and Ashley, just lying there, not moving. He squeezed his eyes shut as he remembered the feel of putting his mouth against hers and then his, trying to give them CPR, pounding on their chests, begging them to please wake up, to not be dead. He thought of Carly – her wild brown hair and soft smiling eyes – and felt a gripping fear like someone had grabbed him around the throat and was squeezing off his air. 'They're going to kill you,' a familiar voice whispered over his right shoulder. When he'd first heard it he was only twelve. He'd assumed that everyone heard voices, a belief that was quickly shot down when he'd told his mother and she'd dragged him to the emergency room and from there to a locked psychiatric ward. It had started as just a grumble, or at times like static on the radio, but then it had started to speak, most of the time just commenting, 'Jerod, brush your teeth,' or 'Jerod, wear the blue shirt.' But sometimes, like now, the grumbling male voice tortured him. 'They're coming to get you. They killed Bobby, they killed Ashley. Carly *is dead. Kill yourself. Kill yourself. Do it now. Put the sheet around your neck, kill yourself. Do it now. Do it now.*'

He heard steps from down the hall and then a key in the steel door. He looked up and saw Dr. Conyors; she was in a gray suit and her pretty face looked angry. He could tell she was mad at him – people often were. He knew that he'd scared her yesterday and he was sorry for that, but she didn't understand, how could she? Behind her was a tall man with a half-scarred face dressed in a brown suit and a male nurse in a short white lab coat carrying a maroon plastic binder with *J. Blank* written on the side.

'Good morning, Jerod,' Dr. Conyors said. 'Are you feeling any better?'

'Yes,' he said.

'I've brought my friend Detective Ed Hobbs of the NYPD today, do you mind if he comes in?'

Jerod looked at her stern expression, and then at the tall detective in the dark-brown suit with the burned face, his eyes seemed kind.

'Sure. I mean it's OK.'

'Any muscle aches?' she asked, as they moved into his room. She took the single bolted-down chair and Detective Hobbs turned his back to the room and stared out at the magnificent late spring morning on the other side. The nurse hung back by the door, the chart open in his hands, apparently waiting for something.

Jerod tried to think, he was sore, but not as bad. 'A little.'

Dr. Conyors shot questions at him, briefly waiting for his answers. 'Any runny nose, tearfulness, muscle cramps, sweats, nausea, diarrhea, chills, anxiety, restlessness . . .' When she'd finished she took the chart from the nurse and wrote a few lines. 'Give him eight milligrams three times a day, that should cover it.'

Jerod wondered at her coldness, it made him feel small and like he'd done something to hurt her. The voice whispered, '*Idiot, idiot, idiot.*' She'd been frustrated with him in the past, always wanting him to take the medicines that made him feel drugged and dead inside. At one point she'd pleaded with him to stop smoking pot, told him it was only making the voices worse. He'd kind of followed her directions; problem was he went from pot to dope, and at least when he'd first started, it was the most wonderful feeling he could have imagined. Those first hits of snorted dope, and the first few times he'd shot it into a vein, the voice suddenly silent and a sense of unimaginable peace and happiness, as though nothing in the world was wrong, and that he was perfectly good, perfectly happy. He waited as she sent the nurse away.

'I'm glad you feel better,' she said.

Jerod sat on the edge of the bed and watched her remove a small tape recorder from her pocket. She turned it on, a red dot blinked and then stayed lit.

'Jerod, I have to tape today's interview. You need to know that it could be used as evidence, and possibly as evidence in a case where you are the defendant. Do you understand? What you say today is not covered under the usual rules of doctor–patient confidentiality. What you say could be used to incriminate you. Do you understand?'

'Yes . . . and no,' he said, wishing she'd at least crack a smile.

She looked at him. 'What do you mean?'

'Am I charged with something? I didn't hurt them. I just found them like that. I would never hurt them.' The tears were close, and not from the dope sickness. He saw Bobby's quirky half smile, Ashley's pretty hair, and Carly . . . her smell, the feel of her next to him in bed.

'I believe you, but you did come into my office with a loaded gun; there are probably going to be charges.'

'I'm sorry,' he said, 'I didn't know where else to go. I'm sorry I got you involved.'

'It's done,' she said curtly. 'Who were they?'

'Bobby and Ashley,' he replied, *please don't be angry with me*.

'Do you know their last names?' the detective asked, still staring out the window, keeping his ruined face hidden.

'Let me think.' His stomach was quiet, and the cramps had gone. He'd agreed to take a small dose of the antipsychotic medication she always pushed on him, it was meant to stop the voice. He never quite understood what she had against the voice, but it wasn't there right now, maybe just a little noise in the background. 'Bobby Dix, and Ashley . . . she was a student and lived in the dorm on 13th Street. She wanted to be a fashion designer. She made pretty things. She sewed me a shirt, no one has ever done that for me . . . and for Christmas she made us all matching scarves . . . I wish I had mine.' He remembered the four of them last winter bopping through the streets of the East

Village, hopping in and out of the shops, buying each other ridiculous little presents like the vintage doll with the hair that could be long or short that Carly had wanted, said she'd had one as a little girl.

'Was Bobby a student too?'

He looked down at the floor, remembering that doll and that time, or just a couple weeks back when Carly had kissed him and taken him to her bed in the room next to Bobby's. Tears slid down, and there was pain in his chest, like someone squeezing the life out of him. *How could something hurt so much*, he wondered, *when there's nothing broken or cut?*

Barrett's train of questioning was broken by the metallic ring of a cell phone; it came from Hobbs's direction. 'How the hell did they let you bring that in here? That should have been checked at security.'

'I told them I needed it and flashed my shield,' he replied, looking at the caller ID and then answering the phone. 'Hey, Bryan, what's up?'

She waited, and watched Jerod trying to read the shifting expressions on his face. Caught in a shaft of light he appeared even younger than twenty-two, something in his face like a tortured angel. She imagined him as a boy and wondered what it must have been like when he had his first psychotic break at twelve and his parents, overwhelmed by the needs of their crazy son, had abandoned him. He was crying now. *Is it an act?* She reached into her pocket and pulled out the small packet of tissues she always carried; she handed them to him.

'What are you thinking about?' she asked, figuring it would be rude to try and listen in to Ed's conversation with his partner, Detective Cassidy.

'They're all gone.'

'Who?'

'My friends, Bobby, Ashley . . . Carly. Carly . . . she was kind of my girlfriend; I haven't seen her in over a week. I miss her. I know something happened to her. Something bad.'

'Tell me about Carly.' She noted the depth of his anguish, the way his face contorted from the combination of physical pain, withdrawal and grief. She tried to throw herself into the interview, finding the rhythm, but her thoughts kept shifting back to her office, and to the long car ride down with Hobbs, as they worked through all possibilities.

'She's really pretty and kind, and when I'm with her she makes me feel like there's nothing wrong with me. She once told me that lots of people hear voices.'

'That's true,' Barrett said.

'I know, but coming from her it made it OK. Coming from you, it's like a doctor telling you that lots of people have brain tumors.' He tried to smile, but it was more of a grimace. 'The four of us would hang out, get high, that place where Bobby and Ashley were is where we lived, except Ashley would go back to the dorm some nights. She made all the pillows and curtains. It was like a home . . . a family.'

'When did you start to shoot heroin, Jerod?'

'Few months,' he said. 'I liked it, especially at first. It made me feel like everything was OK, where I'm OK and nothing's wrong and nothing can hurt me.' He shrugged. 'All those pills you give me . . . none of them make me feel that good. Like I'm at peace.'

'Who gave it to you?'

He looked at the recorder, and then at Ed, still talking on his cell, and shook his head no.

'Were you dealing?'

He wouldn't answer, and she saw a new emotion cross his face – fear. *What do you know that you're not telling?* 'So it was the four of you living in that apartment. Anyone else?'

'I can't,' he said.

'Why not, Jerod? Why can't you tell me these things?'

His blue eyes, moist with tears, met hers. 'It's not safe, Dr. Conyors. Look what happened, they're all gone. I don't want anyone else to get hurt, or to disappear . . . I don't want you to get hurt. You should have let me shoot myself. I shouldn't have dragged you into this. You've been good to me; I shouldn't have called you.'

What aren't you saying? she wondered again, at the same time noticing that the Jerod sitting in front of her, despite his intense emotional state, seemed more rational than the psychotic young man she'd evaluated several times since his release four years ago from his last DFYS group home.

Hobbs clicked his phone off and put it in his pocket. He'd listened to their conversation. 'Why do you think someone would hurt Dr. Conyors?' he asked. 'Jerod, if you know anything, you need to tell us.'

Jerod shook his head, tight-lipped.

Frustrated, Hobbs shot Barrett a look and then pulled a sealed plastic bag out of an inside jacket pocket. In happier times Barrett had kidded Hobbs about his custom-made suits from an 8th Avenue tailor who worked almost exclusively with cops. His jackets had several concealed pockets, side vents for easy access to his gun and handcuffs, and a bit of added roominess in the shoulders and underarms to give him maximum flexibility and to conceal his holster. He opened the bag and held a cell – one of the two that had been in Jerod's possession.

'Do you recognize this?' Hobbs asked.

Jerod nodded.

'Good, there's a video file on here and I want you to tell me if you recognize the girl.'

Jerod said nothing as Hobbs pulled up the file and held the phone a few inches from his face.

Jerod's eyes widened and then squeezed shut; he pushed back on the bed. His mouth opened as though he might scream, but instead what came out was a strangled sound, as though in tremendous pain. 'No!'

'Who is she?' Hobbs gently asked.

'Carly! That's Carly. Is she alive?' He looked up at Hobbs, and through the tears he seemed to feel some new emotion . . . hope. 'Is she breathing?' He scrambled forward and stared at the tiny screen in Hobbs's hand. 'I can't see if she's breathing. Why isn't she moving? Where is she? Please tell me she's OK.'

'I don't know,' Hobbs said. 'She looks drugged, and on a bigger screen you can tell that she's alive.'

Jerod relaxed slightly and sat back wiping his nose with the back of his hand, his eyes on Hobbs. 'Who would do that to her? Who would film somebody who's passed out? Why did they take her clothes off? Why would they do that?'

'I don't know,' Hobbs said. 'But we need to find out. That phone call was my partner. They've made a positive ID on your two friends, Bobby Dix and Ashley Kane. I know that you're frightened, and I know that you're in pain, but we need your help. We need to know where you and your friends were getting dope.'

He shook his head again. 'I can't.'

Barrett's frustration bubbled over, 'Why, Jerod? Someone intentionally overdosed your friends, why won't you help us?'

He looked away from Barrett and back to the cell phone in Hobbs's hand that had the video of Carly. 'I can't,' and he stared down at the speckled gray linoleum floor.

'Jerod,' Hobbs said, his voice insistent. 'Jerod, look at me.'

He wouldn't.

'Jerod, we want to help you. We can help you find your girl-friend.'

He shuddered, and looked at Hobbs. 'Don't let anyone know you have that.'

Barrett felt as if ice had just frozen in her veins. *So that is what they were looking for.* She struggled to keep the mounting anger and fear from her voice. 'Jerod, you called me yesterday to that building. What was it you wanted me to do? Why won't you let us help?' and felt like adding, *And what the hell have you pulled me into?*

The side of his mouth twitched. 'I wanted you to save them. I thought you could save them.' His voice trailed. 'But they were already dead. She might not be.'

For another forty-five minutes Barrett and Hobbs chipped away at Jerod, but he was too frightened. 'Please stop,' he begged, covering his head in his hands and retreating to a corner of his bed.

Barrett looked at Hobbs, shook her head and turned off the recorder. *He's shut down*, she thought, and knew they would get no new information.

As they left his room and headed down the long door-lined corridor, Barrett sensed the quiet weirdness that had grown between her and Hobbs. The car ride from Manhattan to Croton in his unmarked Crown Vic had been focused on the break-in, but under that, there was so much unsaid. She thought back through the near-fruitless interview with Jerod; while he was clearly in agony, she'd never seen him look so . . . sane. She listened to their footsteps, his rubber-soled Oxfords and her walking shoes landing on ancient waxed linoleum. 'There wasn't much in that,' she commented.

'No,' he agreed, leaving it with the one syllable.

'Jerod believes the overdose was no accident,' she added, hoping to spark some normal give and take of human interaction.

'Agreed,' and they came to the outer locked door, 'we'll have to wait for the toxicology reports, and even then they might not be conclusive.'

Barrett swiped her ID across the electric eye and punched in her eight-digit access code. It clicked and Hobbs pushed it open, letting them into the manned checkpoint, where all visitors and staff needed to pass on their way in and out of the high-security hospital for the criminally insane. Behind the counter sat two guards, who passed them their belongings. Barrett grabbed her cell, pager, and large black shoulder bag, while Hobbs pocketed his keys and filled out the paperwork for his firearm, a Detective Glock Model 19.

A red light flashed on her phone and her beeper was chirping at one-second intervals. She'd missed two calls, and the LED readout on her beeper displayed one of the same numbers – an extension at the Forensic Center. The other call was from her mother, at her condo taking care of Max. Like gas on a burning ember, her anxiety spiked. She grabbed the handrail and felt her heart pound in her chest. Cruel thoughts slammed through her mind. *Max is sick. Something's wrong with Max.* She flashed on the stolen picture, had someone done something to him – her mind flew into catastrophe mode – *Someone's taken him.*

'You OK?' Ed asked.

'Not really,' she said as she pressed the redial button.

'You're having a panic attack, aren't you?'

'It'll pass.' She tried to keep her breathing in control, feeling like she might black out, as she mashed the phone to her ear.

'I thought those had stopped.'

'Well, they're back,' and wishing this weren't the topic that led Ed into talking with her she heard the line click and her mother's voice.

'Barrett?'

'What's wrong?' Barrett asked.

'Sweet Jesus,' her mother responded, 'I was just calling to see if you'd be home on time. I can't be late again for work.'

'Sorry,' Barrett said, thinking about George's suggestion that maybe she should go on meds to get her anxiety under control. 'So everything's OK . . . with Max?'

'Of course, my little angel just got changed, and now he's taking a nap. We had a lovely walk in the park, I charged two hundred dollars in groceries on your card and also found the most beautiful fire-engine-red spice rack at William Sonoma. It matches the blender you're going to be giving me. So I'll expect you no later than . . . six?'

'Yes, I promise.'

'Thank you, sweetie, I love you.'

'Love you too, Mom.' She looked at Hobbs, who'd clearly been listening in. 'I think I'm losing it.'

'Naah, it's just first-time parent stuff. I remember after we had Katie, Margaret wouldn't leave her with a babysitter for the first ten months. This'll pass.'

'I hope you're right, and how are the girls?'

'Good,' he said, 'and polar opposites. Katie just wants to play sports and Becky has decided she wants to be a princess when she grows up. It makes their weekends with me interesting – last one was a Yankees game on Saturday followed by a trip to this ridiculously expensive doll store in midtown on Sunday.'

Barrett's pager rang. 'Crap!' She looked at the number, a forensic center extension, and not one she recognized. But the voice that picked up was unmistakable – Jim Cray.

'Dr. Conyors,' he said, 'I wanted to give you an update. I've pulled the security tapes from last night and got in a quick and dirty first round with the cleaning crew.'

'And?'

'You're not going to like this. The only possible witness is a woman with Down's who according to her supervisor – and don't shoot the messenger – "saw a pretty man last night".'

'Bring her in,' Barrett said, 'maybe there's something on the tapes and she'll be able to ID him.'

'Maybe,' he said, his tone doubtful, 'her supervisor says she's a sweet girl and a hard worker, but beyond that we won't get much. And the tapes don't cover your floor, just the front door and observation unit.'

'What about the keypads? Do they have a history? Can we see whose card it was?'

'We could if we had a decent system, but the one that got installed doesn't have a retrievable history.'

'If anything turns up, call me right away.'

'You got it, Doc. Your detective friend called in a crime-scene squad, and they're dusting for prints, but considering how many people have been in and out of your office . . .'

'What about Marla, has she been able to identify anything missing?'

'No, so far it's just your pictures. Either they didn't take anything else, or it's something you and she wouldn't miss. But I'll let you know the minute we get something better.'

She hung up and just stared at her cell.

'What?' Hobbs asked.

She put a hand to her brow, 'I'm so creeped out,' thinking about Max's pictures. 'Why would someone take his pictures and nothing else? None of the usual stuff is gone. The computer, printers, anything with value is still there.'

'They tore the place apart and took the most personal thing they could find,' he said. 'I think it was a message, and I also think they didn't get what they were after . . . Jerod's phones.'

'But how would someone even know I had them?'

'A lot of people know,' he said, ticking off all the possibles. 'The security guards and the cops who were involved in yesterday's incident. Then you've got a couple commissioners in your office and this other doc who wants your job, then we've got Marla, anyone involved with his care on your observation unit yesterday and anyone he might have told. It's quite a list. We can narrow it down some, because it looks like they had an access card, but even there, where there's a will . . .'

'So you do think it has to do with Jerod.'

'Yup,' Hobbs said, 'we're mucking in something ugly, drugs, dead teens, a naked girl in a video . . . who's gone missing . . .' His cell rang. He pulled it off his belt. 'Bryan again,' and he pressed on.

Barrett listened in, feeling as though she were being pulled in too many directions. But the worst part was that this had to be an inside job, someone was watching.

'We're at Croton,' Hobbs said, 'maybe thirty minutes from there. I'm with Dr. Conyors. Hold on.' He turned to her. 'Barrett, we're close to the home of the girl you found . . . Ashley Kane. Bryan was wondering if I'd do the "Your kid is dead and would you mind coming down to the morgue, just to be sure?" visit. Your call. I know you want to get back and see what's going on at the center . . .'

'Sure,' she said, wanting any opportunity that might shed some light on this mess. Plus, since seeing Ed for the first time in months, there was no denying it felt good to be with him. She snuck a glance in his direction, the scarred side of his face toward her. She felt a sudden urge to touch it. *What the hell are you thinking?* she thought, and stared at the floor.

'You got it, Bryan . . . No, I have a set of the pictures. Just give me the address and number, and let them know we're on the way.'

EIGHT

With his eyes on the road, Hobbs asked, 'You're pretty freaked, aren't you?'

Barrett again snuck a glance at his damaged face, the scars much less red than the last time she saw him, before Max's birth. 'I hate this feeling that someone's been in my stuff, looking at things, and not knowing what it is they're after – why take the montage? It's ripping me apart, and maybe that's what they want, like they know my most vulnerable point. I hate this.'

'So who has a grudge?'

'Take a number. My boss can't stand me, I've got Dr. Hugh Osborn filing a hostile-workplace grievance against me, and I'd be willing to bet that Lydia – the social worker that found those dead kids with me yesterday – will bring up some kind of hazardous-duty shit.'

'Being the boss sucks,' he commented and then grew quiet.

'Hobbs,' she finally said, 'we need to talk.'

'Listening,' he said, his jaw tight.

'I'm sorry,' she said, not quite certain where this would go, 'I've been a shitty friend.'

'No argument there,' he agreed.

'You're not going to make this easy, are you?'

'I'm not going to be a little girl about it,' he said, 'but after your "can't we just be friends" speech I thought we were good. And then I don't hear from you for what . . . six months.'

'I didn't want to make it worse for you.'

He turned and looked at her, the good side of his mouth twisting up in a half smile. 'My, but we are full of ourselves.' He focused on the road. 'Here's the deal, Barrett, my timing was for shit. You'd just lost your husband and were pregnant with a baby you didn't know if you were going to keep or not, and suddenly I decide it's time to tell you . . . oh crap. I'd had a thing for you for a long time, but when Ralph was alive and we were both married, I wouldn't think about it. Then Margaret dumps me, Ralph . . . well, that was awful, and not something I would ever have wanted' – referring to the hit-and-run murder of her husband. 'Truth is I'm glad I told you how I felt. Too bad you didn't feel the same; it happens. I'm not going to chase after someone who's not interested, and who I always liked too much as a friend to screw that up. And, so you don't have to worry about any more awkward declarations, I'll have you know that I started seeing somebody a couple months back.'

Barrett felt a lump in her throat, glad that Hobbs was trying to clear the air, but surprised . . . and bothered by that last piece of news. 'Is it serious?' she asked, pretending to be fascinated by the passing scenery on the Saw Mill Parkway.

'Hard to say,' he commented, 'we have a good time.'

'That's nice,' she said. 'I've missed you, Ed. But I thought that if I called you . . .'

'I'd turn into a psycho stalker.'

'That's not what I was going to say.' She glanced at him.

'But it is what you were thinking.' He caught her gaze, smiled and looked back at the road.

'Hey, you got to consider my history,' she said, glad the mood had lightened, *and I should be happy he's seeing someone.*

'Great, so now you're comparing me with Jimmy Martin.'

Barrett froze at the name . . . The thought that flew to her brain, *Speak of the devil and he will appear.* 'Don't even say that as a joke.'

'Sorry, it's just that we used to be able to talk about anything. I've missed that, and now I feel like I got to be careful. I want us to get back to the way we were, and I don't know if it's possible.'

He turned off the Saw Mill and negotiated through the pricey community of Katonah. He checked the address and turned down a road where most of the houses couldn't be seen, only guessed at behind high well-manicured boxwood and evergreen hedges, many with iron gates across winding drives. 'Look for thirty-two,' he said.

Barrett scanned her surroundings as Hobbs slowed to a crawl. 'They don't seem to have any mailboxes visible from the road. I didn't think that was allowed. How the hell does the mailman know?'

'I think,' he said, 'this is the kind of neighborhood that if you don't know the number, you don't belong here.'

'There's twenty-four,' she said, seeing a modest but beautifully maintained white clapboard Victorian farmhouse set close to the road.

'Good, so I'm guessing same side of the street, four further along.' He stopped outside a gated drive, opened his window, and pressed a button on the intercom.

Barrett tried to calm her jitters, the break-in, the missing pictures of Max, and the mention of Jimmy Martin in the same conversation sent a lot of horrible 'what if' scenarios skidding through her brain. *What if he had someone break into my office? What if he knows he's Max's father?* Jimmy Martin, born into a family of great wealth and insanity, had been obsessed with her, had stalked her and killed her husband. Now he was locked away in a forensic hospital, she tried – daily – to forget his existence and how close he'd come to killing both her and her sister. But he'd been locked away before, and with his kind of money it wasn't hard to find people on the outside who'd do his bidding. *What if it was him?*

The white-painted iron gate opened. 'This is never easy,' Hobbs said, as the wheels crunched over the white crushed-shell drive.

With a shock, Barrett realized that while she'd agreed to come along, she'd now become involved in a parent's worst nightmare.

As if reading her thoughts, Hobbs said, 'You don't have to come in.'

'It's OK,' she said, and a stunning white stucco structure appeared before them. It was all gentle curves and expanses of glass, an architect's jewel set in a mounting of specimen evergreens in shapes and colors Barrett had never seen before. In front of those was a sea of deep purple-black iris in full bloom. Beyond the house she caught a glimpse of the Hudson River valley, and understood the reason for the long drive; the view was spectacular. At another time she would have liked to just stand there and take it in, but now there was an open door and a woman in her early forties with short brown hair, jeans, a button-down blue-plaid shirt, and dark-green gardening clogs. She stared at the two of them, seemingly frozen in place.

'Mrs. Kane?' Hobbs asked.

'Yes, I'm Marion Kane.'

'I'm Detective Hobbs with the NYPD and this is Dr. Barrett Conyors, my associate.'

Before he could say more, Mrs. Kane looked him in the eye, she held herself rigid and asked, 'It's Ashley isn't it?'

'Yes.'

'Is she dead?'

'I believe so.' Hobbs said simply, 'I need to show you a photograph. May we come in?'

'Of course.' She looked back into the shadowy house, and appeared to struggle with some kind of decision. 'Would it be OK if we stayed outside?' she asked. 'I was working in the back, I find gardening is the only thing that can take my mind off . . .'

'That's fine,' Hobbs said.

Marion Kane yelled into the open front door. 'John, you need to come out, the police are here. I'm taking them around back . . . you need to join us.'

'Your husband?' Hobbs asked.

'Yes.' She led them down a bluestone walk that brought the view into full sight.

Despite the gloom of their task, Barrett nearly gasped at the gorgeous setting, the sun, the smell of the fresh-cut lawn, a breeze off the distant river. She looked at the house and saw that the entire back was a wall of glass, three stories high. It was the kind of house featured in high-end architecture magazines. It didn't fit with that girl dead in a top-floor walk-up of a Lower East Side tenement. The image of finding her, of placing her fingers against the still-warm flesh, and realizing that this was the girl's home, her mother – it was too real.

Marion Kane led them onto an expansive deck that overlooked the valley. There were several sets of wrought-iron tables and chairs with folded-down blue-and-white-striped umbrellas. Next to one of the tables was a green plastic gardener's pail with a pair of leather work gloves placed on top. 'My husband should be out soon.' She glanced at the French doors, and then sat.

Hobbs pulled out a stiff Manila folder and looked through its contents. He selected a single snapshot and put it on the table in front of Marion Kane. It was a close-up of the dead girl's face shot at the scene.

Marion stared at the image. A strand of brown hair, gray at the roots, fell across her forehead. To Barrett it seemed as though the woman was forcing herself to look, to be certain, to have no doubt.

'Yes,' Marion said in a dull voice, 'that's her.'

They turned at the sound of a door opening. 'Shit.' A middle-aged, thin man with military style salt-and-pepper hair, dressed in a navy suit, white shirt, and no tie was shaking his fingers after having spilled his amber-colored drink on the French doors. He wiped his hand on his pants and squinted against the sun; he walked toward them. 'I'm John Kane,' he said, not sitting, not extending his hand.

From across the table, Barrett smelled Scotch, good stuff that carried the whiff of peat and oak.

Wordlessly, Marion stood, picked up the photo and held it in front of her husband.

He shook his head and stumbled back. Hobbs reached over and grabbed him by the arm; the mostly empty glass tumbled to the deck but didn't break. Barrett stood and helped John Kane into a chair. She looked at the spilled alcohol as it glinted in the sun. *A drink wouldn't be so bad*, she mused.

'We saw this coming,' Marion said, sitting next to her husband and putting a hand on his right shoulder. In her other she held the eight-by-ten photo. 'I had just hoped . . .' Her words trailed.

'She said she wanted to go into rehab . . . again,' John said. 'Or am I jumping to a conclusion. It was an overdose, wasn't it?'

'Yes,' Hobbs said, 'but some things make it suspicious.'

'It was that boy,' he said, his mouth twisted.

'Which boy?' Hobbs prompted.

John Kane's eyes teared, he looked at the tumbler lying on the deck. He got out of his chair, his gait unsteady. 'Marion, you tell them. I need a drink. Anyone else?' He picked up the glass and without waiting for anyone to respond headed back indoors.

Marion watched her husband's retreat. 'He's not always like this, at least not this early in the day.'

'Mrs. Kane,' Hobbs said, 'could you tell us about your daughter, her friends, who she hung out with, what you know about her drug use.'

Marion Kane looked at Hobbs and then at Barrett. 'She was a beautiful girl, and an "A" student up until her junior year. She had it all, looks, talent, lots of friends. She wanted to be a designer and have her own fashion line.'

'What happened in her junior year?' Barrett asked.

'Drugs,' Marion said. 'At first I didn't know why she was acting so strange. Not her usual self. She used to be so happy, always doing extra things at school – designing costumes for the drama club or making decorations for dances. Junior year that all changed. I could almost point to the day, suddenly she wouldn't talk to us, stayed up in her room, on the Internet with her friends, doing God knows what. I'd try to check the history on her computer, but it was mostly emails and instant messages to her friends. It was our cleaning woman who found it. When she showed me, at first I didn't understand what I was looking at. I mean, when I was in college I smoked some pot, who didn't? Even tried uppers a few times when I had to cram for a test, or to see if I could lose weight. But this was . . . it was alien, it didn't belong. It was so ugly and what was it doing in Ashley's room, hidden inside her dresser?'

'What was it?' Barrett asked, noting how Marion had trouble looking at Hobbs, and wondered if it was because he was a cop, or was it his scars.

'It was an old cigar box, just like the ones she used as sewing boxes, only it had needles, drugs in plastic bags, a lighter . . . It looked dirty. I mean I'd always prepared myself for the drug talk with my girls; I thought we had one of those healthy open relationships, the kind I'd wanted with my own mother. But here I was staring at something like on a TV show. My sixteen-year-old little girl was shooting drugs. How could I not know? And where the hell would she get them?' Her jaw clenched. 'It's not like we live in the city. I mean, my God, this is one of the most expensive communities in the state.'

'How did you handle it?' Barrett asked.

'I told John, of course, and he handled it . . . well, in hind-sight, I don't know. He exploded and when she got home from school he was furious. Didn't let her talk, just yelled at her. I tried to step in, but in some ways I agreed. How could she do this to herself? To us? We ended up calling a friend of the family who's a psychiatrist and she helped us locate a facility in Connecticut, which would take her right away. She didn't want to go. We forced her. She was furious, screaming at me, screaming at John. She said horrible things. It was like watching *The Exorcist*. She seemed possessed; this was not my daughter. Even her face – she was vicious. She called her father an alcoholic, which made him furious. It's a miracle we didn't have an accident on the way. They kept her for four weeks. The first week she refused to see us or talk to us. They explained that she was going through a detox and was pretty miserable. When she finally

let us visit, she was exhausted, but at least she looked like my
daughter. She apologized for some of what she'd said.' Marion
bit her lip and looked at the photo again. 'She looks like she's
sleeping.'

'Mrs. Kane,' Hobbs said, 'your husband mentioned some
boy . . .'

'I'm sorry, it's just everything's so strange. I don't know how
I'm supposed to react. I feel numb. They don't prepare you for
this, for having a child who's a . . . junkie. One of Ashley's
doctors that first time sat us down and told us horrible things.
How many kids – good kids, from good families – die each year
from heroin, all of the diseases that go with it. They tested her
for AIDS and hepatitis.' Marion glanced at Barrett. 'When she
got out of that place, I swore that it would never happen again;
I wouldn't let her out of my sight. I searched her room when
she was at school, insisted she give me the passwords for her
MySpace and Facebook pages. I needed to know where she was
all the time, who she was with; I didn't let up. I couldn't stop
myself, but somehow, just a couple months later, the changes
came back. She withdrew, lost weight, her eyes were funny sometimes . . . So back to Connecticut for another month. I was furious,
but when she got out she promised to stay clean. And for the
rest of the year and through graduation she was herself again.
But this is where we made our big mistake. She'd applied and
gotten accepted to half a dozen design schools. Her first choice
was the Fashion Institute in Manhattan; it was her dream.
We figured that she'd been off drugs for over a year, and that
maybe she was done with it – like some kind of phase.' Marion
shook her head. 'It happened so fast. She made it through her
first semester, was excited, sewing up a storm, loving her classes;
it was everything that she'd wanted. At Christmas it was like old
times. She made me the most beautiful green-silk dress and gave
her sister an outrageous scarf, all covered with feathers and . . .
it was just wonderful. But a month later I knew something was
wrong. She sounded tired and the spark was gone. I asked her
point-blank if she was using drugs . . . I couldn't even bring
myself to say the word heroin. She denied it, said she just had
a lot of projects to finish and hadn't been sleeping well. I didn't
believe her and drove in. She was furious and told me that I
didn't trust her, which was the truth. I tried to reason with her
and she screamed at me. Told me she was eighteen, that it was

her life, and that I couldn't drag her off to the hospital anymore.' She looked at Barrett. 'It was the most helpless feeling. I called her dean, the dorm manager. They all told me that there was nothing that could be done unless she was in imminent danger of hurting herself, and that without hard proof that she was using they couldn't search her room.'

'That must have been awful,' Barrett said.

'I called every day. Sometimes she wouldn't even pick up. When she did she didn't say much. I told her I knew she was using. I let her know that I loved her and that whenever she wanted to get treatment I'd help her.' Tears slid down Marion's face. 'I knew something was going to happen. Every time the phone rang my heart jumped, wondering if this was going to be the bad news. And then two weeks ago, we got a call . . . it was three in the morning. She'd been arrested. She was crying and begging us to come to the police station and pick her up.'

From behind them, John Kane had reappeared. His gait was unsteady as he crossed the deck and joined them drink in hand.

Marion looked at her husband, and then at the two-thirds-full tumbler of Scotch. 'I was telling them about Ashley's arrest,' she said.

'We should have left them there,' he responded. 'Might have done some good.'

'Them?' Hobbs asked.

'The boy,' John Kane said, his vowels starting to slur. 'The one who was feeding her dope,' he said. 'Bobby Dix. I bailed out Bobby Dix and my daughter.'

Marion cut in. 'They'd been arrested for possession. The officer who was handling the case said that he could have upped it to possession with intent to sell, but because it was the first arrest for both of them, and because I told him that I'd get her into a treatment program, he'd go with the lesser charge. When I saw her in that cell, she looked like a junkie. She'd lost weight, you could see the bones in her face, and her eyes were like glass . . . empty. She begged me to get her out, and her boyfriend . . . Bobby. She'd never mentioned him before. She said she wouldn't leave without him.'

Hobbs pulled out his packet of photos and placed a second one in front of John and Marion. 'Is that him?'

'He's dead too?' Marion asked. 'They were together?'

'Yes,' Barrett said, not wanting to see the picture, 'they were found yesterday morning.'

John stared at Bobby's image and then at the one of his daughter. His eyes teared up again.

'What happened after you bailed them out?' Hobbs asked.

John choked and started to cough.

'She'd lied to us,' Marion said, watching her husband swig back his drink. 'She'd promised that she'd go into a program. As soon as we left the precinct that changed to, "I couldn't possibly go into a program until the summer." Nothing would make her change her mind. John got angry, she started screaming in the middle of the street – it was horrible – and that's the last time we saw her. She grabbed Bobby by the hand and they walked away.'

'Do you know anything about him?' Hobbs asked.

'Just what she told us, which could have been lies. She said they'd been going out for four months. He was polite, good-looking, and he seemed embarrassed at how angry she got. He even tried to calm her down when she started to yell at us. I assumed he was a student like she was. I remember wondering why he hadn't called his parents to get him. I didn't want to ask too many questions and by that point we were all so tired; I was crying, John was furious. There was nothing we could do and so we drove home, and I started with the daily calls again, and hounding the dorm manager. He was very polite, but said there was nothing he could do.'

'She called Saturday,' John said, his glass nearly empty. 'She told me she was sorry. I told Marion to pick up.' He drained the Scotch.

'She was frightened,' Marion added, 'but she wouldn't say why. She was crying and begged us to take her and Bobby to rehab. I wasn't about to argue. I told her to get a bag packed and we'd be there as fast as we could. She told us she'd be in her dorm room. When we got there she was gone. I thought I was going to lose my mind. I got the dorm manager and made him go around to every single room in that building. No one had seen her, no one knew anything; I knew they were lying. I tried to call her on her cell, she wouldn't pick up.'

She looked at her husband. His eyes were watery. 'Finally,' she said, 'I got her roommate – Taylor – alone. I knew she didn't want to talk to me; she was scared. I remember when Ashley first got to the Institute she'd talked about Taylor; she'd found a friend . . . one who didn't use drugs. Taylor wouldn't say anything and had me go with her into the bathroom. She told me that everything changed when Ashley started going with Bobby. She said he wasn't a student, he was a drug dealer who hung out at the dorm. She said he tried to pass as a student, had an ID that he'd use to get in. But what made her so frightened was she said he wasn't the only one and that lots of kids in the dormitory were experimenting with heroin. I asked her when she'd last seen Ashley, or Bobby for that matter. If she knew where they were staying . . . She didn't.' Marion's jaw trembled. 'The rest of that day and the past couple have been a blur. We went back to the precinct station where she'd been arrested. They couldn't help. We couldn't even file a missing person's report because it was too soon.' She shrugged her shoulders. 'When we couldn't think of anything else, we drove around the Village, the Lower East Side, those horrible parks in Brooklyn where people live in tents. Finally, we came home. I tried her cell, I don't know how many times more, called the dean, the dorm manager . . . Mostly, I think we've been waiting . . . and here you are.'

'Did this Taylor mention any other names?' Hobbs asked. 'Any of the other kids she thought were doing or selling the drugs?'

'No,' Marion said. 'She was too frightened. I think just talking to us took everything she had.'

'No mention of a Carly or a young man named Jerod?' he persisted.

'No.'

Her husband stared out at the distant vista, the rolling hills on the other side of the valley, the river below. A tear dropped, his jaw clenched, and he suddenly hurled his tumbler as far as he could. It sparkled in the sun before vanishing from view. He turned back to Hobbs, and looked at him as though seeing him for the first time. 'Will we need to identify the body?'

'Yes,' Hobbs said, pulling one of his cards from his breast pocket. He turned it over and wrote on the back. 'This is the address for the morgue, and the number. Call before you go, and if you could do it today, or tomorrow at the latest, it would be best.' He straightened, glanced at Barrett and then back at the Kanes. 'We'll go now. If there's anything else you think of, don't hesitate to call. And please accept my condolences; this is something that no parent should ever have to face. I am truly sorry.'

'Thank you,' Marion said, wiping her face with the back of

her hand. She led them back out front and stood motionless as they drove off.

Barrett watched her in the side mirror. 'I can't imagine what she's feeling,' she commented, losing sight of her as the Crown Vic crunched and turned on the crushed shells. She thought of Max, his chubby cheeks and crystal-blue eyes, not wanting to think about what it would be like to have your child's life end.

'Yes,' Hobbs agreed, and they drove in silence, each thinking about their own families. Finally Hobbs broke the quiet. 'Unfortunately heroin is dirt cheap right now and what used to be the most taboo drug has become the thing to do. What Mrs. Kane was saying about that kid dealing in the dorm. That kind of thing happens, but it's usually softer stuff and club drugs – lots of pot, some hallucinogens, hash, E, but not dope. It's also usually one of the students or a group of them that starts dealing out of their room. Invariably somebody rats them out and they get closed down. But this feels different, more organized. You know, I think I'd like to have a word with that girl, Taylor. Interested in tagging along, maybe grab something to eat when we get back to the city?'

'Sure,' Barrett said, wondering a little at the invitation. She glanced at the clock – it was nearly four – and remembered her mother's request to get home on time. If traffic were good, which was a gamble, they'd be back in the city by six, more than anything she needed to check in at her office and see if they'd come up with anything new. 'I need to call home,' and uncertain as to why she felt such hesitation, she pressed speed dial.

'Hi, Mom,' Barrett said. 'How's Max?'

'Still good, dear.' She paused. 'I'm assuming you're on the way home . . .'

'About that,' Barrett said, 'any chance you could go in late tonight? Something bad happened at work and—'

'No, dear, there isn't and it's too late to call Brandon for a sub. I need to get back to my place and change, I've got a blob of spit-up on my shoulder. Not to mention pull myself together into the vision of loveliness my regulars have come to expect. I was counting on you being home by six. What about giving your sister a call? Maybe she could sit?'

'No, Justine's working crazy hours at the hospital right now. She needs to sleep. I'll get home as soon as I can, but it's not going to be much before seven.'

'Barrett,' her mother said in a tone she'd heard only rarely as a child, 'don't do this to me. Brandon is the best boss in the world, but even he has his limits and I can't lose my job. I love you and adore Max, but I've been here since eight this morning and I need you to come home now. Do you understand?'

Barrett was about to say something when Hobbs reached over and grabbed her cell. 'Hi, Ruth.'

'Ed?' Ruth said, all annoyance gone. 'Well, there's a welcome voice. How the hell are you and how come you stopped calling?'

He gave Barrett a look. 'Long story. I promise to get her home by six.'

'I'd certainly appreciate that,' Ruth said, now all Southern loveliness and drawl.

'My pleasure,' and he hung up, before Barrett could retrieve the phone.

'Why did you do that?'

'She has a point. Going back to your office won't make a hill of beans difference, let the crime-scene team finish their thing . . . You can go back tomorrow. Or if you're really feeling desperate to look at it again we could head there after seeing that girl.'

'But I've got Max.'

'So? We'll bring him with us.'

She looked at Ed, about to argue, but realized two things; first, he was right and second, the thought of spending time with him and Max together – even if it involved interviewing a witness – didn't sound half bad.

NINE

Janice Fleet looked across her gleaming mahogany desk at fifteen-year-old Morgan DeFelice – Chase was correct, this little slut was just what the customers wanted, and at the end of the day it was all about the money, and struggling to maintain the Manhattan lifestyle that a hundred sixty-five thousand a year as a commissioner couldn't come close to covering.

But Morgan, with her dyed blonde hair, stomach-baring striped top that revealed a navel piercing with a shiny purple ring, low-rider jeans, and cheap shoes, brought lots of memories bubbling

to the surface – bad memories. She pushed those away, and
dressed in a light-weight Kelly green suit and silk blouse she
was all business. It wasn't easy, this one looked so much like
the first one – Krista – the one she and Avery had taken into
their home nearly ten years ago, the one who'd turned her
life to shit.

'So, Morgan,' she smiled, showing her even porcelain-veneered
teeth, noting how the girl seemed out of place and fidgety in the
tasteful Chelsea office that had once been Avery's. It was where
he provided consultation and performed minor cosmetic proce-
dures. It was also where she caught him screwing Krista – their
foster daughter – in one of the two examination rooms. 'What
kind of work do you think you'd be interested in doing?' It was
evening and the four-storey building, still owned by the limited
liability corporation she and Avery had set up, was deserted, just
her and Morgan . . . and of course Chase, waiting in the next
room. The blinds were drawn and the dark-wood furniture,
shelves filled with books and awards, midnight-blue carpet and
leather couch and matching club chairs and ottomans gave the
room a cozy feel.

'Well,' the girl leaned forward; she gazed at the wall of framed
glossy photos of high-fashion models interspersed with plaques
and awards on the shelving unit behind Janice, 'I've done a lot
of modeling. You know, catalog and runway, but what really
interests me is acting. I know I would have to start small, but
maybe something on Broadway. Work my way up to television
and films.'

'A girl with ambition,' Janice said, noting that her tongue had
been pierced. 'Excellent.' She got up and walked across to the
bar. 'Could I get you something to drink. A soda? A wine cooler?'
She winked, and opened the refrigerator concealed by a wood
panel. 'It is after five.'

Morgan's eyes lit and her tongue darted between her lips at
the mention of alcohol. 'It has so many calories, but I'd love a
cooler.'

'Smart girl to think about that, no matter how thin, you've
got to watch the figure.' Janice removed two bottles of the sicken-
ing sweet pink beverages from the fridge. 'Ice?'

'Yes, please.'

Janice twisted the caps on the two drinks, making sure the
girl heard the whoosh of carbonated bubbles. She clinked ice

cubes into large dark blue acrylic tumblers – breaking glass can be such a bother – and handed one to Morgan.

'I saw you left your bag in the waiting room,' Janice said, loving this part, the setting of the trap, the bait, the steel jaws about to slam down. 'Any chance you've brought your book?' She watched Morgan's face, wondering what shape the lies would take.

'I completely forgot,' she said without pause and took a couple deep swallows of the sugary drink.

'Not even a headshot and résumé?' Janice asked.

'I just had new pictures taken,' Morgan said.

'Not to worry,' Janice said, 'a pretty girl like you,' and she asked Morgan an innocuous stream of questions, to which the girl responded with lies. Telling Janice she was eighteen and had graduated high school. She threw around names of well-known photographers and magazines she had worked with and appeared in.

But by the time Janice got to, 'What was your favorite course in high school?' Morgan's eyes had fluttered shut.

Janice swooped forward and retrieved the rest of the drugged drink before it left yet another stain on the dark carpet. She pried it from the girl's soft pink fingers, noting how the nails had been bitten and would need a bit of work with an emery board.

'OK, Chase.' She knocked on the connecting door and opened it. 'She's ready.'

While Janice drugged the girl, Chase waited in what had been one of the examination rooms for Dr. Avery Fleet's cosmetic and reconstructive surgery practice. It had two doors, one that led to the office and the other to the waiting room and reception desk. He sat in the semi-dark and made a rapid series of phone calls – seven in total, the numbers all memorized. The phone was a top-of-the-line prepaid cell with light-up buttons, speaker phone, conference calling, and camera and video capability, just like the one that had gone missing. It would be used for tonight only and then he'd pulverize it with a hammer and send the plastic and metal guts through a cross-cut shredder. It was what should have been done with the last one. 'Yes,' he said into the cell, 'in twenty to thirty minutes. Very good.' He hung up and called the next.

Through a slit in the closed blinds, he looked out at the mostly residential street, three stories below. The block was undergoing massive change, with many of the old brownstones and parking garages being demolished and replaced by high-rise pricey condo complexes. This little brownstone that Avery had shrewdly purchased for his practice – and apparently for some extra-marital activities as well – for just three hundred thousand dollars nearly thirty years ago was dwarfed by all the new construction.

Janice had it done over after Avery's death, the examination table gone, the sleek stainless-steel cabinets, autoclave, and sink all gone. Chase had taken many of the surgical instruments for himself; she would have just thrown them out, tens of thousands of dollars of precision German steel, unused boxes of syringes and needles for administering Botox, he'd even kept the cartons of purple propylene gloves, and sutures with which he practiced tying knots. He felt a hint of nostalgia. There was no glamour left, even Avery's exquisite artwork – Pre-Raphaelite master-pieces – Janice had boxed up and sent to auction. He'd been furious with her, seething that she'd not given him one of the glorious canvases that showed beautiful Renaissance men and auburn-haired women, drawn with intense realism, their perfectly proportioned faces aglow as if lit by rays of sun. She'd said that she couldn't, that there couldn't be anything traceable between the two of them.

Now, waiting for Janice to finish prepping Morgan, he sat silent, imagining the room as it once had been, and picturing himself in the role of the surgeon, the central fantasy shifting subtly over time as the details filled in. Powerful, handsome, successful, and rich; he'd have it all. He'd be married by the time he finished medical school. His wife would be beautiful, although he doubted she would be better looking than he, and intelligent. She could also be a little older – like that Dr. Conyors. Before he'd ransacked her office – an exercise in futility as the cells were nowhere to be found – he'd looked her up on the Internet. She was one very hot woman, which was further confirmed by the picture he had of her with her newborn – even then, after the stress of childbirth when most women are drained and look like hell, she'd glowed with a dark beauty as she stared at her baby. Janice, who clearly despised her, had even called her 'pretty'. But that wasn't the best of it, she was a doctor and a director of a facility. It would be useful to have a spouse who could support them both. But his prospective wife couldn't

be too old; he wanted children, two of them, and Dr. Conyors
with her new baby and breast pump was obviously fertile. He'd
found the news story of her dead husband and wondered why
there were no other family pictures anywhere in her office – it
seemed a wrong note, but maybe she didn't want people to know
too much of her private business. He wondered what her reaction had been when she found her office all torn up, would she
be frightened? Janice had wanted him to be discreet . . . oh well,
sometimes she couldn't get her way, and the longer he'd looked
for the cells the more furious he'd become. What had she done
with them? Did she even have them?

He heard Janice's knock. And then her backlit silhouette
through the open door. 'She's ready. Are you done?' she asked.

'Yes, they're all waiting.' He followed her into the office. He
looked at Morgan slumped in a leather chair, her head had fallen
back; her mouth hung open and she was snoring. The girl had
wasted no time; she'd called Janice within an hour of leaving
his office. She was young, younger than any of the others, exactly
the kind of girl Avery Fleet and so many other men found exciting.
He'd idolized Avery as a man who'd achieved everything that
Chase wanted – power, money, respect . . . at least that's what
he'd once thought. The truth of his double life had been revealed
in layers, like an onion coming undone, after his death.

'Get her ready,' Janice said.

Chase noticed eagerness in her eyes, a glitter as though this
weren't just about the money – money that she never split fairly.
'How much will she bring?' he asked, tipping the girl's chair
back and dragging it across the rug toward the leather couch.
'You know she kind of reminds me of—'

'Don't,' Janice warned, as she pulled a wine-colored velvet
spread from out of a cabinet and draped it over the sofa.

He waited while she smoothed it out and then he lifted the
drugged girl and set her down.

'The minute she walked in the door,' Janice said, 'it was like
going back in time; she could have been her sister.'

'I know; I've been her counselor for the past couple years,
but it was only recently I made that connection.' He knelt and
pulled off her shoes, noting the poor quality and how the blue-
plastic heel on one had pulled away from the sole. Timing his
words so that he could catch Janice's expression, he added, 'Just
like Krista Brent.' He looked up, noting the lines in her face, the

pucker around her mouth and under her nose, and the hollows in her cheeks as she winced. If Avery had still been alive he'd have done something about that, probably several somethings – a total lift, Botox on the forehead, and a chemical peel to tighten the pores.

He unsnapped Morgan's jeans, pulling them and her purple nylon thong off, while Janice worked away at the striped top, with no bra underneath. 'I'd always wondered,' he said, 'do you remember that night you and Avery took me to dinner?'

'Of course,' she said warily, as she stepped back and took an appraising view of the naked girl. She shook her head, 'These need to go,' and snapping on propylene gloves, carefully removed the iridescent-purple belly-button ring, and a series of earrings, three on one side and two on the other. 'At least there are no tattoos.' And careful not to gag the girl, she opened her jaw, lifted her tongue, and pulled off the backing for the ball-shaped piercing and then the stud. 'Disgusting,' and she put it and all of Morgan's clothes into a black plastic garbage bag.

'That would have been close to the time you took in Krista.'

'What are you getting at, Chase?'

From one of the built-in cabinets behind her desk he retrieved a red-plastic tackle box and set it on the coffee table. He clicked it open and lifted back the top tray, which held an assortment of cosmetics. In the bottom was an array of makeup brushes and tubes of foundation. He glanced at the girl and pulled out a shade slightly darker than her skin, squeezed out a generous amount onto a soft pad. 'Maybe I'm wrong, but I always wondered if you'd been considering taking me in as your foster child.'

'You weren't wrong,' she said, stepping back as Chase rapidly worked over the girl, making any small pimples and blackheads disappear; he gently made up her face, being careful to give her as youthful an appearance as possible with the barest touches of blush on her forehead, the apples of her cheeks and chin. For lipstick he used a translucent pink gloss

'So why didn't you?' he asked, thinking he already knew.

She looked at Chase as he rearranged the girl to appear as if she'd fallen asleep on the couch. 'It was Avery. He liked you, said you had great potential, but he thought you didn't need us, that you'd make it through on your own. Krista, on the other hand . . . he felt she'd been "horribly used by the system". He wanted to rescue her.'

'He wanted to fuck her,' Chase said bluntly, and he went to retrieve his briefcase from the other room.

'In hindsight, perhaps. Although, he'd said the affair hadn't started until after she'd turned eighteen.'

'You believe that?' Chase asked as he set up the cells on Janice's desk, all fully charged and on speaker, with the single number to be dialed preset and ready. The last one he'd use to send the video stream.

'No, I don't. I knew Avery for over twenty years. In the end he was just a cliché.'

'Mid-life crisis.'

'Yes, and a pervert and a child-molester. He got what he had coming. Are you ready?' she asked.

'In a second.' He finished setting up the phones, while keeping Janice in his periphery. There was something in the tone of her voice; she hated this subject, while he found it fascinating, how in one afternoon both of their lives had been transformed. 'So he was all those things, and a highly successful surgeon. If you'd not walked in on the two of them fucking, it would have kept going. It might still be going on.'

'Maybe, maybe not.'

'He said something.'

'He said lots of things, and because I didn't say a word he figured it would all work out, that I'd just roll over. Give him a divorce, watch as he married that little tramp, lose my career, my house, probably my license because after all I was supposed to protect that girl from men like Avery. Can you imagine the headlines? For God's sakes I was the Commissioner of Family and Youth Services. He would have used all of that to buy my silence.'

Chase systematically checked the phones, even though he'd already completed the setup. 'He actually said he was going to marry her?'

'I don't know why we have to go over this. Yes, he said they were in love and that he no longer loved me. He told me that he'd never loved me.'

'And then you just left them there and went to work.'

'Chase, drop it. Are you ready?'

He nodded, turned on the video, and adjusted the focus. He thought back to the day eight years ago, and how different Janice had been at his weekly session. At the time she was the newly appointed commissioner, but had kept him and a couple other patients in an effort to not lose touch with the reality of the children and teens she was supposed to serve. That day she'd had a blank look, one he associated with 9/11, everyone walking around not certain of where they were going or what they were supposed to do. Janice had just found her husband screwing their foster child; her world had cracked open, and to keep from falling apart, she'd gone to work. For Chase it had been an opportunity unlike any other. He'd sensed her pain and given her everything she'd needed; it had started with 'What's wrong?' Half an hour later she'd cancelled the rest of her appointments and meetings for the day. Beneath her shock he'd seen the rage, and like a good therapist – God knows he'd met with enough of them – he'd brought it out. *'He'll get everything, the money, the house, the pretty young wife. You'll get nothing.'*

'So what am I supposed to do, kill him? Kill them both?'

He hadn't flinched as he'd given her his greatest gift, a glimpse inside his mind where everything was possible, and all of the rules that held everyone else inside their ticky-tacky little boxes didn't apply. *'It's what he deserves. It's what they both deserve. But do it fast. The minute one other person knows about this, it will be too late,'* he'd told her. By the following morning Dr. Avery Fleet would be dead from an unintentional drug overdose and Krista Brent – a troubled girl – had run away from home, as she had done many times before, never to be heard from again.

Now, he looked at Janice, sitting behind her desk, powerful, wealthy, and dependent on no one . . . but him. He turned on all the phones and dialed. She waited until they'd all picked up. 'Good evening,' she said, 'I hope everyone is well. Are you all receiving the video and can you hear me?' She paused until four male and three female voices responded with a broad range of accents, Southern, Asian, Middle Eastern, British, and German. 'Good, I'll remind you of the terms of sale. Payment is by bank wire, the account number will be provided to the winning bidder at the end of the auction. Payment must be received within an hour of auction's end, and the merchandise must be picked up within three hours. As you are aware, we do not provide a shipping service. Failure to comply with either term of sale voids the transaction and the auction will be repeated . . . of course without the offending bidder.' An Asian woman and the Brit chuckled. 'Questions?' There was silence. 'Excellent, I'm sure you're all eager to see what's on the block this evening.' She nodded at Chase, the Bluetooth function on his phone glowed as he zoomed in on Morgan's sleeping face, her delicately parted lips. And slowly he panned back revealing more and more of the teenager, who just this morning had been complaining about every portion of her wretched life. He hoped she'd bring a lot of money, and could care less that bad as the girl's life had been, it was about to get a whole lot worse. He imagined himself in the role of the high-fashion photographers who had once shot his pictures; he let the camera play over Morgan, checking how she was framed in the tiny LED screen. He was conscious of the lights and the glow on her skin; the hot spots and the shadows. He made her beautiful, and was barely aware of Janice in the background.

'I have an opening bid of one hundred thousand,' Janice said. 'Do I hear one ten?'

TEN

It was night and Jerod had turned off the only light in his cell-like room, with its locked door, bolted-down furniture, and wire-meshed window. There was a full moon and it spilled silver light across the waxed floor. The voice in his head was barely there, mostly a noise with no clear words. His thoughts were jangled and while he no longer felt the horrible aches of withdrawal, he wondered if he would survive. Images of Carly tortured him, her by his side, taking his hand as they walked, at times almost skipped, through the East Village. The night she'd entered his room and asked if she could sleep, 'just sleep', with him. He'd been barely able to breathe as she settled next to him on his tumbled nest of blankets and sleeping bags. He'd not wanted to scare her, and held back despite his powerful longing. The smell of her hair, the way it tickled his nose. 'Hold me,' she whispered, and he did, wrapping an arm around her as they spooned. He knew that she'd been through bad times, all of them had. He'd caught snippets of her story, not wanting to push or to pry. She'd been taken from her home because her mom smoked crack and her father had left when she was still a baby. He'd seen her bare arms – usually kept covered – when she'd shot up. There were old scars tracking up her wrists and forearms; they weren't needle marks; she cut, she told him she did it with a razor blade, or if she didn't have one anything she could find, even her fingernails. He stayed awake that entire night, even though he knew it would make the voices worse. He listened to her breath and could tell the point at which she fell asleep. He wondered if in the morning she'd be horrified to find him next to her. She wasn't. Tears squeezed from his eyes as he remembered how she'd woken; turning lazily into him, smiling and giving him a dry kiss on the lips, 'My breath is gross,' she said, and rested her head against his chest.

The memory faded with the sound of footsteps. A female guard looked through the small window in the door, knocked, and softly called his name. 'Jerod, I need to take you to the infirmary. You need to have your admission physical.'

'OK.' He got off the bed, noting a dull ache in his chest.

The guard stood by the door and waited for him to put on his hospital-issue no-tie rubber-soled slippers. 'They should have done this when you arrived,' she said, 'but it's always like this. Just go ahead and dump on second shift.'

He recollected that a doctor had come into his room earlier in the day and quickly listened to his heart and lungs and made him stick his tongue out, but maybe this was something else, so he said nothing.

He followed the guard through the eerily quiet ward, all the rooms locked. He sensed the others in their cells, everyone watching through tiny windows or lost in their own thoughts or dreams. The guard unlocked the door that led to the nursing and security areas. In front of the nursing station he saw a row of monitors, each one trained on a patient's room. The nurse on duty wasn't looking at any of them, but was absorbed in a paperback that had a beautiful woman with fangs and a lot of cleavage sinking her teeth into a handsome man's neck on the cover.

'This way,' she said, 'it's kind of a hike.'

He lost track of the twists and turns, the staircases they went down until finally they came to a brightly lit examination room. Inside, a sandy-haired man in his late twenties wearing a lab coat was standing by a stainless-steel counter; he was leafing through a blue plastic binder with J. BLANK written in bold letters down the spine. He looked up, his eyes bright. 'Oh, good, you got him. Hi, Jerod.' He stood and put Jerod's chart on the counter. He extended his hand. 'I'm Dr. Nader, if you could take off your shirt and slippers I'll give you a quick physical.'

Jerod did as instructed, catching the reflection of his tall skinny frame in the glass-fronted cabinets. He sat up on the examination table and watched while the young doctor washed his hands and slapped on a pair of gloves – he seemed nervous.

The doctor glanced at the guard. 'You can wait outside if you want.'

'You're sure?' the guard asked.

'Yeah.' The doctor made eye contact with Jerod. 'I don't think Jerod is going to cause any problems.'

The guard left the room and Jerod felt a shiver of something not right about this doctor. It was in his eyes, too bright, but maybe it was just the lighting, and Jerod always had to be careful because it was easy for him to get paranoid. Maybe it was just his imagination that the chatty young doctor seemed jumpy. He followed all of the rapid-fire instructions. 'Follow my fingers with your eyes, shrug your shoulders, smile, frown.' He felt a shiver spread across his bare flesh as the doctor examined his injection sites.

'When did you last shoot dope?' the doctor asked.

He had to think, it was still Tuesday, he thought about Bobby and Ashley, mumbled, 'Few days.'

'How big a habit did you have?'

'I don't know, couple bundles a day. However much I could get.'

'They giving you methadone?'

'No,' Jerod said, wondering why the doctor didn't know this.

'Interesting,' he flashed a light in Jerod's eyes, 'look straight ahead.'

It was then Jerod made the observation that the doctor's eyes weren't right. His pupils were tiny, almost not there.

'OK,' the doctor said, as he again leafed through Jerod's chart. 'There it is. You're on Buprenorphine.'

Jerod nodded.

'Good, and it looks like it's keeping you comfortable, that's great. OK, now all that's left is to get you a flu shot and we can send you back to your room.'

Jerod waited as the doctor unlocked one of the overhead glass-fronted cabinets and pulled out a box that contained small glass ampoules. From one of the drawers he grabbed a plastic-wrapped syringe and drew up a small amount of the liquid. He then methodically put the box back into the cabinet, locked it, and threw all of the wrapping materials into a red hazardous-material container mounted on the wall. Approaching Jerod with the loaded needle, he asked, 'Any allergies?'

'I don't think so,' Jerod said, feeling his paranoia swell as the doctor swabbed his shoulder with an alcohol wipe before the needle made contact with his shoulder.

'You're going to feel a little pinch.'

He wanted to run, and the voice screamed, '*Get out, Jerod!*' but he held rigid as the tiny needle sank into his flesh.

'All done,' the doctor said. 'You can put your shirt back on.'

The voice shouted in Jerod's head, like someone standing just behind him, '*That was stupid, Jerod. Now you're in for it. Now you're in trouble.*' He tried to ignore it as he pulled on his brown pajama top with the words PROPERTY OF CROTON FORENSIC HOSPITAL stamped on the front and back. He barely heard the doctor call for the guard, telling her that he was ready to go back, as the first finger of discomfort hit and then blossomed into a searing pain, like a knife that ripped through his gut.

The guard appeared as Jerod clutched his stomach, doubled over, and vomited. At first nothing came and then he heaved again and again, his supper and then dull greenish bile flew out of him. His eyes teared and he gasped from the pain that seemed to start in his gut and then spread through every bone in his body.

'What's wrong with him?' the guard asked, trying to avoid the puking man.

'He said he was starting to feel sick,' the doctor said, putting his hand on Jerod's forehead. 'He's burning up. We need to get him to the hospital . . . Now! You call the ambulance, and I'll see if I can get him stable.'

Jerod tried to stand, it was hard to breathe and his heart pounded way too fast. The room shifted, the glass cabinets, the doctor all spinning at crazy angles. He shivered as the nausea came again. He tried to vomit but nothing came, he gagged and spit, his jaw ached. He looked up at the doctor, who was standing back by the counter, just watching him.

'What did you do?' he gasped.

'Not a thing,' the doctor said, not moving to help or even offer him a basin or water to wash out his mouth.

The female guard returned with a pair of burly aides. They helped Jerod into a wheelchair. She grabbed a pink plastic bedpan and put it on his lap, as he heaved and retched, now only bringing up the tiniest bits of brown bile. 'The ambulance should be waiting,' she told him.

To Jerod it was all white noise and pain, the voice now screaming, *'Stupid, Jerod. Real stupid. Stupid stupid stupid stupid.'*

'You're going to be OK,' the guard said, as they wheeled him out. 'It's going to be fine.'

Dr. Jack Nader, in his final year of residency training, watched and listened for the retreating footsteps to vanish. He pulled his cell out of his lab coat's breast pocket and dialed. 'Marky, it's me. He's on his way to the hospital . . . no more than ten minutes. I don't feel good about this. When can I get my stuff?'

He hung up, glanced around nervously, closed the door, and then reached deep into the inside pocket of his lab coat and retrieved a small Ziploc bag filled with ten white pills.

He thought how he'd no longer have to count these so carefully. *Only ten left, only eight left, only six left, will they have more? Will I have enough money?* His entire life, since the dental surgery three years ago, revolved around his Oxies and Roxies, Percocets, Vicodin, Dilaudid. Even working as the on-call doc at Croton, a moonlighting job that left him drained and exhausted for his daytime assignment, was just so he could have enough cash. At ten pills a day, five to ten dollars a pill, he was burning through thousands a month. Every time he tried to cut down or quit, he'd get sick and depressed. Never going more than a day without a pill, before he'd call Marky, begging. At least he hadn't shot dope . . . although he'd come close. It was cheaper than the pills, but that was the one line he swore he'd never cross – he'd never shoot. But in his heart he knew it was just a matter of time, constantly needing more to not get sick.

He shook two pills into the palm of his hand, and popped them dry. After tonight he'd be set . . . at least for a while. Marky had just wanted this one little favor and in exchange he'd have pills for a year. 'I've got a friend in there,' Marky had said and had given him the information on Jerod. 'I need you to get him out. He's also got some stuff of mine, so when he goes make sure it's with him.'

Dr. Nader picked up the phone and called security. 'Hi, this is Dr. Nader. The man that just went to the hospital – Jerod Blank – won't be back tonight. If somebody could arrange to have his belongings transported to the hospital that would be great . . . No, it should be tonight. Thanks.'

It's not like that Jerod kid had done anything really bad, he told himself, he'd read the chart. He wasn't a murderer or anything, getting him out of here wouldn't hurt anyone.

He felt the bag. Now only eight pills left. He'd meet Marky tomorrow and get more, get lots. He promised himself that he wouldn't take more than ten a day; he made plans to cut down. Maybe take one pill less a day every week – *I should be able to handle that. And after that,* he thought, *I'll quit. I'll really quit.*

ELEVEN

B arrett hadn't been inside her condo thirty seconds before her mother started in. 'What's wrong, dear?'

It was a simple question, and as she bent down to pick up Max from his Pack-N-Play, 'Long day, Mom,' she said, hoping that Ruth, who was rapidly surveying the living room and gathering up her belongings, would let sleeping dogs . . . cower in corners. It was also a day that wasn't nearly over, and she hoped her mom would be out the door before Hobbs showed up. 'And I'm sorry that I'm late. I know you wanted to go home before your shift. It's just . . .'

'It's OK, Barrett, at least I'm not going to be late for work, I figured this might happen so I hand-washed the puke off my shirt and used your blow dryer . . . good as . . . well, good enough, and thank God for low lights.'

Barrett felt a surge of gratitude as she cradled Max, and followed her mother's rapid progress. 'I can't thank you enough for helping out.'

'Well, that's what grandmothers are for.'

'You sure don't look like one,' Barrett said, taking in her

mother's curvy figure in skin-tight jeans, a black T-shirt with the Night Shade logo, and burnt-red sling-backs with four-inch heels.

'Yet another advantage of unwanted teen pregnancy – you get to be a grandmother before fifty.' Using the mirror by the front door, Ruth piled and twisted her thick auburn hair into a purposefully untidy bun, setting it in place with rhinestone-studded hairpins. She pulled out long tendrils and twirled them with her finger, making quick curls to hang loose on either side of her face. Glancing at the clock she pulled out lipstick and quickly put on her face. 'I look like day-old crap.'

Still holding the baby, Barrett came up behind her and looked at their reflections. 'You look beautiful. Course . . . none of the men in the Night Shade are really going to notice.'

'You're so wrong,' her mother said, 'and I wish you wouldn't make stereotypical judgments about my patrons – and besides it's not just men. Many of the women find me very attractive.'

'Is there something I should know?' Barrett asked, catching her mother's eye in the mirror.

'Don't think I haven't considered it,' Ruth said, 'with my record with men, it's a damn shame I'm not wired to be a lesbian . . . and how did the conversation shift from your bad day to me?'

'I'm fine, Mom.' She looked away, and her eye caught the blinking light on the phone.

'Who called?'

Ruth cast a worried look at her daughter. 'Those people about the hearing for Jimmy Martin, seems they really want to talk to you.'

'That's all I need.'

'Sweetheart,' she said, pursing her lips and dabbing a bit of the same blood-red lipstick on the apples of her cheeks, 'if it's one thing Conyors women know about, avoiding stuff doesn't make it go away, just makes it fester.' She smiled and using her deepest Southern drawl added, 'Like a big ol' boil.' She caught her reflection and then looked at her watch. 'I'll do the rest on the bus.' She grabbed her bag, went over to Barrett and Max, rubbed her nose against his, and hugged her daughter. 'I'll see you in the morning.' And she was out the door, her high heels clattering down the stairs.

Still in her work clothes, Barrett closed the door – she was exhausted and the thought of the day not being over was depressing. It would be so much nicer to just stay in. She put Max down. 'It's OK, sweetie.' He started to cry. She quickly stripped off her blazer and unbuttoned her shirt. He watched her, now making goo sounds as he waited to be picked up. As she nursed, she took in her surroundings, so familiar from the green-and-white-striped sofa, two armchairs upholstered in rough-woven beige, the framed family photos, her wedding picture with Ralph, Justine's graduation pictures from medical school, the galley kitchen, and her ebonized Mason and Hamlin grand piano that had once belonged to Sophie. She'd not played much over the past year, not since . . . There was no getting away from him. Her mother, as usual, had hit the nail square, there was no running from Jimmy Martin and what he'd done to her. He was still alive; she'd seen videos of him in his super-max cell at Croton. For the second time in his life he'd avoided prison and gotten a not-guilty by reason of mental defect. They said he would never be released; they'd said that before. And like every long-term patient at Croton, every six months he would go before the release board and they would have to determine if he was well enough to be discharged back to the community.

She looked down at Max as he suckled; he had Jimmy's blond hair and blue eyes. He was a beautiful baby . . . like Jimmy had been. 'What have you done, Barrett?' she said aloud. She had nearly terminated the pregnancy, and only three other people knew the truth – Hobbs, Justine, and Houssman; they'd all encouraged her to go through with the abortion. And now . . . 'Hi, Max.' He was in a blue-flannel one-piece, his skin soft against hers. At four months, he was getting big, no longer the passive bundle of flesh that just ate and pooped. She rocked and held him, her gaze resting on her wedding picture with Ralph, her in a white-silk flapper dress, him in tails – a carnation in his lapel; he'd not been a perfect husband, but she had been hopelessly in love. She looked down at Max, contentedly suckling, making squishy gurgle noises. In a couple months she'd be able to start him on solid food, and a couple months after that he'd be weaned. She'd told everyone, including Ralph's parents, that the baby was his. If the blond hair and blue eyes didn't darken, the lie would be impossible. Ralph had been half Cuban with swarthy skin, liquid brown eyes, and full lips that knew how to kiss, to smile, and to tell her lies.

When Max had his full, she burped him and gently placed him back down; she looked across at the piano. Music had been her first passion, a full scholarship at Julliard turned down in favor of pre-med and then medical school. But life as a concert pianist was too uncertain, she had people depending on her, and becoming a doctor had been the practical thing.

She crossed the room and walked up the single step to the raised area in the center. There was a thin layer of dust on the closed keyboard. She lifted it back and sat down. What to play? She let her fingers drift down to the keys. Without thinking the notes of an Erik Satie tone poem – one of Ralph's favorites – wafted through the room. She glanced across at Max, who appeared to be asleep. The music felt good, calm, and peaceful, and then the phone rang. She tried to ignore it, but the ring was joined by her pager's metallic bleat and then the doorbell. 'You have got to be kidding.' She stopped playing as her cell phone joined in.

Startled by the noises, Max let out a cry. 'It's OK, baby.' Barrett stepped down from the piano and lifted him out of his pen. Holding him tight, she glanced down at the caller ID on her cell. The number was unfamiliar but above that was the ubiquitous State of New York ID, which meant it was from one of the facilities or agencies. Letting the landline ring, she picked up her beeper and saw a Croton extension on the LED readout, as Hobbs's voice came through the downstairs intercom, asking her to buzz him in.

With Max nestled in her arms, she walked across the room and hit the button. Behind her, she heard the answering machine pick up, and then Hugh Osborn's voice. 'Dr. Conyors . . . It's Dr. Osborn. I have to speak with you about my evaluation, I've been leaving messages, and I would appreciate you doing the courtesy of calling me back.'

With everything inside of her screaming to not answer the phone, Barrett unlatched the door for Hobbs and picked up the receiver. 'Hello, Hugh.'

'Dr. Conyors, finally,' and he launched into what for her was a dead topic. 'I need you to redo my evaluation. I've asked around and everyone else got better reviews. It's clear that you have something against me. I don't know what I did to deserve this, but it's unfounded, in all my years in state service I've never been so insulted or so . . .'

Before he could say more, the pager went off for a second time, and Max, who had finally quieted, let loose with a piercing scream. 'Look, Hugh,' she said, having to almost shout to be heard over the baby, 'it's late; I'm not changing your evaluation. You know what you need to do to improve the next one. And as I told you multiple times, you have every right to go to the union. And please do not call me at home with this again. Good night.'

As Barrett, not waiting for any response, hung up, she saw Hobbs, dressed in jeans, T-shirt, and a leather jacket, his tall frame filling the doorway. When could he have found the time to go home and change? Or was he like her keeping several changes of clothes at the office?

'You OK?' he asked, looking at her holding a screaming Max whose face had turned an alarming shade of red.

'Been better, can you take Max?'

'Sure,' he said, depositing his jacket on the couch.

'Please take that thing off.' She pointed to his shoulder holster.

'Afraid the kid might get ideas?' he quipped, while unbuckling his sidearm.

'Now is not good for jokes,' she said rubbing a hand over Max's back and trying to calm him.

'What's going on?' he asked, taking Max in his muscular arms.

'I don't know, but I am about to find out.' And her beeper sounded for a third time. 'All right, already.' She dialed the Croton extension. 'This is Dr. Conyors, someone trying to reach me?'

'Yes, Doctor. It was me.' A woman's voice spilled hurriedly over the line. 'We've had a security breach involving one of your patients.'

Barrett's first thought was Jimmy Martin, but the woman on the other end went on, 'Jerod Blank got violently ill and was taken to the hospital. Apparently he'd faked the whole thing, because he somehow managed to run away. We have the local authorities looking for him and they need to speak with you for information about the patient.'

'You have got to be kidding. How did this happen?' This was too bizarre. Jerod was intelligent and certainly resourceful, but with his heroin addiction and schizophrenia he was not the type to mastermind an escape from Croton.

The guard went on with the details. The more she said, the less sense it made. 'I saw one in his chart this morning,' Barrett grumbled. 'Why would he have a second one?'

'The on-call doctor said there wasn't one in the chart, and it had to be done within twenty-four hours of admission.'

'This is a huge screw-up,' Barrett said, wondering where Jerod could have gone. She didn't even want to consider the horrible press this could generate. The local community was still enraged by a recent incident when an inmate had escaped and killed his ex-wife.

'I'm sorry, Dr. Conyors, but you don't have to use that tone with me. I'm just doing my job.'

'OK, so who needs to talk to me, just give me the name and number.'

She fished paper and pen from her shoulder bag, and wrote down the info for the Croton police sergeant. Not stopping she dialed, and got through. 'I'm Jerod Blank's admitting psychiatrist at Croton, I was told you needed to speak to me.' She quickly gave him the overview – 'No, he's not violent' – choosing to ignore yesterday's incident with the gun. 'The only one he's ever harmed has been himself. He does need to be found as he's the only witness in a case that could possibly turn into a double homicide . . . Yes, it's very possible that he did not act alone . . . No, I have no idea as to who might have arranged this.'

As she hung up, her cell went off.

Hobbs, who having two children of his own was no stranger to babies looked up from the couch where he had managed to calm Max, who nestled on his chest, his tiny body held fast in hairy arms. 'Not good,' he commented.

'Tell me something I don't know,' she said, and picked up her cell. Her gut turned at the sound of Janice Fleet's tightly clipped words.

'I'm sorry to call you so late at home, Barrett,' her boss began, 'but we were never able to complete our business yesterday and I needed to be certain that you were fully prepared for tomorrow's conference.'

What is she talking about? And then she remembered the meeting with the two commissioners . . . and Hugh, and their talk of some kind of interagency emergency something or other that would involve way too much manpower from her agency.

'Yes, of course. I haven't checked in with my office this afternoon. I'm sure my secretary has all the details.'

'Barrett,' Janice warned, 'it starts at eight in the DFYS downtown building. It's important. I need you there the whole day, and you have to represent the department with some workable solutions. I know you have other priorities, but those come second. Am I understood?'

'Of course,' Barrett said, seeing no way out. 'I'll be there.'

'Please see that you are. Good night.'

Holding the cell, Barrett let out a strangled scream. First Hugh and then this . . . almost like the two of them had planned it.

Hobbs, now playing peek-a-boo with Max, who seemed entranced by the big detective, said, 'I spoke with the crime-scene team, and their computer guy. Someone was on your computer last night, but the only password used was yours.'

'It wasn't me.'

'I know, but according to our resident geek it's not that hard to get, from going into the hard drive and looking for frequently repeated code. After that he kind of lost me. But we know that whoever went into your office knows something about computers and has more than a few IQ points.'

'Did he say what they were looking for, or what files they went into?'

'Your patient records.'

'Great! The single most confidential thing there is! Whose records were breached?'

'Didn't say, but they're probably the most recent in your history. Also, there were traces of talc on the keyboard, so it's likely they used gloves. What we need to do is have you boot up. So I thought we'd check out your office first and then shoot over to interview Ashley Kane's roommate?'

'It's a plan,' she said, also remembering there had been mention of dinner and that the whole outing reeked of a date, albeit a twisted cop–shrink kind of one. 'Let me check something first.' She punched into her phone's history screen and compared the numbers for Hugh and Janice – they were different.

'You still up for this?' Hobbs asked.

'I guess,' she said, realizing that more than anything she needed a friendly voice and someone who wouldn't ask her to do things she didn't want to do, or criticize her, or bring up topics that made her flesh crawl. 'You sure you don't mind me bringing Max?'

'Naah, the little monster kind of grows on you; I always thought it would be fun to have a boy, not that I'd ever let my girls know.'

'You're good with kids,' she noted, seeing how easy he was with Max. She knew he had two daughters and an ex, but seeing him in her condo, holding Max . . . *What are you thinking? He's dating someone. That ship sailed, and don't you dare bring it up. You hurt him once, Barrett.*

'Love kids, probably why I stayed with Margaret long past the time we should have split. This joint-custody thing blows.'

She fixed the straps on the navy BabyBjörn sling over her shoulders and the buckle around her middle. 'For the first few weeks I was petrified, he was so tiny,' she admitted. 'I kept thinking I'd hurt him.'

'They're sturdier than they look,' he said, and then, keying into something in her expression, 'What's wrong?'

'What's not? My boss is looking for ways to can my ass, I've got a doc at work I don't trust as far as I can throw him, Jimmy Martin is coming up for his six-month review and I think they want me to testify . . . Someone broke into my office, my patient just ran away from Croton, and a couple days ago I found two dead teenagers . . . Not a good week. And you're sure this isn't some kind of child abuse, dragging him along like this?'

'Naah, however, should you strap the kid in Kevlar and use him as a shield . . .'

'Not funny,' she said taking the now sleepy Max and arranging him in the sling.

'Yeah, it kind of was, considering the way you dragged that social worker into that crack house yesterday.'

'Thanks for reminding me. I've a bad feeling that I've not heard the end of that. Here, do you mind taking this?' she asked, handing him the soft-sided bag she used for baby supplies.

'It hasn't been all bad,' he commented. 'You did call me.'

'True,' she said, 'that's one for the plus column,' and then quickly added, 'I've missed you, Ed.'

'Ditto, just don't do it again.'

TWELVE

Barrett raced up the broad steps of the conference center two blocks from City Hall Plaza. She was half an hour late, and wondered if that would be another shot of ammo Janice would lob her way. This was the last place she wanted to be. Her thoughts still on the scary interview she and Hobbs had had last night with a terrified Taylor Osborn. The eighteen-year-old had painted a picture of rampant drug abuse inside the dormitory, only instead of soft drugs like pot and alcohol, the drug of choice had become heroin. Sadly, the girl had given them little concrete, but Hobbs thought he'd be able to get the narcotics squad to try tracing the source of the dope from the dorm to its point of origin, although as he reminded her, 'Those kind of investigations can take months . . . even a year or more.' But the thing tearing her up was Jerod. She feared the worst, and the more she thought about his escape, the more it seemed someone had broken him out, someone who did not have his best interest at heart. One thing Hobbs had said last night was also digging away at her: 'Why does this Jerod kid get to you so much?' It was the kind of insightful question she'd expect from Hobbs or Houssman, and she knew that there was something about Jerod that had her pushing above and beyond where she'd normally go for a patient – especially one of hers with a long criminal history. There was something about him and it went beyond her belief that underneath it all he was a good person. Something about him that she couldn't yet get her finger on.

Inside, the soaring lobby hummed with hundreds of voices as people clustered in groups, drinking coffee and orange juice while balancing blue-paper plates of bagels and mini-Danish. She recognized a few faces, higher-level managers, the commissioner of corrections, police administrators, the chief juvenile judge . . . She saw that this was meant to be a big deal, or at least appear that way.

Across the ceiling a blue-and-gold banner had been hung, clarifying that she was at the NEW YORK STATE INTER-AGENCY TASK FORCE ON AT-RISK YOUTH. Along one side of the massive entryway were cloth-covered tables that matched the banners, with coffee urns, pitchers of OJ, and tiered trays of pastries and bagels. To her right was a long bank of tables with a second banner – *Registration*. Relieved that nothing had yet started she found her name on the sign-in sheets for last names beginning with the letter 'C' and put her initials next to it. A woman seated across, looked at the sheet and rapidly wrote Barrett's name in black magic-marker on a peel-off tag that now proclaimed *Hi, my name is Barrett Conyors, MD* – and handed it to her. 'Here's your packet,' and she handed her a thick blue folder, the same color as the tablecloths, with her name on a sticker in the upper right corner.

With the tag stuck to the lapel of her navy blazer, she was about to head for the buffet, having raced from the house without having had a bite to eat, when a bell chimed three times.

Undeterred by the signal, she snagged a cup of coffee and a poppy-seed bagel with cream cheese. Balancing her bag and light breakfast, she turned and followed the flow of attendees into the auditorium. A sign overhead informed her no food or drink allowed inside but as no one else seemed to care, she followed suit.

Inside she immediately spotted Hugh's well-groomed head in the front row. He was looking around expectantly – hopefully, not for her. And not wanting to take that chance she headed toward the back, and spotted the TV cameras. *Great*, she thought, realizing that this was going to be televised on the government's cable channel. She also ran a mental calculation on what this shindig must be costing. There had to be over five hundred state employees in attendance, most of them toward the higher end of the pay spectrum. The day would run the taxpayers a quarter million bucks – hopefully something would come from it.

Her eyes landed on a couple empty seats in the last row. She turned to her right, nearly spilling her coffee on a short woman with white hair, 'Excuse me,' and made a beeline, just squeezing through to one as a tall man in black jeans and blazer grabbed the other. Relieved to be far from the cameras, she sank back into the chair, coffee and bagel still intact, and quickly glanced at her neighbor. He smiled back, and she found herself staring at one of the most beautiful men she had ever seen . . . possibly the best-looking man ever.

He smiled over perfect teeth, and extended his hand. 'I'm Chase Strand – DFYS.'

'Barrett Conyors,' she said, balancing her bagel on her lap and hoping she wasn't about to drop her coffee, or otherwise embarrass herself. *God, he has gorgeous eyes – almost gold.* They reminded her of a painting she'd seen of a dark-haired Persian boy that hung at the Met.

'Quite the turnout,' he commented. 'Of course, my supervisor made it clear that attendance was not optional.'

'Yes,' she said, reaching for the distraction of the blue binder that she'd wedged into the outer pocket of her bag, 'there's a lot of that going around.' She flipped it open and felt him watching her. She looked back, wondering what had gotten his attention, and thinking that he could easily have been on the cover of a magazine.

'*Dr.* Conyors?' he asked.

'Yes, how did you know?'

He pointed at her lapel. 'Your nametag. What kind of doctor?'

'Psychiatrist,' she said, wondering at his interest, while sneaking a peak at his nametag, which showed him to be a counselor. She also noted the absence of hair on the expanse of throat and chest that showed through the open two top buttons of his dark-green shirt. 'I work in forensics,' she added, wondering if this handsome young man would even know what that was.

'Really, that's interesting. So the "not guilty by reason of mental insanity" people?'

'Exactly, and quite a bit more,' she said, taking a sip of coffee and noting how dry her mouth had become. 'And you're with the Department of Family and Youth Services.'

'I'm a counselor . . . at least for now.' He flashed a smile that was merry and mischievous.

'And then?' she asked, feeling the contagion of his joy and wondering just how young he was. She was guessing twenty-two, maybe twenty-three, twenty-five tops.

'I start medical school in the fall.'

'Really? Congratulations. Where are you going?'

'NYU, I just got my acceptance letter. I also got into Columbia, but it's easier to stay downtown.'

OK, she thought, *accepted to two of the best medical schools in the country, crazily handsome and smart*, and as the lights started to dim, *Maybe this conference won't be a total waste . . . of course he could be gay. Does he shave his chest? And for God's sake, Barrett – way too young!*

Sneaking the occasional glance at him, and suspecting he might be doing the same back, Barrett half-listened as the Governor got up to the spot-lit podium and made his opening remarks. He stressed the critical importance of this initiative, how change must come, how each and every child entrusted to the state must be given the opportunity to . . .

She felt a shiver as Chase turned and whispered close to her ear, 'I don't like to be a cynic, but I wonder if this might all be a terrible waste.'

'It's almost impossible,' she whispered back, 'so many variables with each of these kids and not well suited for top-down solutions that a lot of suits make at a conference.'

'One size does not fit all,' he responded, as the moderator introduced the keynote speaker for the morning session.

Barrett's attention was suddenly pulled to the podium by the mention of her boss's name.

The moderator, a consultant whose firm had been given the task of pulling together what was clearly a major conference, gushed through Janice's accomplishments. 'We are thrilled and honored to have with us today a woman who won't just tell us about the problem, but will help us chip away at a series of harsh realities to find core solutions that can make a difference in the lives of real children. Dr. Janice Fleet has not just talked the talk, she has walked the walk, from her years with the Department of Family and Youth Services, where she obtained seven- and eight-figure federal grants, while always maintaining a clinical caseload, to her ground-breaking achievements opening Mother's Milk, an internationally recognized string of drop-in centers for at-risk, runaway, and throw-away youth. The Mother's Milk centers have set a standard on getting services into the field. Every year Mother's Milk provides tens of thousands of homeless and at-risk youths with critical medical care, food, social support, housing services, legal aid, or just a friendly ear, always with the motto – *We do not judge.*

'It was a sad day for the department when she left to take on her current position as the Commissioner for Mental Health. However, as she's here to tell us today, this move does not represent an abandonment of her commitment to our youth, but is the next critical step in building bridges to support our most vulnerable youth.

'We are very grateful that she is with us today as we undertake this most important task. I give you . . . Dr. Janice Fleet.'

Barrett wondered why Janice hadn't mentioned she was the keynote. Then again, she had been somewhat preoccupied with Jerod. She felt a twinge of guilt as she watched her boss take the podium in a burgundy skirt suit, her blonde hair worn up, and her cream blouse open at the neck. 'I'd like to thank all of you for having me here . . . and for being here. I'm also a bit worried, because I'm not certain that I have any great expertise . . . or answers.'

Her candor surprised Barrett as Janice freed the microphone and stepped from behind the podium to the front of the stage.

'I'll tell you what my approach has been, and this could turn into the shortest talk ever. What I know to be true in terms of working with these kids is that everything must happen at the level of the individual child or teen. This doesn't mean you can't think in broader terms about program development, resource allocation, and all of that other stuff that we administrators like so much.' There was a round of polite laughter. 'End of the day what matters and what makes a difference is how well that case manager connects with that child. Is there enough food in their belly? Do they have a safe place to sleep at night? Is somebody harming them, and how do we intervene and not make things worse? Because as someone who's worked for years in state agencies, I know that even the most well-intended intervention can make things worse. Children want to be with their parents, they need to be with their parents, and yet we're often faced with situations that are too dangerous and too damaging.' Janice looked down at the floor, and then back out at her audience, seemingly scanning the faces, and smiling at people she recognized – including Hugh. 'Sometimes I hate talking about this stuff, because it can quickly get to that point that seems overwhelming, almost paralyzing. But then I come back to what I know is true, and works. Everything we do, without exception, must center on that one child or teenager, never losing focus of who they are, what they've been through, what they need, and perhaps most importantly finding out what they want. It's not a new approach, and it's certainly not something that I lay claim to. I like the expression "meet the person where they're at" that's been coined by the Harm Reduction movement and I also think the motivational approaches that have been so well studied with substance abuse and dependence are getting to exactly the same point. It's about practicality and doing what works. If someone shoots dope and doesn't want to stop, how can you help them? Well, maybe by focusing on what they do want . . . a place to live, a chance to get back into school, a job, friends, a girlfriend, medical help, clean clothes.' She paused, and shook her head. 'This was the approach I took when establishing Mother's Milk. All of the case workers, and even the volunteers, were trained to not judge these kids and young adults who have been through so much. Everything they do – even the bad things – makes sense. They turn to drugs to numb the pain, the crimes they commit are for food, drugs and clothing . . . and sadly some of the crimes that will get them locked up are the very ones that were perpetrated against them as children. When I first started out in this field, I would never have believed that I'd get to this point. But now, when someone tells me that one of our clients is a sexual predator, my first thought is that they are likely also a survivor of trauma and sexual abuse; sadly, I am almost never wrong. That had a great deal to do with my shift from my first love at DFYS to my current position with DMH. Our kids grow up, and how they make the transition into adulthood . . .' She paused and looked down, there was brutal frankness in what she said next. 'It's not going well.'

In spite of her reluctance to be there, Barrett found Janice's words moving and on target. She espoused a matter-of-fact approach and the only one that would make a difference in someone's life.

'Powerful stuff,' Chase whispered, as Janice finished.

'Indeed,' Barrett said, and wondered why she'd responded like a Jane Austen heroine. She'd also started to notice more about Chase, at whom she was trying hard not stare. His black leather boots were trendy and expensive. She wouldn't have put money on it, but having prowled the discount racks at Prada, they had the distinctive flare of the designer. Perhaps knock-offs, but even so, what did that say about the man? No wedding ring. Metrosexual? Gay? His jacket, too, perfectly tailored, not a wrinkle across his broad shoulders. The guy was into fashion, but counselors for the DFYS, especially young ones, weren't that well paid – forty or fifty grand tops.

Next speaker was Commissioner Carlos Martinez – Janice's replacement at DFYS – armed with a PowerPoint presentation. Mostly statistics and charts about high-risk kids aging out of the youth system – they were grim. Thirty percent arrested at least once in the year following their release; over seventy percent had serious mental health problems, and roughly the same number into problems with drugs and/or alcohol. 'As desperate as all of that is,' he continued, 'this is the part that we have got to do something about. Ten percent of these kids will be dead within three years of leaving our . . . care. This was in the morning paper.' Barrett shot forward in her seat as he flashed a black-and-white scan of a newspaper article – it had today's date, a crime-scene photo that showed the bodies of Ashley Kane and Bobby Dix. Her heart raced and she thought of Jerod, and felt a rush of helplessness; she shouldn't be here, she should be trying to find him.

She glanced to her left and saw that Chase too had been disturbed by the photo. She revised her inventory of him: *Gorgeous, smart, knows how to dress and has a heart. Way too young, Barrett, don't even think about it – has to be gay.* Her ruminations were mixed with thoughts of Hobbs, of how right it felt being back with him, and of how strange it felt to know he was dating someone.

Chase felt Barrett startle in her seat as the grainy photo of Bobby and his troublemaker girlfriend filled the screen. Up to now this had been hot; getting a firsthand look at the beautiful Dr. Conyors, neither her pictures – both the ones online and the framed montage now in his desk drawer – nor Janice's description had done her justice. He glanced at the podium as Commissioner Martinez talked.

'Robert . . . Bobby Dix . . . was one of ours,' Carlos Martinez said. 'He left his group home on his eighteenth birthday, and was dead before his twentieth.'

'Sad stuff,' Chase commented, letting his words waft toward Dr. Conyors.

'Very,' she said.

Chase felt her gaze flit over his perfect profile. This part of things was just like fishing, the bait drifting on the surface, letting out the line, waiting for that first bite. He sensed her attraction, from the dryness in her throat to the furtive glances, as though needing to confirm that he was really that beautiful.

'At least he's not shifting the blame,' she added, as the commissioner candidly laid out the failures of the system.

'That comes later,' Chase said, catching her eye. He smiled. 'The whole agency is obsessed with documentation and covering your ass. Pretty sad, actually.' He loved the color of her eyes, somewhere between gray and blue, hard to be sure in the dim light . . . she wore almost no makeup, just a hint of lipstick, her skin was flawless, but her clothes were a catastrophe, at least from his perspective. She was in a navy off-the-rack skirt suit, with a mannish button-down shirt – it was clear she did not like to bring attention to herself, even her jewelry, tiny gold earrings and a plain gold chain around her neck, was a study in understatement.

He turned back, wondering at the body she was concealing, *Is she still nursing?* and relieved that Bobby's photo had been replaced by snapshots of other dead youths, none more than twenty or twenty-one. Commissioner Martinez gave brief histories of each, how long they had been wards of the state, how they had lived and how they had died – mostly through drug overdoses and suicide, but there were homicides as well. Chase recognized a few of the faces; one – like Bobby – had been part of the family, but he'd gotten too old and a little sloppy. Bored with the well-intentioned dribble, he let his gaze wander toward Janice, sitting on the stage, her hands folded in her lap, a look of fixed concentration on her face as she nodded in approval with the commissioner's talking points. In the front row he spotted the man whose electronic passkey he'd used a day ago to gain access to the lovely Dr. Conyors' office. He was nodding along with Janice, and every few seconds would turn in her direction. Obviously one of her lackeys; he wondered if he'd slept with her, or was it just the usual kiss-up at the office to get ahead?

'Potent,' Dr. Conyors said as the lights turned up, signaling the midday break.

Chase used the back of his sleeve to wipe away an imaginary tear, as all around him he saw people reaching for tissues. He looked at her, and cocked a half-smile. 'Dr. Conyors, I am thoroughly depressed,' he said.

'Yeah, and it's Barrett,' she said.

'Chase,' he said, extending his hand and taking hers in a gentle shake. Her fingers were long and there was strength in her grip.

She turned away, and smoothed a long bang from off her brow as she opened up her packet. 'They want us to divide up in work-groups,' she said.

'Which one are you in?' he asked, even though he already knew.

'Criminal and legal dimensions of at-risk youth.'

'What do you know,' he said, 'me too, probably because two-thirds of my caseload is budding young thugs and thugettes. It seems I'm always bailing somebody out.' He shook his sleeve back from his right wrist and glanced at his watch. 'We've got fifteen minutes to find room D132.'

OK, Barrett thought, catching the Movado logo on the black dial that had four gold dots to denote the three, six, nine and twelve, *let's add money to the list, and I bet those shoes aren't knock-offs. Wealthy girlfriend? Boyfriend? Family money?*

'You want to grab some coffee?' he asked. 'And I don't mean that boiled crap downstairs. There's a Starbucks around the corner.'

'And every corner,' she added, but fresh air was suddenly very appealing. 'Let's go.'

Pushing their way into the emptying throng, they drifted up the stairs of the auditorium. She walked just behind him, and noticed how others turned to look at him – mostly women, but a few men as well. He took the stairs with an easy grace and she guessed his height at around six two or three – about the same as Hobbs. She had the oddest thought, that this was a man without flaw. His thick, almost black wavy hair left no flake of dandruff on his jacket that gave a silhouette of broad shoulders tapering to a narrow waist. He looked back at her, a stray bang across his forehead. He pointed toward an opening in the crowd, and reaching back to grab her hand they shot through.

The physical contact, his warm hand strong in hers, but not dragging her, felt easy and sexy. There was an awkward moment as they made it to the top and he let go of her. 'I hate crowds,' he admitted, 'I just had to get out of there. I hope you don't mind.'

'Not at all,' and they headed down to the lobby and outside.

'God, what a gorgeous day,' Chase said as they caught the first whiff of the slightly cool June day. Purple and yellow irises were in full bloom in the carefully tended beds of the municipal building and across the street the small park was an explosion of new green leaves, and pink and white bridle wreath.

Barrett couldn't resist. 'I like New York in the spring.'

Without pause, Chase responded, in an off-key baritone, *'What about you?'*

Thank God, she thought. *Finally a flaw, he's tone deaf. But he knows show tunes . . . gay gay gay. OK, so he's gay, probably has a wealthy boyfriend and will make a nice buddy for this miserable conference.* 'So how did you get dragged into this?' she asked, as they headed for coffee.

'I'm kind of a department golden boy,' he said, catching her off guard. 'You see,' and he threw an odd look, almost as though he were testing her, 'I was one of those at-risk kids.'

'What do you mean?' she asked, realizing she might have been way off base with her first impressions.

'Foster care of one kind or another since I was three.'

'I'm sorry, Chase, I had no intention of prying.'

'You're not, it's one of those things that either you try to keep hidden or you let just be a part of you, and people either can deal with it or they can't.'

'I imagine it must give you amazing insight in working with these kids as their counselor,' she said.

'It does, because I know exactly what they've been through. Or if I haven't been through it myself, I was around kids who'd had the same horrible things happen to them.'

'Do you enjoy the work?' she asked.

'Mostly,' he said, 'it's nice to see that some of them can pull it together, try to make it past the horrible hand they've been dealt. But others . . .'

'I know,' she said, her thoughts drawn back to Jerod and Hobbs's question – *Why does he get to you so much?* 'I've got one now that I'm working with, you see all the potential and then all of the obstacles and you don't know if they'll ever make it. Or if you can really make any kind of difference.'

'It definitely gets to you, and I think if I did it too much longer, I'd become one of the department burnouts. So what about this kid makes him special?'

'The usual mess. A psychotic disorder – probably schizophrenia – but when he's on his meds, you'd never know. And the trouble he gets into with the law is all petty stuff, then there's the horrible childhood, the bad things that happened to him when he was in foster care . . .' She stopped, realizing how enjoyable it would be to discuss Jerod's case with someone like Chase, also how wrong and a breach of confidentiality.

'He's one you think you can save.' He held the door for her at Starbucks, and they both ordered large lattes with extra shots of espresso. They spoke little inside, but when they got out, Chase said, 'Can I ask *you* something personal?'

'OK,' she said warily. 'I do reserve the right not to answer.'

'Understood.' He sipped his latte through the hole in the plastic cover, *just like letting out fishing line*. 'You are without doubt one of the most attractive women I have ever met, why no wedding ring?'

He saw her recoil and wondered if he'd pushed too fast.

She paused. 'I was married,' she said.

'Divorced?'

'Widowed,' she said simply.

'Kids?'

'OK, buster,' she said, 'I thought you said one question.'

'Sorry,' he smiled, 'I'm just curious.'

'I have a son . . . Max.'

'Excellent name, how old?'

'Four months.'

'Really?' coloring his voice with surprise, and pretending to choke on his latte. He coughed a couple times, and used the napkin to wipe his nose. He stopped and looked at her, not too much to be creepy, just enough so she could know that he admired her figure. 'You gave birth four months ago?'

'Sure did,' she said.

'I have so many questions,' he continued, noting the rise of color in her cheeks, 'but I have a feeling I've gone over my quota.'

She laughed, as they came back to the steps of the conference center. 'Boy, I don't want to go back in,' she said.

'We could play hooky,' he offered.

'Uh-huh, I don't know how your boss will take that, but mine will be auditing all of the sign-in sheets to make certain I didn't miss a single session.'

'Mine's the same,' he said, 'plus I'm supposed to represent the department as not being one giant screw-up. I am an example of how the system can work; their shining star.'

'So, shining star, do they know you're leaving?' she asked.

'No.' He glanced up at the massive marble-fronted facade and steps. 'And that's complicated.'

'Because?'

'OK . . .' He lowered his voice, and thought, *After the compliments come the secrets, let me be the man you want.* Or as Janice called him 'her chameleon', but even she didn't know how true that was. 'If you nark me out, I will find you and do horrible things that only an *at-risk* adult could do.'

'I won't breathe a word.'

'It's a somewhat big deal,' he said. 'The department paid for my undergraduate degree one hundred percent. It was through a scholarship program that no longer exists. In principle it should have worked, but I think the results with the exception of me and half a dozen others weren't so great. In exchange for promising a year of service to the department for each year of college, they paid for everything. Even a monthly allowance, which while it wasn't great, did take care of the mac-and-cheese two boxes for a dollar on sale at Gristedes. And don't get me wrong. I am extremely grateful, but what they don't know is that while I was taking all of the social-work courses, making it look as though I'd go on for the master's, I was also busting my butt to get in all the pre-med requirements.'

'You've not finished your four years of payback,' she said, realizing her guess at his age couldn't be far off, and further upgrading this gorgeous man's intelligence; pre-med with all of the chemistry, calculus, organic, micro, bio, and physics was hard enough, but to do it as a double major. *This dude has serious IQ points.*

'I have another year to go.'

'You're twenty-four?' she asked.

'Five, and now who's prying?'

As they headed up the stairs, she figured the age difference. She was thirty-three, thirty-four in July, which wasn't that far off. It was a solid eight or nine years, *and what the hell are you thinking about anyway*, she reminded herself. She thought of Hobbs, although he said he'd moved on, and then of Ralph, just over a year since he was run down coming home from the symphony.

Back inside there was an excited buzzing of voices as everyone pulled facility maps from their folders and went in search of their respective rooms. 'I think it's close,' Chase said, and again she noted how people snuck glances at him, a couple doing semi-comical double-takes, as if uncertain of what they'd seen. It was also one of those rare times where she tuned in to the looks *she* attracted from men. Most days it was something she shoved to the back of her awareness, always damping down her looks with a minimum of makeup and ultra-conservative clothing – mostly suits that she could wear to court. She'd learned to keep her eyes forward when walking the streets of New York, not acknowledging the frequent head turns, never making eye contact. But now, because of the proximity to Chase, she wanted to let herself meet the glance of the man with the graying hair who smiled and then looked away – obviously married – and then the social-worker type in the khakis, plaid shirt, and Birkenstocks who grinned widely when she returned his look.

Chase turned and caught the exchange. 'Friend of yours?'

'No, just another schmuck who got pulled into this.'

'Hmmm. I think this is ours,' he said, looking at the number next to the door.

The room was classroom size with chairs and tables arranged in a circle and a modest buffet on one side with coffee and hot-water urns. A smiling redhead in a green suit with a green-edged nametag – denoting that she was one of the consultants – greeted them. She looked first at their nametags – blue-edged. 'Hi,' she gushed, extending her hand first to Chase, 'I'm Monica Fitzsimmons, I'll be your facilitator.' The woman's high-wattage smile made Barrett's teeth ache, and she did her best to be pleasant as the woman squealed, 'Dr. Conyors! You're our forensic expert, how thrilling that must be!'

Fortunately, Monica had spotted the next arrival and moved on before Barrett could respond.

Chase steered them to purple-and-gray upholstered office chairs close to the door and under his breath mimicked Monica's voice and whispered, 'How thrilling.'

'Don't,' she warned, trying to hold back a giggle.

'No really,' he persisted, his imitation uncanny, 'just thrilling!'

She glanced down at the agenda on the table. 'Oh no,' she whispered.

'What?' he asked.

'You've not been to many of these, have you?'

'It's my first,' and then pitched his voice to a low growl. 'I'm a virgin.'

'Yeah, right.' She pointed at the top of the page. 'Opening exercises are never good.'

She wasn't wrong, and as soon as Monica had checked off the last name on her list, 'OK, it's time to start. Everyone in your seats, and let's get to work!'

It could have been worse, at least Hugh had been assigned to another group and the opening exercise wasn't a total waste. It involved going around one by one, saying your name, the agency you worked for, and why you were at the conference. The twenty or so people in her group were either counselors – like Chase – or upper management. Someone had actually given some thought to this, bringing together the people who worked with the kids and the people with enough administrative juice to make some changes.

Monica kept things moving, and the woman had an endless supply of flipcharts and markers, taking down points and ideas while keeping up an energetic stream of 'excellent', 'outstanding', 'perfect'. She was also adept at steering them back to the topic of how and why so many of these kids got involved with the legal system.

An hour into the session she'd created an agenda, and at the very top she'd written – *Dissect the problem.* As Chase was nonchalantly slipping Barrett a note, Monica turned to her. 'Dr. Conyors, as a forensic psychiatrist, maybe you could take the first go at this.'

Barrett looked up from Chase's note, which had a single word on it – *Lunch?*

'It's not simple,' she said, hiding his note under her hand, 'and the people I evaluate who've been part of the system represent a sub-population. Although the more I hear today . . . maybe I need to rethink that. Basically, I work with adults who have both some form of mental illness and criminal behavior; the vast majority also have substance-abuse problems. By the time they get to me, it's more damage control and for those with truly dangerous or predatory behavior – like rape and pedophilia – it's about containment, and the level of risk that any community can tolerate in terms of putting them out in the world.'

'OK,' Monica said, indicating that Barrett wasn't quite giving her the information she wanted, 'let's go backwards. From your perspective, how is it that they've ended up in your office?'

Barrett looked around at the faces, men and women whose working lives were spent with these children. There'd be no need to dummy this down, if any group could get it, they would. 'It starts early,' she said. 'Most of the young adults in the high-risk groups – the ones who've committed crimes, or display illegal sexual behaviors, or are involved with other high-risk activities like prostitution and substance abuse – have been through a series of traumas and separations, most starting at an early age. They get taken from home, put into foster care, then another foster home, at some point they're molested, maybe at several points, they get shifted to a group home, they start to latch on to any adult who pays them attention or flatters them, but that's all behavior we see on the outside. It's what's on the inside that's more important to understand. With all of this disruption early in life, and I'm even talking about babies and before the child is able to talk, important developmental milestones are delayed or might never occur at all.'

Several men and women had started to nod in agreement, as Barrett forged ahead into what had always been a hot topic in theoretical psychology. 'Without a stable parent, the child never creates that hugely important bond. He never sees the reflection in his mother's eyes that lets him know things are going to be OK, and equally important the underpinnings of empathy and compassion will not form. Without those, without understanding that hitting Mommy makes her feel bad and in turn makes you feel bad, the building blocks of what we consider morals are gone.' As she spoke, she thought of Max and how little time she got to spend with him; she was also acutely aware that Chase was staring at her. 'Without those the child's behavior as he grows up is pretty much guided by making himself feel good, regardless of the feelings of others – "I like your Game Boy, I want your Game Boy, I'm going to take your Game Boy, and if you get in my way I'm going to hit you." While some may be able to model socially appropriate behavior by watching and learning from others, it will be applied externally, almost like putting on a suit of clothes. Underneath there will be no true compassion or ability for empathy. This doesn't mean one hundred percent that the kid is going to grow up to be a sociopath, but we've certainly laid the groundwork.'

'If what you're saying is accurate,' Monica said, 'and judging by the expressions I see around the room, I suspect you've hit the nail on the head, then wouldn't it be true that where we can have the most impact is with the very young?' And she turned her attention to a balding man in khakis and a polo shirt who was the director of a safe home where children who had just been removed from their parents' custody were put until a more permanent solution was found.

To Chase, Barrett's words had the effect of a light switched on. Yes, he'd heard this before and studied Attachment Theory in the psych courses he'd taken, but that had just been theory. She was talking about him and his childhood; it made sense, and gave him a queer feeling of being exposed. She missed one or two vital points, but that could be forgiven. She didn't realize how his total lack of empathy gave him power and detachment. It made him strong, like a cat that feels no sadness for the prey it toys with and then kills.

He whispered, 'OK, beautiful and brilliant . . . please tell me you'll have lunch with me.' Janice was frantic for him to finish the Jerod thing; it wouldn't be hard to find out what Barrett knew, and if necessary have her meet with an unfortunate accident. If it involved the boy, that would be best – he'd already barged into her office with a loaded firearm, it wouldn't be a stretch for crazy boy to do something . . . well, crazy. At this point he knew Jerod was with Marky, probably doped to the gills; it wouldn't be hard to stage something and get them both out of the way. Although the more time he spent with the beautiful psychiatrist, the more that kind of plan seemed wrong.

'I can't, I'm booked.'

'A date?' he whispered, seeing in Dr. Barrett Conyors an exquisite possibility. Women like her were rare, and despite her beauty and intelligence she carried the scent of self-doubt; women like that, once under his thrall, could be controlled. As a doctor, even one employed by the state, she had to be making close to a couple hundred grand a year – it could be enough.

'Hardly.'

He knew she was attracted; it was just a matter of gently reeling in. 'Another time?'

'Maybe.'

'Dinner . . . tonight?' He smiled, and saw the slight intake of her breath, how her pulse had quickened.

'Maybe.'

'OK, you two,' Monica said, her expression one of mock exasperation, 'I have exceptionally good hearing, and while I do love a good shipboard romance, please save it for the break.'

Barrett blushed. Chase grinned, knowing he'd not been wrong. An older woman seated to her right whispered, 'For God's sake, go to dinner with him. If not for you, do it for me.'

THIRTEEN

Janice felt Chase's breath hot on the back of her neck, his strong arms circling around her front. His fingers deftly unclasped her lace under-wired bra. She needed this, and hated that she did. His face nestled in the back of her hair, his hands cupped her full breasts that with each passing day sagged a bit more.

'Nice,' he growled, pressing his hardness into the small of her back.

At least she still aroused him, although she never quite knew what went on between his ears. Even now as he pulled her playfully toward his massive modernist leather bed, raised up on two steps – like a stage – in the middle of his TriBeCa loft, she wished her thoughts would shut up. *Surrender, don't think about the age difference, or the spider veins in your legs, or how goddamn handsome he is. Or how when you looked out from the podium you saw him flirting with Barrett Conyors – you told him to do that.* A groan escaped her lips as his tongue slid down the side of her neck and circled the soft flesh of her earlobe. Her back arched. 'Hurry,' she whispered, knowing there wasn't much time in the conference lunch break.

'You want this?' His teeth pulled at her ear, balancing shades of intense pleasure and the beginnings of pain as he nipped playfully at her diamond studs.

'Hurry.' She turned into him and threw her arms over the rolling muscles of his back, letting them slide down to the firm mounds of his ass. She needed him inside of her, his hardness, the proof that he was hers, that she was still attractive, that she could have a man as gorgeous as Chase.

He did not disappoint; he never did. From his rock-hard cock to the way he stroked her body, whispering the words that let her know he found her desirable and exciting.

'So beautiful,' he said as the last rolling wave of pleasure coursed from her toes to a tingling at the roots of her hair.

She lay back, savoring the moment of post-coital quiet, of having her mind be at peace, even though it wouldn't last. She watched the ceiling fan overhead as it lazily spun against the zinc-patterned ceiling of this former warehouse that had been converted into large, trendy, and expensive lofts – far more expensive than what an agency counselor could afford. The air was softly scented with citrus zest. His furniture was leather-upholstered modern Italian chairs and couches, with frames of welded nickel that had cost their previous owner thousands and even tens of thousands of dollars. 'Dom had beautiful taste,' she said, remembering her long-time friend who had succumbed to the ravages of AIDS three years ago.

'Yes,' Chase said, rising up in bed, his muscled torso glittering with a sheen of sweat. 'And he was very good to me. You both were.'

Janice kept quiet, the topic of the arrangement she'd set up with Chase and her sick friend, the architect Dominic Hilliard, had been one of urgency and convenience on all parts. Dominic had needed live-in care and Chase, who was about to be discharged from the department, albeit with a full scholarship, needed a place to live. 'You took good care of him,' she said. 'Even at the end. And then when his family swooped down.'

Chase's tone darkened. 'They wanted nothing to do with him when he was alive, but they all became real interested in what he had. I'm lucky to have come away with this; he wanted me to have more; he'd said so. Which reminds me, my cut from the girl we sold?'

Janice wished he'd turn away as she retrieved her bra and panties, and dressed carefully. She caught her reflection in a massive nickel-framed mirror that ran lengthwise over the black granite in the open kitchen. It was like some horrible ultra-realist painting, her hair in disarray, the lace of her bra visible through her unbuttoned blouse, Chase like some naked god rising from the sheets in the background, and there on a red-leather chair – part of a furniture line that Dom had designed – was her pocketbook filled with a wad of hundred-dollar bills in an envelope. Quickly doing up her blouse and smoothing back her hair with her fingers, she retrieved the bag and pulled out the envelope.

'Thanks.' Chase came up beside her, still naked, the smells

of their lovemaking – and citrus – pulsing from his warm, hard body. She couldn't help but watch as he weighed it in the palm of his hand, and then opened it. 'Is this all?'

'It's fifteen grand,' she said, her tone neutral, bracing herself for his petulance and anger.

'The girl went for one forty; I need more. I deserve more.'

Janice turned away, hating this. 'What's the status of the boy? And Dr. Conyors? This was fun,' she said for malicious effect, 'but you were supposed to find out the extent of the damage and fix it.'

'It's being taken care of,' Chase replied, coolly.

'That's what you said before, and look at the mess.' She again saw her reflection. Damn Dom and his love of glass and mirrors. Almost like he wanted to see the progression of his flesh as it decayed. She didn't want to risk looking at Chase, knowing that when he was angry or frustrated his face became a blank mask, and what lay beneath was scary and beautiful and cruel.

'Marky picked up Jerod last night. By the end of the day we'll know everything he told Barrett – Dr. Conyors, we'll know where the cell phones are. She started to talk about him; she's worried about him, seems to really care.'

'Good,' Janice said, putting on her jacket. 'And then no more Jerod? And if you think she suspects anything . . . we can't risk that. You'll have to take care of her.'

'Yes,' Chase said, 'and that should all be worth something.'

'We'll see.' She turned to look at him. 'Get dressed, we have to go back to the conference . . . Do you think she's pretty?'

'Extremely,' Chase said, 'and not the type to advertise it either. Almost no makeup and a haircut that looks like it was done at a barber shop. It's hard to believe she has a new baby; it's clear that she's in amazing shape.'

Janice wondered if Chase were deliberately hitting her soft spots. Her own struggles with infertility, the endless visits to the specialists, Avery's obvious disappointment at her not being able to give him his own children. 'What does she know?'

'Too early to tell. I'm going to try and get her to have dinner tonight. We'll see what we see.'

Janice felt her anger boil as she stared at Chase and his flawless body. 'Do you plan to fuck her? Is that it?'

Chase met Janice's gaze, his expression blank, almost peaceful.

'Janice,' he cocked an eyebrow, 'we both know that it's not about what I want.'

She took a step back and nearly stumbled on her heels.

He didn't break his gaze. 'What I do want, what I need from you, is more money. I'll take care of the Jerod business and find out just how much the lovely Barrett knows. You will compensate me for that.'

'I told you, we'll see.' She turned, her breath caught in her throat. At the door she looked back at him, he'd walked to the kitchen and was selecting an orange from out of the blue glass bowl. She fled into the hallway and toward the industrial elevator; her insides jumbled. Why didn't she just give him more money? She knew that the taxes and monthly upkeep and common fees on his loft were staggering. Dom had left him the place free and clear, transferring the title well before his death, all of the legal work had been ironclad. But the money Dom had wanted Chase to have he never got, his family had seen to that. They'd contested the will and drawn Chase as little more than a prostitute taking advantage of a dying man.

Janice couldn't tear her thoughts from Chase as the elevator carried her down. Out on the street she hailed a cab to take her back to the conference. She knew that she could have, and possibly should have, given Chase a bigger cut. She also knew why she hadn't. She thought of one of the many conversations she'd had with Dom about Chase. She'd known when she had hooked the two of them up that there was the strongest of possibilities Dom would try to seduce Chase. What she hadn't counted on was the bond that had developed between the two men. Chase had cared for Dom, patiently ferrying him through the endless doctors' appointments, staying by his side during his three last hospitalizations for pneumocystis pneumonia, and the scare when they thought a parasite had infected his brain. But one conversation in particular stuck with her. It had been near the end. Dom had wanted to hang on at least until Chase's college graduation, and knew that it was unlikely. He'd asked Janice to keep an eye on him. 'You don't think it to look at him, and I do like to look at him,' Dom had wheezed through the oxygen tubing he was forced to wear. 'He's like a baby that desperately needs to be held and fed . . . just not too much.' At the time Janice had taken it with several grains of salt, just the ramblings of a dying man. 'But you know about that,' he'd added. 'You're the mother in

Mother's Milk, feeding all those kids, trying to wean them off the tit. That's what we are, giant tits filled with beautiful milk. But if you give them too much . . . they just up and leave.'

The cab quickly traveled the short distance back to the conference. Up ahead she spotted the tall, lean figure of Dr. Conyors, and her heart raced. The woman was nothing but trouble, too smart and too curious. This Jerod thing was way too close for comfort, and this awful sense of dread. Everything she'd worked so hard to achieve would come undone. It would be so much easier to be rid of her and have someone like Hugh in charge of the forensic center. She clicked open her bag and gave a twenty to the cabbie. While she waited for her change and receipt, she checked her reflection in the rearview mirror. She put on a blank smile, and hoped she didn't look like a woman who'd just had a roll in the hay with her much younger lover. She told herself that if Chase handled Jerod and got rid of Dr. Conyors she'd give him another fifteen, but not more than that, just enough to keep him fed and to keep him coming back.

Chase stood naked in the shaded window, one hand holding the orange firm as the other sliced through the skin with a stainless-steel peeler. He watched Janice get into the cab. *How old she looks.* Not that it mattered, except she'd brought him only enough money to make it through the month; he was sick of it. He looked down at the perfect piece of fruit in his hand and then at the rind, which he'd deftly opened flowerlike into six even sections. He slowed his breath, not wanting to give in to the mounting anger that could rob him of reason. His rage simmered as he threw out the fruit and grabbed a sealed pre-threaded suture from a kitchen drawer. Cupping the peel together in the palm of his left hand, he let the curved surgical needle enter the fleshy rind at the top, where all of the sections had once connected. He was practicing purse-string stitches, a technique that could pull together a complex open wound. If drawn too tight, the patient would be left with an angry pink scar, if done to perfection the skin would knit together as though it had never been damaged. The peacefulness of the act, of focusing on holding the right tension, eyeballing the edges of the cut, making certain they were aligned just so. The needle entered the flesh, curving in and out of the petal-shaped wedges, weaving together the purse string and then pulling it slowly together until the rind resumed

its original shape. He then grabbed a second fresh suture and
needle and worked a whipstitch down the sides. Each time he
entered the skin he went through a pore of the dimpled surface,
knowing that on human flesh there would be no residual scar.
He replayed the long-ago conversation with Dr. Avery Fleet at
that restaurant with Janice. Dr. Fleet had told him how as
a medical student he'd known that he always wanted to be a
surgeon, to be the very best, and about how he'd practice tying
knots with citrus rind. The next day, Chase had swiped three
oranges from the kitchen of his group home, got a small sewing
kit, and started a practice that he would do each day, at least
one orange a day, sometimes half a dozen. It helped him, made
him not think, got the screams that sometimes rose inside
of him to shut up, just focus on the needle, the thread, and
the flesh. He used to throw them out when he was done, but
Dom asked him to keep them, he liked to watch the way the
skin dried and they became like shriveled heads, filling the air
with orange tang. He needed to calm himself, to not hate Janice
and want to hurt her, to get back to the conference and to
Barrett . . . not that much older than he was, successful, had
a child, she was a doctor. She could help him with so many
things, and they had so much in common; they would look
good together. He liked the way men tried to catch her eye, a
couple even doing double-takes, checking out her face, and
the lithe body she kept hidden under her conservative suit
and button-down blouse.

His fingers flew down the seams of the skin; he'd finish one
more piece, and get dressed. His cell rang. He tied off the
suture and picked up. It was Marky.

'What does he know?' Chase asked. 'What has he told the cops
and that shrink?'

Marky sounded nervous. 'He says he didn't tell them anything,
but they asked lots of questions about where the dope came from.
He swore he'd given no names. He said they had the phones.
I'm so sorry, Chase. He said something else that didn't make
any sense.'

'What's that?'

'He said there was a video of a naked girl on one of the
phones. I didn't know what he was talking about . . . He said it
was Carly, the girl who used to hang out with Bobby and Ashley.
He kept asking me where she was, like I knew anything about it.

He was crying and said she was his girlfriend and that he had to find her.'

Chase felt his stomach lurch. He pictured the girl – Carly Sloan, eighteen years old. She'd been one of his patients and he'd given her Janice's number when she'd faced the terrifying prospect of having to leave her group home, with no money, no family that gave a shit about her, no place to go . . . nothing. 'What did he tell them about her?' Chase asked, trying to think how this could be traced back to him or to Janice.

'I don't know,' Marky said. 'Do you want me to find out? I just gave him three bags and he's nodded out. Just tell me what you want me to do, Chase.'

'Sssshh,' Chase cooed into the phone. 'It's OK, Marky, I'm not mad at you, but I have to know everything. We need to know where those phones are, although . . . the damage may be done there. And I need you to make certain that Jerod does not get away. Do you understand?'

'Yes . . . I've got some super F . . . When can I see you?'

'Soon. Call me when you've gotten everything out of him. We can hook up after.'

'I miss you so much,' Marky said, his voice calmer. 'I'm so sorry I fucked up.'

'It's OK, baby.'

There was a pause on the line. 'I love you, Chase,' Marky said. 'Oh fuck no!' he blurted and the connection went dead, as if he'd dropped the phone.

Chase held the phone and waited. Seconds ticked and bad thoughts streamed into his brain. He glanced at the kitchen clock shaped like a sunburst, and watched the second hand go around one whole rotation. He pressed redial and waited for Marky to pick up. He glanced at his partially reconstructed orange, thinking of all the reasons why the line could have gone dead – low battery, lost connection . . . Marky fucking up. He hit redial again. This shit couldn't keep happening.

He had to get back to the conference. He felt his rage and wanted to punch something, or someone. 'Stop . . . stop, get dressed, go back to the conference.' He told himself that Marky had let his cell go dead. 'Focus.' He reminded himself that he needed to make sure that Barrett would meet him for dinner. That helped, and he retrieved his black briefs, and wondered what her body would feel like under his, how her breasts filled with milk would feel in his hands. He punched his arms through his shirt, needing some way to vent off the anger that made his cock tent against the cotton of his briefs as he pulled up his zipper.

Fully dressed, he headed down the four flights of stairs and then pushed through the side-alley door, letting it slam hard behind him. 'Fuck Marky! Fuck Janice!'

He still had ten minutes, and as he walked his head was filled with a confusing mix of all the things that could go wrong, as well as some interesting new ideas. First was that Janice had grown cheap, stringing him along month to month, like he was one of her stupid little dogs. And he was taking way too many risks with the kids and the dope and the auctions; it was too hot, and just a matter of time before it would come crashing down. If they had the video of Carly, how long before someone traced her back to DFYS . . . to him? If Jerod had blabbed they'd know about the family and the kids selling dope in the dorms. Already they could have them under surveillance, setting traps . . . 'Just focus,' and he drafted a mental list of all the things and people that needed to change. Take care of Jerod, Janice, Marky . . . Things needed to change, it was time for the next rung of his ladder – in a few months he'd start medical school, the defining step toward becoming a surgeon. Problem was, he still didn't have enough money – not by a long shot. There had been Dom, now there was Janice . . . and she was cheap, demanding, and old. It was time for someone new, someone who could help him up to the next level. It was time to clean house, and a phrase flashed through his mind – *out with the old and in with the new.*

FOURTEEN

Huddled in the back of Marky's funky little van, Jerod knew he had to get away, that Marky would kill him, just like Bobby and Ashley. He pretended to nod out, the rubber tourniquet dangling from his upper arm, the needle rolling around the truck's rubber mat, his T-shirt wet with the wasted dope. The voice had come back, almost as though it knew its existence was tied in with Jerod's ability to save himself. '*He's going to kill you,*' it said. '*He killed Ashley. He killed Bobby . . . He killed Carly. He's going to kill you. He's going to kill you.*'

He'd known it when Marky appeared in the busy emergency room dressed in surgical scrubs and lab coat. At first he'd not recognized the man who doled out dope on a weekly basis to all the kids selling in the dorms; his spiked blond hair was under a brown wig and he'd taken out his earrings and his nose ring. Jerod didn't really know Marky, other than seeing him at the apartment where Bobby, Ashley, Carly, and the others crashed. His Sunday visits brought the whole house together, everyone there, wanting dope, cash, hoping for something extra.

'I'm carrying,' he whispered, taking Jerod's metal clipboard from the end of his stretcher. 'Do what I tell you and I'll get you out of here. Get you all the dope you want. Make you feel good.'

Jerod was in agony, whatever the doctor at Croton had given him had thrown him into unbearable torment. The mention of dope was all he needed to hear; it would make everything better. The pain, the nausea, the chills, the knowledge that life like this wasn't worth living and that death might be better. That doctor had given him something to make him dope sick, and suddenly here was Marky with dope. He was being tricked, he needed dope, but that's not what made him play along.

'Hurry,' Marky whispered, closing the curtain on the emergency-room cubicle, 'lie back.' And he handed Jerod jeans, T-shirt, and running shoes. 'The doctor wants you to go for an ultrasound,' he said in a louder voice, 'thinks it could be your gallbladder or maybe kidney stones.'

Jerod had thought to say no, to scream for help; he didn't. He knew that going with Marky could mean death, but that didn't matter as he stripped off his brown Croton pajamas and pulled on the new clothes, it was her . . . Carly. If he had any hope of knowing where she was, of maybe saving her, Marky was the only connection. He wondered if Marky had made that video, and how good it would feel to punch him out.

'Lie down and look sick,' Marky said, and he threw a sheet over him and pulled back the curtain.

Seated outside was a young Croton guard working away at his monster Sudoku puzzle. He looked up as Marky pushed the gurney through the opening.

'We'll be back in about fifteen,' Marky said, 'the doctor wants an ultrasound of his abdomen.'

'I should go with you,' the guard said, not getting up.

Jerod shivered, and not needing to fake things, started to retch. 'I'm going to puke,' he said.

Marky grabbed the pink plastic basin and stuck it under Jerod's chin. 'Turn to the side if you vomit,' and then to the guard, 'Your choice, but I don't think this one's going anywhere.'

'I think you're right, fifteen you said?'

'Could be half an hour depending if there's anyone ahead of us.'

'I'll be here,' he responded and resumed his puzzle.

Jerod said nothing as Marky wheeled him toward the elevators, and pressed the up button. On the second floor, he pushed the gurney out and wheeled him toward a deserted stretch of offices. 'Get up,' he said. 'Let's go.'

Jerod followed Marky, on achy rubbery legs. The pain was intense, deep in his hips, knees, and ankles. He heaved again but all that came up was bile and spit. Marky took him to the far end of the corridor. 'I'll get you a fix as soon as we're in my car.' And then they headed down a stairwell, and out a side entrance to the visitors' parking lot. It was after 2 A.M. and the lot was mostly deserted and dimly lit.

Marky's truck was parked well away from overhead lights. Jerod thought it was a strange car, a boxy mini-truck, red with black trim, like something in old movies. The seats in the back had been pulled up and were fixed to the ceiling by hooks and the floor was a rubber mat. 'There's a couple bags in that box back there, help yourself . . . then we talk, but wait till we're out of here.'

Marky shed the lab coat and put a leather jacket over his scrubs and then zipped it up, and put the vehicle into motion.

Jerod wondered if this was how it would end as he opened the metal cookie tin, saw three bags of dope, a clean syringe, tourniquet, spoon, matches, and a candle shaped like a cartoon character. 'What do you need to know?' he asked, hoping that just maybe Marky had some reason to keep him alive.

'A few things.' He stopped at the booth, handed the attendant his slip, and paid the five bucks.

Jerod thought to shout out, to get free from Marky. He glanced at the dope and the silly candle like the ones a lot of the kids liked when they were cooking up a fix. He couldn't remember the name of the cartoon, he'd seen snippets on TV with a character shaped like a yellow sponge who lived underwater.

'OK,' Marky said, as he turned up the road and away from the hospital, 'start by telling me what you did with the cell phones you found on Bobby.'

Jerod shot the bag of dope, and then a second, and tried to answer the questions. 'The cell phones were with my stuff,' he said, thinking about that video with Carly. 'Where's Carly?' he asked. The pain in his joints melted away, a feeling of being OK, of everything being all right, shot from his arm, to his belly, and hushed the voice, just a whisper now, '*He's going to kill you. He killed them all. He's going to kill you.*'

'I don't know where she went,' Marky said, as he drove down I-684. 'Just gone.'

Jerod knew that Marky had to be lying. 'Where could she have gone? Who took that video of her?'

'What the fuck you talking about?' Marky said.

'There was a video on Bobby's phone of Carly.' Jerod started to cry. 'She was naked and somebody had done something to her.'

'I don't know what you're talking about and I don't care,' he said. 'Just another strawberry, either she'll turn up or she won't. Maybe she was making pornos. Maybe she had something going with Bobby.'

'You know something,' Jerod pressed, not about to take the bait. 'You know where she is.'

'Maybe I do. Maybe I don't. Tell me what I need to know and maybe I'll tell you something about her . . . What did you tell that lady shrink? What did you tell her about the kids and the dope?'

'Nothing. She doesn't know anything,' he said, wondering how Marky even knew about Dr. Conyors. *What have I done?* She'd been good to him, had tried to help more than once. '*He's going to kill her,*' the voice said, adding her to the growing list.

'Does she have the cell phones?' Marky asked.

'I don't know, I don't think so,' Jerod lied; wanting the questions to move away from Dr. Conyors. He'd assumed that Marky was taking him back to the city, but after half an hour's drive he turned off 684 onto 84 heading west into Jersey or Pennsylvania.

Wanting the questions to end, Jerod reached for the third and last bag of dope. He cooked it up in the back of the truck, doing everything exaggerated and loud so that Marky would know what he was doing. He tied on the tourniquet and slapped his arm, raising the good vein in the crook of his elbow. He pressed down on the plunger, desperately wanting the dope, but instead letting the needle filled with the milky liquid dribble down his arm and into the fabric of his T-shirt.

He yawned and leaned back against the truck wall; through the window he glimpsed the first pink and purple lights in the sky. He closed his eyes, and tried to steady his breath, the voice getting louder, taking on a rhythm, '*He's going to kill you. He killed Bobby. He killed Ashley. He killed Carly. He'll kill Dr. Conyors.*'

Hours passed and exhaustion overtook him. He fell into a half-drugged sleep and when he awoke daylight streamed through the truck's skylight and dark-tinted windows.

He heard Marky swear, and then the vehicle left the highway. He felt it slow and then come to a stop. He cracked his lids and saw they'd come to a gas station.

'You awake?' Marky whispered.

Jerod kept still.

'You awake?' And Marky got out of the truck.

Jerod couldn't tell how long he'd been asleep, and chanced a look through the van's back windows. They were at a busy truck stop with eighteen-wheelers; a diner and a fast-food burger place. He got up slow and looked around. Marky had locked the doors, but there was a latch on the tailgate. Trying to make no sound, he pulled at the release. It clicked open with a crisp metallic twang, the top flew up and revealed a second latch.

He heard Marky. 'Oh fuck, no!'

Jerod grabbed the latch and pulled. He pushed the tailgate down and stumbled out the back. His sneakers landed hard on the asphalt; the sun burned his eyes.

Marky grabbed at the back of his T-shirt— 'Get back in there!'

Jerod twisted free and ran. At first he thought his feet would give out, but he spotted the restaurant in the distance and bolted with Marky close behind. The voice in his head screamed, and so did he, 'Help me! Somebody help me!' He ran into the restaurant, still screaming. And then he stopped, his gut knotted, barely able to catch his breath, his muscles cramping from withdrawal. He looked back and saw Marky, just outside the door, his van still at the pumps with the back open.

A middle-aged waitress in a baby-blue uniform with a plaid apron and matching cap came over to him. 'Honey, what seems to be the trouble?'

He shivered; gooseflesh popped on his arms. He made eye contact with Marky, standing just outside the restaurant, and saw fury and fear.

'You look sick,' the waitress said. 'You sit right here.' She led him to a just-emptied booth at the counter next to the cash register. He didn't take his eyes off Marky.

The waitress followed his gaze. 'Friend of yours?' she asked.

'No.' He felt in his pockets and realized that the jeans he was wearing weren't his. He had none of his stuff. 'I need to make a call,' he said. 'I have no money. I don't have anything.'

The waitress looked around at her mostly full tables. She shook her head, and pulled out her cell. 'Use mine,' she said, 'and I'll get you something to eat when I get a chance.'

'Thank you.' He watched as Marky turned from the restaurant and stormed back to his van, slamming the tailgate and overhead doors closed.

'What's your name, honey?' she asked.

'Jerod,' he said, feeling a ray of hope as Marky drove off. He just wished he could see where he'd gone. Did he get on the highway or was he just waiting, waiting for him to leave?

'Well, Jerod, I'm Lois,' she said. 'You call your mother or some relative to come and get you and I'll bring you some . . . pie?'

'Thank you,' he said, and tears started to flow.

'Oh, honey,' she laid a hand gently on his back. 'There's no reason to cry, everyone has a bad day, just make your call, eat some apple pie, and things will look a whole lot better, you'll see.'

FIFTEEN

Walking back to the conference from the subway, Barrett tried to hang on to her half-hour at home with Max – an island of peace in the middle of her day. Her thoughts were short-circuited by her cell.

'Dr. Conyors.' Marla's wispy voice. 'I hate to interrupt you, but a call just came that I thought you'd want to know about.'

'Yes?'

'It was Jerod Blank. He sounds like he's in trouble; he said he needs to speak to you.'

'Did he leave a number?' she asked, feeling a rush of anxiety as she put her shoulder bag down on a bus-stop bench.

'Yes, but he said it was a borrowed phone and he didn't know how long he'd be there.'

Barrett grabbed a pen and yellow legal pad from out of the bag, and scribbled down the number. 'How long ago did he call?'

'I just got off the phone with him. I told him I'd call you right away. I hope that was OK.'

'It's fine. If he calls again, ask him where he is. Tell him I'll send someone right out to get him. Or tell him to call 911 and have the police pick him up. I got to go . . . and Marla, please stay by the phone, I might need you to help out with this.' She hung up and immediately dialed the number. It rang three times before a woman with a Jersey accent picked up. 'Hello?'

'Hi, this is Dr. Barrett Conyors, I was given this number for a young man named Jerod Blank.'

'Kind of cute, big head of funny hair, and in some kind of trouble?' the voice replied.

'That's the one.'

'Just ran out of here . . . and I do mean ran,' the woman said. 'Didn't even stay for his pie, which is surprising 'cause he looked kind of green around the edges.'

'Where are you?' Barrett asked.

'Bella's Diner. It's off 84 in Port Jervis.'

'That's about an hour out of Manhattan?'

'Just about.'

'Did you see which way he went?'

'Hard to say, I was getting him something to eat, turned my back, he was gone, and my phone was on the table. At least he didn't take it.'

Barrett wished he had, at least that way she could have talked him into staying safe someplace till she could come for him, or have someone pick him up.

'I could tell he was in some kind of trouble,' the woman offered. 'There was a young man, medium build, brown hair, stood outside, seemed real upset and stormed off in one of those little two-tone Hondas everyone's driving.'

Switching into Hobbs mode, she asked for the details. 'What color was it?'

'Kind of a red wine with black trim.'

'And the man?'

'Young, early twenties, and the funny thing is I thought his hair might be a wig, kind of lopsided. Wore dark wrap-around glasses, looked like money. I just assumed they were friends who'd had some kind of fight. It's not that, is it?'

'No, and if Jerod comes back call the cops and tell them he just escaped from a New York forensic hospital. He hasn't done anything bad, but they need to take him into custody and keep him safe. Is there anything else you can think of that might help me find him?'

There was a pause. 'I couldn't say for certain, this is a busy place and all, and there's a lot of ways out of here, but he said that he didn't have any money, so I bet he hitched a ride with one of the truckers.'

'Which means he could be anywhere.'

'Sorry I can't be more help; if I think of anything or he comes back I'll be sure to do as you say.'

Barrett thanked the woman, got her name, and hung up. She pulled up Hobbs's cell number and pressed. She gave him the update, while trying to fight down a growing sense of frustration.

'My guess,' Hobbs said, 'he'll head back to the city. He's either going to try and find you or find dope. And nice as you are to him, I bet he'll find a fix first.'

'Which sends him right back into harm's way. Shit! Ed, we're dealing with something big, and these kids are just disposable bits. I'm at this stupid conference right now . . . maybe not so stupid, but well intended and pointless, and I shouldn't be here.'

Ed chuckled. 'No, really, Barrett, how do you feel about it?'

'What about the narcotics squad,' she asked, 'are they finding anything . . . like who's setting up these kids to sell dope in the dorms?'

'Whoa,' Hobbs said, 'don't look to narcotics for the answer. They're interested in working back as high up in whatever organization as possible. They don't move fast.'

'What about the girl, then? Jerod as good as ID'd her. She can't have just vanished off the globe.'

'My guess . . . she's doing Internet porn,' he offered. 'Maybe she doesn't want Jerod to know or . . . possibly against her will. Someone drugged her, stripped her . . . God knows what else.'

'I don't know,' she said. 'It's disgusting to contemplate, but what comes to mind is white slavery. She was being displayed, like something for sale.'

'Not so far-fetched. White slavery is real . . . especially for wholesome-looking girls. Occasionally they find these kids years after the fact, they're either dead, or so traumatized that they wished they were.'

Barrett looked down the street as fellow conference attendees streamed back from their lunch break. Mostly state employees, or else working for non-profit agencies that were funded by the state. 'Ed, three of the four kids – Bobby, Jerod, and Carly – were products of the foster and group-home system. The only one who wasn't was Ashley Dix, who just happened to fall for drugs and the bad boy who could get them for her.'

'You don't think it's a coincidence.'

'I don't know, but I have a feeling that Jerod might. There's stuff he wasn't telling.'

She felt a gentle tap on her shoulder. 'Hey, Barrett.' She turned to find herself staring into Chase's eyes. In the bright sun, they had specks of gold and amber. 'Hobbs,' she smiled at Chase, finding it hard to catch her breath, 'give me a call later.'

'You got it, and I'll see if I can do a bit of street work. If my hunch is right, the kid is going to be like a homing pigeon back to his supply.'

'I hope you're wrong,' she said, 'call me if you find him.'

'Problem?' Chase asked, as she put her cell back into her bag.

'Just some kid who got himself into big trouble.'

'The one you were so worried about?'

'Yeah.' She broke from Chase's gaze.

'Anything I can do to help?' he offered. 'If he was one of the department's recent graduates I might be able to access his records.'

'Aren't those sealed?'

'In theory.'

'But not in reality.'

'Not so much,' he admitted, 'especially since they scanned everything and made it electronic. Maybe he has some family or something that he'd try to go back to.'

Why would he think that? she wondered, like he knew something.. Before she could ask, she spotted Janice in sunglasses, stepping out of a cab. For an instant she hoped she'd not been seen, but Janice nodded in her direction as she smoothed down her skirt, and headed toward them. 'Barrett, so glad you're here.'

Not that you left me a choice, she thought, her jaw tense. 'It's interesting,' she said, keeping the futility she felt about such projects to herself.

'Amazing how many people they roped into this,' Janice replied. She sighed, 'It's too big, but it's what the Governor wanted.' She looked at Chase. 'I'm surprised to see you here.'

'You two know each other?' Barrett asked.

Chase nodded at Janice. 'I don't care if she knows,' he said, and then added, 'She was my counselor when I was in foster care. Now that she's a big commissioner, you'd never know it, but she is an amazing therapist. If it wasn't for her, I know that I wouldn't be here right now.'

'Please,' Janice said, and then to Barrett, 'You've got to watch this one, he knows how good-looking he is, and he uses it.'

Her tone was light, but it threw Barrett – was this some kind of peace offering? *Show up to the conference and I won't be such a bitch.* 'I liked what you said up there, frank, to the point.'

'Just words,' Janice said, 'but that goes with the job, and I do understand that the patient always has to come first. So whatever happened to that kid who broke up our meeting?'

'It's a mess,' Barrett said, and stopped herself from adding, *he's gone missing and someone is probably trying to kill him.*

'Sorry to hear that,' Janice said, and then looked back toward the broad steps of the administrative building. 'We're going to be late,' she said, sounding less than eager.

When she turned, Barrett noted how crumpled her silk shirt had become – and it wasn't all that hot. Her skin was flushed and up close her makeup was clumped, revealing the mesh of fine lines around her mouth, eyes, chin, and nose – almost like she'd taken the break to go work out and hadn't showered and applied fresh foundation, just slapped on some lipstick. It felt odd and too convenient – Chase asking her about Jerod and then Janice . . . and now this coincidence, that she was Chase's counselor. 'Actually, he's gone missing,' Barrett said, keeping her expression neutral and wanting to see what reaction she'd get.

'You think he's in trouble?' Chase asked.

'I do.'

'Jerod, wasn't it?' Janice asked.

'Yes,' Barrett said, starting to feel like a mouse batted by a cat's paw. They were both too interested. 'When they gave your introduction,' she said, wanting to shift the focus, 'I'd not realized you set up Mother's Milk.'

'I was extremely young then . . . and naive. If I'd known then what I do now, I probably wouldn't have done it.'

'Why not?' Barrett asked, trying to find her footing with this different-acting Janice.

'I bit off too much,' she said. 'The need is endless, just a stream of kids dumped onto the street with no place to go, no skills, half of them don't even have a high-school diploma. It's amazing they didn't fire me when that first center opened. Almost every day the cops were there, because it became a hub of drug activity, some of the kids started turning tricks from the park across the street . . . it was a big mess.'

'But you turned it around,' Chase said.

'Eventually . . . but that's how we learn.' She looked at Barrett. 'You get thrown into something and you sink or swim. I so don't want to go back in there.'

'Really?' Barrett was thrown. 'I thought this was . . .'

'A big deal,' Janice said, glancing up the stairs, 'I know, I'll eat my words. We have to be here . . . I was still in my twenties when I'd been through my third Governor's Blue Ribbon Commission on the problem of these kids. I was excited at the first one, determined to see something come out of the second, and by the third realized putting a lot of administrative types and state workers into a room won't solve anything; it's doomed from the start.'

'Why's that?' Barrett asked, shocked that she shared Janice's views, or that her boss would be so candid. *Who is this woman?*

'Let's face it, we make our living off the tragedy of these kids, or in the case of the Department of Mental Health, the adults they grow into. If the problems were ever truly addressed, there'd be a lot of people out of work – the unions would never go for it. To be blunt, the agencies mostly serve themselves. Our employees want nine-to-five jobs for problems that happen around the clock.'

'But not Mother's Milk,' Barrett said. 'My understanding is they're open twenty-four–seven every day of the year.'

Janice smiled. 'I didn't use union labor . . . or state workers.'

'Then, how?'

'I spun it off as a non-profit, half of the staff are volunteers, and I worked my butt off getting the funding – mostly grants. At this point they're self-supporting; I just sit on the board, really have little to do with them.'

Barrett looked at Chase, and realized that he had to have been one of Janice's last patients. 'Do you miss the direct work?'

'At times,' again glancing up the steps and the stream of conference-goers headed in. She turned back to Barrett. 'And that's your struggle right now, isn't it?'

A cell phone rang. 'Not me,' Barrett said, still wondering what ulterior motive Janice had in this sudden shift.

'Mine,' Chase said, pulling it out of his jacket pocket. 'I've got to take this,' he said, and quickly walked back into the small park across from the DFYS building. He stood behind the reddish trunk of a beech tree, his body mostly blocked from sight.

'You were his counselor,' Barrett remarked. 'He kind of argues against your point that the department can't help these kids.'

'Touché, but Chase is unique. Have you known him long?'

'No,' she said, again feeling that this was some kind of game, only she didn't know the rules, 'just met this morning. He told me that he plans on going to medical school.'

'Yes,' she replied, looking toward the park and what little of Chase she could see. 'He's ambitious and has the brains to pull it off, that's rare.' She cracked a smile. 'I bet you want to know if he's dating material or not.'

'Too young,' Barrett said, struggling to find her footing.

'Please, single men that good-looking, who aren't gay; I'd say if he's interested, go for it.'

At which point Chase emerged from behind the beech. Whatever the call had been had clearly upset him, even though Barrett could see he was trying to appear calm. 'Trouble?' she asked.

'One of my clients . . . I have to take care of this,' he said. He looked at Janice. 'Please don't rat me out.'

Janice looked at Barrett. 'You want out of here too, don't you?'

'I do,' Barrett said.

'Fine, you did your duty. I'll get Hugh to carry the torch.'

Barrett's impulse was to say, 'Hell no,' but with Jerod on his way back to the city and someone after him she wasn't about to argue.

'Which way you heading?' Chase asked. 'Maybe we could split a cab,' and before she could answer he'd spotted one and ran to flag it.

'Dr. Conyors . . . Barrett,' Janice said, 'I hope everything works out with Jerod.'

Barrett's every instinct was that something was way off with Janice, and she had to think it had something to do with Chase. Obviously the two had a history, but it wasn't that. She tried to put words to the fuzzy impressions racing through her brain.

A yellow taxi pulled up and Chase held the door. As she slid in, she caught a worried expression on Janice's face in the passenger-side mirror. She had mouthed something at Chase, the lines around her lower lip pulled taut.

Barrett twisted on the bench, trying to get a better look, as Chase scooted in next to her. 'What was that about?' she asked.

'What?'

'What you just said to her.'

'An old joke,' he said. 'She's a great lady, and if it wasn't for her . . . well, she was a big help to me when I really needed it.'

Barrett looked back as the cab pulled away. Janice was on the sidewalk staring at them; she caught sight of Barrett and quickly smiled.

Yes, Barrett thought, Janice was worried about something and the plastered-on smile seemed fake. She mulled over one of her favorite truisms – a gift from Hobbs – *when things don't add up, there's always a reason.*

'So I was hoping,' Chase said, 'that we could clean up our respective messes and maybe get together after work, have some dinner. As I recall you'd left things at "maybe". Can I push that into a yes?'

'Why not,' she said as the cab crossed Houston.

'You like ethnic?'

'Love it.'

'Indian?' he offered.

'That would be nice,' and they made plans to meet at one of the popular Indian restaurants in the East Village.

'You can drop me here,' he told the cab as they headed up 1st Avenue and hit 14th Street.

As he got out, leaving Barrett with one of his cards that had his cell phone and office numbers, she realized that something else didn't fit . . . and Chase's list was growing. *How the hell did he know that sharing a cab would work?* Had she told him that the forensic center was also on the East Side, had he guessed, or had he known?

'I'll see you at eight,' he said, giving her a smile so dazzling that it momentarily wiped doubt from her mind . . . a brief moment, and as the taxi moved toward her 34th Street office, timing the lights as only a seasoned cabbie can do, she knew there was more to Chase than a handsome face, and as seductive as all his pieces were, like Janice's pasted-on smile, something didn't fit.

SIXTEEN

C hase's thoughts raced wildly; he felt excited, on fire. Bits of plans slid into place, new contingencies flashed through his mind only to be replaced by other options as he entered the dingy regional DFYS office building. One false step over the next few hours could destroy everything he had spent the last twelve years building. He would need to be seen throughout the day and evening to create a seamless alibi – every moment of his time accounted for. He smiled and briefly flirted with Nadine, the pretty half-Asian secretary assigned to him and half a dozen other counselors. He retrieved his phone messages, and flipped through them, deciding which would be turned into the emergency he'd used as an excuse to leave the conference.

'This is a real mess,' he commented to Nadine, holding one of the message slips. 'We're going to end up having to find a safe home for Danielle Waters before the weekend. I really hoped this one was going to work out. Oh, well . . .'

'Again?' Nadine replied, as she leaned forward, letting Chase get a view of her firm breasts, sweetly framed by the outer edge of a lacy lavender bra. 'Didn't you just place Danielle a couple weeks ago?'

'It's not working . . . crap. Well, there goes *my* afternoon.' He retreated to his office at the end of the hall. He closed the door, pulled out his cell, and booted up his computer. He pictured his ladder, having somewhere read about the importance of visualization; his goals were clear and solid in his mind. The next rung – medical school – was almost in his grasp, and as he'd needed to do before, everything below had to be cut away. It had been true for Janice's husband, for Dom, and now for everything and everyone that could connect him to the mess with these kids and the dope. It was turning into a nightmare, and for what? So Janice could keep working through her issues with her dead husband, stockpiling cash, so that she'd never be at the mercy of anyone ever again.

The call that had made him leave had been from Marky; once again Jerod Blank had escaped. The more Chase thought about this, the more he realized that Jerod, who had never met him, was not the problem; it was Marky. And Janice was wrong about Dr. Conyors . . . Barrett. She was beautiful, intelligent, and could be his next meal ticket – *out with the old, in with the new*. He unlocked his desk drawer and looked at the framed photo-montage he'd taken from her office. The only image of her was in the center, holding her newborn, her dark eyes looking lovingly at her child, her bangs cutting a shadow across her exquisite cheekbones. He studied the surrounding pictures of the baby, blue-eyed and perfect. He wondered at her dead husband, a musician whose pictures he'd looked at on the Internet – not blond, not blue-eyed. *What have you been up to, my lovely?* He envisioned his upcoming dinner with her, he would become the man she'd always wanted, he'd make her feel desired, special. He played back their conversations at the conference, the ease with which she'd opened up over coffee. What would it be like to feel her full lips pressed against his? He stared at the picture and imagined the baby was theirs – he'd be in the picture, by her side, two gorgeous parents and a beautiful child. Janice wanted her dead; jealousy had clouded her judgment. It was Janice who was the liability. She'd given him all that she intended to, and now she just used him for sex and as some kind of lackey; there was no equal exchange. Yes, she'd helped him immeasurably, but lately . . . not so much.

On impulse he picked up and dialed his grandmother's nursing home. He asked for her aide. 'Dorothy, could you put the phone up to Grace's ear?' he asked, having done this before, knowing she could understand, but not communicate, other than through blinking. He waited until the aide had done as instructed. 'Grandma, it's Chase. I have good news and you were the one person I wanted to tell. I've found the woman I want to marry. I'll tell you all about her when I come out this weekend. She's a doctor and she's beautiful and smart and she's the one I want; she's perfect. Her name is Barrett, and I know you're going to love her.'

He heard movement over the line, and then Dorothy's voice, 'That's great news, Mr. Strand.'

'Any reaction?' he asked, picturing his grandmother, in that dreary room.

'She's blinking,' Dorothy said, 'just once . . . and once again. I think she's happy.'

'Thanks, Dorothy,' and he reminded himself to put a couple hundreds in his wallet before his weekly visit. 'Dorothy, do you ever do private-duty work?' he asked, a new possibility flashing to mind.

'Some,' she said, 'you thinking of breaking Miss Grace out of here? You know she'd need twenty-four–seven care and Medicaid won't pay for that in the home.'

'I know, just a thought for the future.'

'Well, count me in,' she said, 'I just love our Miss Grace . . . she's no problem at all.'

As he'd been talking, he'd punched Jerod Blank's name into the department's database, entered his security code, and printed out several typed summaries. He'd pass these along to Barrett at supper. She probably already knew the contents, but he'd said he'd help. He needed to show good faith. She needed to see his caring, concern, and intelligence. He stuffed the pages into a folder and dropped them into his briefcase. Next, he dialed the female director of one of the three local safe houses used to hold kids for brief periods after they'd been pulled from their families, or from foster settings that hadn't worked. As a counselor he was skipping steps and going straight to the top, but the few times he'd met the house's director – Jocelyn Flanders – she told him to call her 'any time if you need help'. In a few brief moments he'd completed a complex bureaucratic transaction that would normally take weeks. The safe house had a female bed, and they'd hold it for Danielle. In the next hour, Chase dove through a stack of paperwork, made calls back to Nadine, the safe house, and arranged for Danielle's transportation later that afternoon. 'A fine day's work,' he whispered, again dialing his secretary. 'Nadine, there's no way I'm getting out of here before eight tonight, can you let security know I'll be up here working?'

'Poor Chase,' she said, 'do you want me to order Chinese?'

'Naah, I'll grab a sandwich at the deli at some point.'

'Chase, you are so committed to these kids. I hope Gretchen appreciates all you do for them. You know, I'd be willing to stay and help out . . .'

'Nadine, that is so sweet, but it's just a lot of phone calls and paperwork. There's really nothing anyone else can do, but thanks.' And he hung up, before she could create another possible reason to stay, or meet after, or . . .

For the next three hours he worked feverishly to ensure that everything was done perfectly with the transfer to the safe home, and in between he set up the rest of his evening.

He started with a call to Janice, still at the conference. 'I can't talk,' she said, and then called him back fifteen minutes later.

'Marky has become too much of a problem . . . he let the kid get away again. I've got it under control, but I can't deal with this level of incompetence,' Chase said.

'Agreed,' she said. 'Handle it.'

'Of course. I'll stop by your place around . . . five-thirty? Does that work, pick up some of the special F – I gave the last of it to Marky. Maybe a little visit?'

'I'd like that,' she said, 'it's been one hell of a day. You get anything out of Dr. Conyors?'

'No, but I'm working on it . . . I'm meeting her for dinner.'

There was a long pause.

'You still there?' he asked, knowing that the mention of his dinner with Barrett had thrown her.

'What are you playing, Chase?'

'Nothing. Don't get paranoid.'

'Dinner? What, you're going to fuck me and then go for her?
Two in one night, is that the plan?'

'Janice, sometimes you're out of your freaking mind. You
wanted me to find out what she knew. This is the way I know
how to do it. If you've got a better solution, by all means tell
me. I have no intention of sleeping with her, but we need to
know what happened with those cells.'

After hanging up, he brought a stack of paperwork to Nadine.
'Could you copy these for me, three sets, and put them into some
kind of folders?'

'Sure.'

Back in his office he called Marky, who was still on the road.
'Hey, doll, sorry I got all over you about that kid. Any chance
you've found him?'

'Not yet, but I will. I promise, Chase, I'm so sorry.'

'Sshhh. It's OK, end of the day, what does he know? Hung
out with a couple dead junkies. No biggie.'

'He knows me,' Marky said nervously. 'He knows I'm the one
who hands out the stuff and gets the cash. I mean he could point
me out or something. I should have done him. I should have just
done him and made sure.'

'Can't change the past,' Chase said, realizing how much of a
smoking gun Marky was, how reckless this whole enterprise had
become. 'You can only change the future. If you see him you
know what to do. And if you don't he's probably gotten his ass
far out of town and out of our hair. Either way, problem solved.
Life goes on, business goes on,' and dropping his voice, 'love
and sex and rock 'n' roll.'

'Can I see you, Chase?'

'Sure, I'm at the office. I got the stuff for the week and I've
also got a little side job I want you to do. Low risk, high yield,
but I'll tell you about that later. Where are you right now?'

'Heading back on the Saw Mill.'

'Perfect, meet me at the Night Shade at seven, but I'm going
to need you to do this other thing first. No screw-ups. Then
maybe later you can come back to my place . . . if you want.'

'Fuck, yes, just tell me what I need to do. I really want to
make this up to you.'

'Sounds good . . . Here's the deal . . .'

At four-thirty, he called Nadine as she logged off for the day.

'Just checking, you let security know I'm going to be here really late?'

'All done, they said it shouldn't be a problem, just let them know when you leave.'

'You're awesome, Nadine . . . and hot. See you tomorrow.'

She giggled. 'You bet, and try not to stay too late. There'll still be plenty of screwed-up kids in the morning.'

'Sweet.'

She laughed and hung up.

He looked at the clock above his office door. He grabbed a clementine from out of the bowl on his desk, peeled it, tossed the fruit, and started to stitch. He completed three tidy seams, using self-dissolving suture that in human flesh would leave almost no scar. He fantasized about Barrett, the age difference didn't matter. He pictured the two of them moving into his loft; he'd be a perfect stepdad to Max, and maybe even set up some kind of room for Grandma Grace. They'd sell Barrett's apartment and that would be enough to support them while he got through medical school. They'd have a child . . . maybe two, and then he'd go into practice. Everyone would look at him and know he was the perfect husband and father, they'd talk about his sacrifice in caring for his grandmother.

Somewhat high from his daydream, he checked the clock again, four forty-five, fifteen minutes after day's end; the building would be largely deserted. He cracked open his door, and looked down the hall. No lights coming from any of the other counselors' rooms. Nadine's computer was off and she was gone. Taking no chances, he changed into jeans, black T-shirt, and scuffed-up running shoes. He pulled on dark glasses, leather jacket, and a Mets baseball cap and headed toward the back stairwell; it was a favorite hangout of the smokers who had repeatedly dismantled the smoke alarms, security camera, and the siren on the outside door, paying no heed to the memos that warned of dire consequences for such behavior. He stepped into the alley, which reeked of cat pee and cigarettes, and closed the door behind him, making sure it didn't latch.

He had fifteen minutes to make it to his first stop, *half an hour to get this done*. He moved fast, and kept his eyes on the sidewalk in front of him. As he headed north and then west he dialed on his cell. 'Hi,' he said, as a man picked up. 'This is Chase Strand on the fourth floor, I just wanted to make sure

Nadine told you I'd be here real late . . . great, thanks. Yeah, it always hits the fan at the end of the day. So if you hear someone up here swearing; it's just me . . . Yeah, sure, I'll check out when I leave.'

So many things could go wrong over the next few hours, he had to stay focused. He was banking on a shitload of a human nature, but mostly on himself. He knew the one chubby security guard he'd just spoken with rarely made rounds, and certainly wouldn't be stomping up and down the back stairwell.

Up ahead was Janice's brick-and-glass condo building on East 18th. Slouching down and with his hair tucked under the cap, he bounded up the short flight of steps and inserted the key he'd had made into the security door. Holding it open with his foot, he looked around, dropped the key into a small white envelope with the letter K on it, and taped it next to the bank of mailboxes, where a number of notices and flyers for local restaurants had been posted.

Bypassing the elevator, he sprinted up six flights, moving with catlike grace, barely breathing hard as he exited the stairwell. He rang the buzzer, and heard excited barks and the clicking nails of her dogs. He heard her pull back the cover to the fish-eye, and he pushed back his cap and tilted down his glasses.

She opened the door and the three white dogs tried to squeeze past her. 'How did you get up here? I didn't buzz you in,' she said.

He smiled, letting the dogs sniff him as he entered her apartment and took off his cap. 'Someone let me in,' he lied. 'I seem to have that effect on people.'

SEVENTEEN

Barrett didn't know what she hoped to accomplish as she and Hobbs headed to the tenement where she'd found the two dead kids on Monday. Riding next to him through the rapidly changing neighborhoods of the East Village and the Lower East Side, she compared the comfort she felt with him to the fuzzy rush she got from that Chase guy. She knew there was something wrong with that man, something below the surface . . . but what a fine-looking surface it was.

'Son of a bitch!' Hobbs swore as a motorcycle zipped past on his right, just as he was about to take the turn south on Avenue A. 'Guy's going to get himself killed.'

'One man's death is another's kidney donation,' she said, coming back to the task at hand – find Jerod.

'That's dark,' Hobbs said.

'Hey, in medical school we called them donor cycles, especially for those brilliant souls who don't wear helmets.' She snuck a glance at Hobbs, intent on the craziness of New York City driving. 'You think there's any chance we'll find him?'

'No clue, but one thing about junkies is first and foremost they need their fix. He'll go to where he thinks he can find it.'

'Even if that could kill him,' she said.

'Yup, even that.'

'That's the crazy thing about heroin,' she said, 'it's like demonic possession. Jerod is a sweet guy; I genuinely like him. He cares for others, worries about hurting people, but the minute he starts to get dope sick, it's as if there's someone else inside of there – someone desperate and ugly. All he wants is dope, and he'll do what it takes to get it.'

'Yeah, but at least with him, he's not mugging people.'

'No, mostly shoplifting. But if it weren't for the drugs, I don't think that would be an issue. It used to be pot, which was bad enough because it made his paranoia ten times worse, now he steals just so he can get enough for his next fix.' She felt her breath quicken as they turned onto the block where she'd found Bobby Dix and Ashley Kane. The six-story building's security door was held open by a rock.

'The kids are back,' Hobbs commented as he parked the gray Crown Vic – a vehicle that screamed cop – in front.

In the empty lot next door half a dozen teens were playing hoops in a well-cared-for pocket park. Hobbs got out and Barrett followed. 'I got some information on this building,' Hobbs said.

'And?' she asked, feeling that they were being watched, not just by the teens playing ball, but by the whole block. She caught a curtain being pulled back from a window on a second floor, and there was something else that caused her nerves to rev, a hunch that people here were waiting for something to happen.

'For starters, the apartment where you found those kids was

rented fourteen years ago to a Melanie Jacobs; who's been living in California for the past four. Ms. Jacobs did not want to talk to me, but when I mentioned the local police would pay her a visit and that defrauding the city's housing authority was an extraditable offense . . .'

'It is?' Barrett asked as she looked up, noting a few cracked windows and how the entire building seemed like a throwback to another decade in this block that had been sandblasted, rehabbed, and transformed into expensive condos and coops.

'Not for this kind of small potatoes, but anyway she told me how she'd put an ad up in the student center. She said some blond guy named Marky gave her five grand in cash for the lease. And miracle of miracles, she's been paying the rent every month with a cashier's check, even got a new lease last year.'

'You lost me,' Barrett said, following Hobbs as he walked toward the kids playing hoops. 'How could she . . .'

'It's not her; it's a scam. Anyone can get a cashier's check and put whatever name on it they want. As long as the landlord – or in this case the holding company – gets the rent they don't give a shit. And getting a lease, unless they're looking to clear out the building, isn't that hard. Get a fake ID, sign your name and there you have it.' Hobbs's steel-toed wingtip kicked at a small Ziploc baggy on the ground, and then he pointed out a little uncapped root-beer-colored bottle. 'I can't believe you actually went into this place without an escort.'

'Yeah, so you've mentioned one or twenty times . . . Let's show those kids Jerod's picture.'

'Worth a shot,' he said.

He reached into his breast pocket and pulled out his detective shield as she pulled out an eight-by-ten of Jerod, from a stack that also included pictures of Bobby Dix, Ashley Kane, and an old fifth-grade photo of Carly Sloan.

The six teens, five boys and a girl, mostly Hispanic and none older than fifteen, had stopped their game and watched Barrett and Hobbs approach. As Hobbs held out his shield and introduced himself, a lanky boy crossed his tattooed arms across his chest. 'We didn't do nothing.'

'I know,' Barrett said, 'we're looking for a friend who's gone missing.'

The lone girl, her long black hair tied back in a red bandana, laughed. 'Yeah, you got friends in our building? Don't think so.'

Barrett lifted the first photo from off the stack. 'His name's Jerod Blank. You ever seen him?'

The tall kid looked at the photo and then back at them. 'What happened to your face, man? It looks like the shit my mom feeds the dogs.'

Hobbs didn't pause. 'Someone blew up my car; it's burn scars.'

'No shit,' the girl said, detaching herself from her friends to get a closer look. 'Can I touch it, mister?' she asked, smiling over even white teeth.

'Cora, you are twisted,' said a chubby kid who couldn't have been more than thirteen.

'Shut up, Gordo,' the girl said, showing no fear as she walked up to Barrett and Hobbs. 'Can I?' she asked.

Hobbs, who had a good six inches on the girl, leaned forward. 'Sure.'

She put her right hand gently on the side of his face, touching down with the pads of her fingers, her eyes meeting his briefly. 'You don't have a beard anymore on the side that got burned – there's no whiskers.'

'No, they had to take skin from other parts of my body to fill in the parts that were too messed up.' He smiled. 'I miss my moustache.'

'Did it hurt?' the girl asked.

'A lot.'

She looked at Barrett. 'You his girlfriend or something?'

Barrett responded, 'Something,' and held the picture toward the girl.

'Crazy boy,' she said, looking back at her friends, who were edging closer. 'Don't be so chicken-shit, that's what they want. No one says anything and they just act like they own you,' she said. 'That's crazy boy. Cute, but you know something ain't right. Sometimes you see him talking . . . and there's no one there.' She looked at the other pictures in Barrett's hand. 'Who else you got?'

There was something defiant in this girl, and Barrett noted how she'd occasionally glance back at the building. Barrett flipped through the pictures, making sure Cora and the other kids could get a good look.

'Those two I seen,' offered a light-skinned boy with freckles, blue eyes, and red curly hair. He looked to Cora, as though wanting her approval for having spoken.

'They took out two dead ones a couple days ago,' Cora said. 'Which ones were they?'

Barrett held out the pictures of Bobby and Ashley.

Cora nodded. 'Yeah, we seen them. My mom says the whole top floor is junkies and crack-heads.'

The fat kid snorted, 'Your momma should know.'

'Shut up, Gordo!' Cora said, and barely looking at him, cuffed him on the ear.

'They sell it on the street?' Hobbs asked.

'No. Not here,' she said, and looked up at the top floor.

Barrett turned to follow her gaze. 'There's something happening up there, Hobbs.'

He turned as well, and pulled out his cell.

As he called for backup, Barrett bolted toward the stairs and the open door.

'Don't even think about it,' Hobbs said, still on his cell.

Ignoring him, and feeling an urgent need to do something before Jerod went the way of his friends, she ran in.

'Barrett, don't,' Hobbs yelled, as he raced after her.

'There's shit happening on the roof,' Cora shouted after them. 'They can get off that roof onto the one next door.'

Barrett's senses switched into the fluid state that Sifu Henry, her kung-fu teacher, had instilled in her. He called it 'wide focus' and it overrode fear and doubt. She flew up the stairs hearing Hobbs two flights below as he followed. The building reeked of fried food and dogs and urine; she strained to hear what was going on above, a door slammed . . . voices of people in a hurry.

She ran flat out, grabbing at the scarred oak railings and using them to propel herself, swinging up each landing, making a mental note of the passing floors.

When she got to five, just below where she'd found Bobby and Ashley, she heard a male voice. 'Come on!' He sounded frightened. 'Move it! Hurry!'

A girl pleaded, 'I need it.'

'Leave it!'

A door slammed overhead and Barrett pounded the stairs to get there. She heard Hobbs from below. 'Barrett!'

'Hurry!' She ran the final two flights and came to the roof-access door. It was closed, and she heard scraping against the other side, like something being dragged across a tar roof.

She twisted the knob; it was unlocked. She pushed with her shoulder; it gave a half-inch.

'Move it!' the male voice said, from the roof side of the door. 'Now!'

She pushed again, and felt frustration well – they'd barricaded the door. 'Jerod!' she shouted. 'It's me, Dr. Conyors.' Not sure if he was even out there. 'Wait for me! Don't run.'

She saw the top of Ed's head. 'Hurry up. I can't get it open; they're getting away!'

Hobbs turned the final bend and looked up at her. He bent to catch his breath. 'How many and are they armed?'

'How should I know? We've got to get the door open.'

'Crap,' Hobbs said, making it up the last half-flight to the roof door. 'If you get me killed, I'm never talking to you again.'

She said nothing as the two of them threw their weight against the door. 'On my count,' he said, 'one, two – three.' It opened a good four inches. 'Again, one, two – three.' This time they got another half foot, and before Hobbs could stop her, Barrett wiggled through, scraping her shin on the heavy air-conditioning unit that had been shoved against the door.

Outside, she squinted against the bright western sun that caught her full face. She looked around, trying to get her bearings, heard the girl Cora shout up from the little park. 'There! They're running away!' She pivoted at the sound of a sneaker scraping on metal and saw a man's hand disappear down a ladder on the other side.

'Wait!' she shouted, and sprinted toward the fleeing youth, a hope kindled. Perhaps it was Jerod. When she got to the edge she looked over, and sure enough, there he was, not moving, his arms hugging the ladder. On the roof next door a dark-haired young man looked back at him, 'Come on!' And then he saw Barrett. 'You're so fucked,' he said, and took off across the second roof.

Barrett could see another three teens scurrying across the rooftops. They were all dressed in the kind of clothes you get at Gap, Abercrombie's, or one of the other chains that peddle youthful individuality but deliver a homogeneous mix of distressed denim and shirts with the store's logo. They moved fast, like roaches when the lights go on, there was no way Hobbs or any of the backup that was now pulling up down the block would catch them.

'Jerod,' she said, keeping her voice soft. 'Jerod, it's me. It's going to be OK.'

'I didn't run away,' he said, looking up at her.

'I know and I'd love you to tell me what happened.'

'I will, can you get me some of those pills?'

'Sure,' she smiled. 'You realize I don't have them on me.'

He climbed up, a twisted grin on his face. 'You're not holding?'

'No, I'm not,' and she gave him her hand as he stepped back onto the tar-paper roof.

'I am so screwed up,' he said, looking at her. 'I tried to get a hold of you, but I couldn't wait. I thought maybe if I came back somebody would know something about Carly . . .' His smile vanished. 'No one knows shit, or else they're lying.'

Hobbs had finally made it through the door; he had his gun in hand. He took in Barrett and Jerod. 'No one else?' he asked.

She pointed across the rooftops heading east. 'All gone, like a herd of mall rats.' She stopped and looked at Jerod, in his new jeans, bright red Converse sneakers, and trendy striped polo shirt. 'Who's been getting you these clothes?'

He hesitated.

'Don't even think about it,' she said. 'You held stuff back and look where that got you.'

'He tried to kill me,' Jerod said. 'I thought he might, I almost thought that I didn't care . . . I do. I don't want to die and I don't want to be a junkie.'

'Good,' Barrett said, trying to figure out how and where she could keep him safe. 'But please just answer the questions. Who buys the clothes? They look new.'

'Marky. He tells them where to shop, what to get. They were supposed to look like college students. He's the one who gave Bobby and Ashley the killer dope. He broke me out of the hospital, he gave me a few bags, and all night just asked questions.' Despite the heat that pulsed up from the black rooftop, he shivered and pulled his arms in tight.

'We've got to get him out of here,' Hobbs said.

'But where?' she asked. 'I don't think he's safe at either the center or back at Croton.'

'That leaves lockup,' Hobbs said.

'Please don't put me in a cell,' Jerod said. 'I'm already sick and it's going to get a thousand times worse.'

'We need to keep you safe,' Barrett said, trying to come up

with something, 'and if you're serious, we have to think through how we can get you detoxed.'

She ran through options, batting each one away as either unsafe or impractical. The kid had no insurance, so a private facility was out of the question. Croton and the forensic center had major leaks, one of which nearly got him killed, and the same could be true for any of the state hospitals. Jerod was an escapee from Croton, although no charges had yet been filed about his gun-waving episode, a jail cell might keep him safe, but no way he'd get the treatment he needed. The one place that popped to mind that would actually work was wrong, dead wrong . . . and yet. 'Hobbs,' she said, 'I need you to talk me out of something.'

He shook his head. 'Right, like that's something I've ever been able to do.'

EIGHTEEN

Janice looked at Chase in her doorway, and hated herself. He'd covered his hair in a baseball cap and had on shades; it was something of a disguise. He'd been to her apartment only a few times, always against her better judgment, but years into this relationship she knew that it was all against her better judgment, and yet . . . just looking at him made something ache inside.

She let him into her comfortable two-bedroom, two-bath apartment and watched her three precious darlings swarm his ankles. He closed the door, put his black leather briefcase on the floor, and knelt down to pet each one, saying their names, 'Taffy, Lily . . . Buttercup.' Buttercup, the smallest of the three white shih-tzus, butted her head against his hand, and nipped playfully at his fingers when he tried to pull back. 'You look pretty,' he commented, still crouched among the excited dogs.

'We shouldn't meet here,' she said, glad that he'd noticed the effort she'd put in. Her softly draped Grecian pale-blue dress floated to mid-calf, and exposed a generous expanse of cleavage and back. Her hair was down and she'd run a curling iron through the ends. The lights were dim and cast amber shadows that hid the fine lines around her eyes and mouth. When she glanced in the mirror . . . from a distance, she caught traces of the beautiful woman she'd been a decade or more ago.

'I was careful,' he said. 'We have to talk.'

'Fine, but first let me feed my babies. Lily, Taffy, Buttercup, let's have a treat.'

The fluffy little dogs wagged their tails as Janice led them into the galley kitchen off the hall. She reached up into a cabinet, pulled out three cans of gourmet dog food, put them in matching pottery bowls, and placed them on separate mats at the far end. 'Did Marky take care of that boy?' she asked, closing the kitchen door and leading Chase back to the living room, with its plush ivory carpet and overstuffed furnishings, all in soft shades of white and peach, all purchased after Avery's death.

'That's what we need to talk about. It's time to pull up stakes. We're taking too many risks. Between this Jerod catastrophe and that damn videophone . . .'

'I see,' she said, feeling as though her brain were split in two whenever he was around. One part of her needed to focus on business, while the other clamored to lock herself on his full lips, to strip him naked right there in her all-white cocoon. She moved in close, catching the whiff of orange. 'And how will you keep up your loft? I know your expenses . . . and your tastes. What will you do for money? The scholarship is well and good, but you still need at least ten K a month for the taxes and maintenance fees.'

'True, I'm going to have to put it on the market. Do what everyone else does, live within my means.'

'Really.' She didn't buy it. 'Drink?'

'Sure.'

'So you're going to sell Dom's loft . . . that should keep you solvent for a while. Of course the capital-gains taxes will take a chunk, but even so.'

'No,' he said, 'I'll get the one-time credit.'

'So you've really thought this through.' She played along, wondering what he was up to, as she turned her back and poured two generous Scotches from a Swedish crystal decanter. 'You never answered my question, Chase,' she said, handing him a drink, and placing a hand on the front of his leather jacket. 'What happened to the boy? Did Marky finish it?'

'Yes.' Chase took the drink and got a clear look at her. *God, she's old.* His mind raced, as he thought through all the potential missteps, needing to keep track of everything he touched. 'Jerod is no longer among the living, but this whole mess made me realize we have too much at stake. These kids, all of them, are just a bunch of loose ends that need to be tied up.'

'I thought you said that Jerod had run away.'

'He did, but he got him back and mixed some sufentanil in his dope. Went to sleep and didn't feel a thing.'

'I don't need the details, just that it's done.'

'The details bother you,' he commented. 'It's exactly what we did with Avery and Krista.'

'No,' she said, giving him her annoyed face, where she scrunched up her mouth as if tasting something bad, 'it's unnecessary and unpleasant . . . So tell me what your big plans are to "pull up stakes".'

'Nothing fancy, but we need to think it through. I need to know that you'll be OK with it.'

'People will be upset,' she commented; he could tell she wasn't taking him seriously. 'Our customers will not be happy, there's going to be a lot of puking kids in the dormitory . . . not to mention our suppliers. You think they'll just say, "Oh, fun doing business, have a nice life"?'

'Good,' he said, 'I'm glad you're here to help me think through the details. And not to be pushy, but you did say you'd give me another fifteen K when Jerod was out of the way . . .'

'Of course,' she said, 'I assume you want that now.'

'I would.' He kept his expression blank, just the hint of a smile.

'Stay here; I'll get it.'

'So,' he continued from the couch, 'the customers will just be out of luck, oh well. It's not like there aren't a few thousand dope-dealers in the greater Manhattan area. We were just very good at a niche market.'

'And the suppliers?' she asked.

'I've had Marky handle all the pick-ups for the last three years,' he said, letting his voice drift toward the bedroom where she'd gone, 'and before that I was careful that they never saw my face. They've always met a blond guy with sunglasses, as far as they know it's been Marky the whole time.' He eased up from the couch, and silently put on propylene gloves and then dug his hands back in his jacket pockets.

'And the other business?' she asked. 'Our little auctions?'

He moved slowly toward the bedroom, the door was open and he heard her from inside her spacious closet. He stood outside the bedroom, his ears strained for the sound. Making his voice softer, as though he were still on the couch, 'You like those,' he commented. 'I can't help notice how turned on they get you.'

'I don't know what you're talking about, but the cash is good. I can survive without the other, and maybe you're right; it's gotten too risky.'

He heard the steel click, and closed the remaining distance of thick carpet on silent feet. A gloved hand slid from his pocket. He caught sight of her back, one hand on the wall, the other pulling the handle of the safe. He felt something akin to nostalgia as he raised the small handgun and silencer, and in a single fluid motion pointed it at the back of her head, steadied it with his other hand, and pulled.

There was a wet cracking noise, and his hands jerked back. Excited barks erupted from the closed kitchen, and a dull thud as Janice's knees buckled and she fell down and then forward, one hand still on the open door of the safe. As she tumbled, he grabbed at the door, fearful that it would close and lock. Her fingers grasped weakly at his, the nails searching for the flesh of his wrist, but found only gloves, and then they fell away.

He counted to ten, reached down, and checked her pulse. He felt a little something against his gloved fingers, and then nothing. 'Bye-bye, Janice,' he said, as he stepped over her and looked in the safe. Inside, he saw neatly stacked bundles of cash, bearer bonds, some jewelry boxes, and the flat leather cases that held her collection of gold coins. It had become an obsession with her since Avery's death – liquid assets. The financial ruin her husband left, his secret double life, making her into a woman possessed. 'Never again,' she said as she was confronted with the lies and the near-financial ruin that followed his death. Her gold coins – imminently liquid – were a temptation, but he knew that he had to stay on script. Deviations would only create problems – devil's in the detail. He glanced at his watch. He'd been here less than twenty minutes. He stepped away from the safe and grabbed a heavy floral terry-cloth robe from the rack. He looked at the entry wound on the back of Janice's head, a nickel-sized circle of dark-red ooze. He tilted her head to search for the exit wound, hoping there wasn't one. Unfortunately, there was. 'Too bad,' he muttered, as he quickly wrapped her head in the robe, made sure it would stay in place by lashing it on tight with the belt, and then dead-lifted her over his shoulder. He carried her to the hall closet, and while balancing her with one hand, pushed back a row of coats. He stepped in, leaned forward, and let her drop down among the umbrellas, outerwear, and cardboard boxes where she kept the wooden leaves for her dining-room table. In the kitchen the dogs were going crazy. He thought briefly of killing them, but that seemed too harsh even for him. They'd done nothing wrong, they had no guilt. Janice, on the other hand, if there were in fact a God, would have much to answer for. He looked down at her crumpled body, her blue eyes open and staring at the wall. 'Sorry,' he said, pulling down a couple coats to conceal her body and then closing the door.

He retrieved his briefcase and returned to the bedroom. He took the stacks of cash – $10,000 per bundle, two hundred twenty in all. He also took a small leather notebook that contained her pass codes and the numbers of her Cayman Island accounts, as well as the stacks of bearer bonds that had to be worth another hundred K. Lastly, he took a small wooden box that contained glass ampoules of sufentanil, a synthetic opiate used by surgeons that was a hundred times more potent than heroin. He then rearranged the jewel cases and the boxes of heavy coins, so that someone looking into the safe for the first time wouldn't think anything had been taken. He snuck a quick glance at the coins, Krugerrands, antique American eagles and double eagles. The three boxes weighed pounds each and some of the antiques were rare and worth tens of thousands. He felt his rage, at how much she'd kept from him – *Got what she deserved*, and despite what he'd told himself, he grabbed one of the coin cases and shoved it into his briefcase. He then closed the safe, careful not to have it latch, and moved back through the living room. He picked up his glass of Scotch and wiped down any surface he might have touched. He emptied the liquor down the bathroom sink and washed it away. Quickly drying the glass he replaced it in the living-room hutch. Standing there, he looked around. *What have I missed? What have I missed?* It had been just half an hour; right on schedule. He tried to calm himself. *It's perfect.* He mentally retraced his every step through her apartment – no loose ends. This evening into night would mark the start of a new life – one rung falling away as the next appeared. Bye-bye, Janice, with her crumbs of money, saggy breasts and veiny thighs, bye-bye. The vision that took shape in his mind's eye was glorious and heady, the successful surgeon Dr. Chase Strand and his beautiful wife, Dr. Barrett Strand.

With his hands still in the purple hospital gloves, he peered through Janice's fish-eye – the hall was clear. He turned the knob, and keeping the door on latch, headed out and down through the stairwell

NINETEEN

Ruth was the first to give voice to what all four of them knew was a big problem. 'Dear,' she said, while busily preparing a pitcher of iced mint tea in Barrett's galley kitchen, 'it's not my business, and I'm sure you have your reasons . . .' She looked around at Hobbs, who was on his cell, the boy with his wild hair and skinny arms covered in tattoos who was so clearly sick, and then her daughter, with her untucked shirt and navy suit that looked as though she'd worn it while playing some contact sport . . . in the mud. 'I've never known you to bring home a patient.'

'I don't want to get you in trouble,' Jerod said. 'This is nice and all, but you shouldn't do this. You've got a baby here . . . What if . . .' He looked at Max, who was staring back at him from the crib on the far side of the couch. 'You can't take risks like that, not for me.'

'It's OK,' Barrett said, as her mother came around with the iced tea. 'They don't know where you are, or where I live,' she said, realizing that might not be true. More importantly, this plan to keep Jerod from harm was way outside the rules of her agency, not to mention the bounds of professional ethics.

'No luck,' Hobbs said, clicking his cell back onto his belt. 'I can't get the manpower. Schmitt said I could keep him in lockup, but beyond that he couldn't free up anything more. Low priority.'

'Not good,' Barrett said, realizing they were on their own.

'No,' Jerod said, 'I'd rather stay on the street than get you in trouble.'

'Stop it,' Barrett said, trying to think through to the next step.

'What did we see up there, Jerod? How many kids live in that building?'

'Maybe ten,' he said, his eyes on the small bottle of pills they'd picked up from the pharmacy. 'They've got the two apartments on the top floor.'

Barrett looked at Jerod; he was shivering and sweating at the same time, and the hairs on the back of his arms were sticking up like porcupine quills. 'Put two of these under your tongue and leave them there.'

He reached forward. 'You got to find Marky,' he said. 'He's the one who collects the money and drops off the dope. But there's somebody behind him.' His fingers rested on the top of the bottle.

'Who?' Hobbs asked.

'Don't know,' Jerod said, as he pressed down with a shaky hand on the cap and looked in at the tiny but potent pills. He looked up at Barrett, and then at her mother. Tears squeezed from the corners of his eyes. 'How sick will I get if I don't take nothing?'

'Real sick,' she said, 'you know that.'

'Can it kill me?' he asked.

'No, not as long as you can keep some fluid down.'

'How long will it last?'

'Few days, the first two will be the worst, it'll be a lot easier with the pills, we can get you off more slowly.'

He put the cap back on the bottle and pushed them away. His hands covered his face and he leaned forward. 'I don't want to be a junkie. I just want this to be over.' He started to dry heave. 'I don't want the pills. Take them away.'

Barrett put down her tea and settled beside him on the couch. She put an arm around his shoulder, and felt like telling him to just take the damn pills. 'You sure you want to do this cold turkey? You're going to be miserable.'

He nodded and rocked in place his head still in his hands, his rough braids making a curtain in front of his face. 'I can't keep doing this shit,' he said. He bit his lower lip. 'If I hadn't shot up she'd still be here.'

'Carly?' Barrett offered.

With his head inches from her coffee table he looked at her, his lashes wet, his mouth twisted. 'It's my fault. If I hadn't been nodded out I would have been able to stop them. I could have saved her.'

'Stopped who?' Hobbs asked, kneeling next to him.

'I thought it was a dope dream,' Jerod said, 'now I know it wasn't. It had to be real. There were two of them, Marky, and some other guy. I hadn't seen him before.'

'Did you see his face? What did he look like?'

'It was fuzzy, but Marky was into him. He's gay, and this guy was like telling him what to do. I remember thinking that was weird; people don't tell Marky what to do. He kind of orders everyone around, but not this guy. Told him to be careful with her, that he couldn't bruise her. He was talking about Carly, like she was a piece of furniture. They took her.'

'Was there anyone else there?' Hobbs asked.

'It was the four of us – Bobby, Ashley, Carly . . . I'm the only one left. That's why they keep trying to get me. I'm supposed to be dead. That's why you shouldn't keep me here with your baby and your mom. It's too much.' He sobbed. 'There's got to be somewhere else. You shouldn't do this. I'm just a fucking junkie. Maybe you *should* put me in a cell.'

'My place,' Ruth said.

'What are you talking about?' Barrett said, noting the determined line of her mother's mouth.

'Barrett, I don't know all that's going on here. Because Lord knows you keep things from me . . . your sister too. But I sure as hell know if you brought a patient to your house that something is wrong. I also know that if anyone finds out – like your boss who called here twice this afternoon looking for you – you're out of a job . . . Am I wrong?'

'How secure is your place?' Hobbs asked.

'Please,' Ruth said, 'it kept out my ex-bastard-cop of a husband when he thought he'd come and drag us all back to Georgia. And Sophie and Max were no slouches when it came to home security, back in the days when having a store and living on the Bowery meant something; they never once got robbed. We can leave the gates down on the first floor; it's pretty secure. There's no easy roof access, and no one knows who the hell I am, unlike my almost famous daughter.'

'It doesn't suck,' Hobbs commented.

'That's settled, then,' Ruth said, and proceeded to pick up Max's large Thomas the Train tote bag and then headed toward Barrett's bedroom.

'He's going to get very sick,' Barrett said, 'you're not going to be able to leave him alone.'

'Fine,' she said, 'I have tonight off anyway, it sounds like you and Detective Hobbs are up to your ears, so I'll take Max and Jerod for the night. We'll figure out what comes next in the morning.'

'You want a ride?' Hobbs asked.

Ruth stopped packing and looked at Hobbs and then Barrett. 'No, we'll get a cab. I think you two have things to work on; we'll be fine.'

Five minutes later Ruth had packed up the baby. She passed Jerod the tote and walker and they were out the door and into a cab.

'What are we missing?' Barrett asked as she watched the taxi from the window.

'Marky,' Hobbs said. 'He's the link to whoever is behind this. Although whenever you talk dope, it's a chain, and it can be a long one. That's why narcotic's operations take forever; you're always trying to work your way back as high up as possible. This Marky guy and whoever's bossing him around are just two links, the dead kids are the final link.'

'Here's the part that's gnawing at me,' she said, 'and it's so way out you're going to think I'm certifiable.'

'As opposed to your normally sane behavior of running into crack houses and getting abducted by sociopaths?'

'Cute . . . Here's the deal. All these kids were products of the DFYS system.'

'So, them and tens of thousands more?'

'What if someone within the department gets it into their head that these kids have real value . . . as dealers, maybe even as fodder for the sex trade or even white slavery? They're disposable, don't have families that care . . .'

'We've been here,' Hobbs said, 'what's the leap to our perp or perps?'

'I think they made a mistake when they broke into my office, because it was a big tip of their hand. It had to be someone high enough up who would know that I'd been Jerod's doctor, who would have access to a key card, know where my office was, and . . . Call me paranoid, but the person that leaps to my mind is my boss.'

'The commissioner? That is a leap.'

'She used to be the Commissioner of DFYS, and years back she set up a string of drop-in centers that did good work with the kids on the street. So maybe not her directly, but someone close to her . . . like Hugh Osborn. Or . . .'

'Or?'

'I go to this conference . . . I have no choice, Janice lets me know if I don't show it'll be considered insubordination and finally give her the grounds she needs to get rid of me. So I show up and this ridiculously handsome young guy sits next to me in the auditorium. Turns out he's something of a golden child for the DFYS, and . . . was also one of Janice's patients when he was a kid growing up in foster care.'

'OK, connections, but still not off the chart.'

'Yeah, but something happened when she saw the two of us together. Almost a complete personality shift, and this is the weird thing, after making such a big deal about my being there, she was fine with me taking off in a cab . . . with this Chase guy.'

'Really? And what exactly were you doing getting in a cab with him?'

'He said he had some kind of emergency back at his office and offered to split the cab . . . course he knew that I worked uptown . . .'

'It's still weak, but maybe there is something. Much as I hate dealing with these top agency types, it's time for a chat with your boss . . . It might be good for you to be there, kind of keep it informal, less of an investigation and more of a, "By the way do you think anyone in your old department might be preying on their clients?" '

Barrett glanced at her watch. 'I can't.'

'Because . . .'

'I sort of have dinner plans.'

'The ridiculously handsome guy you think might be a white slaver and drug lord?'

'Yuh.'

'You are a piece of work, Barrett.' Hobbs did not sound happy and he shook his head. 'I guess this gives you your chance to see if he's all that he seems.'

'I suppose,' she said, unable to shake the intimacy of Chase's smile, his amber eyes, and the way those eyes seemed to drink her in. Her gut told her he was bad news, but another piece of

her was flattered and knew how easy it could be to fall for such
an attractive man. She glanced at Hobbs; he was looking out her
living-room window, the scarred side of his face turned from
her. Why was he suddenly so cold? She had to change the subject.
'You never told me who you were dating.'

'You don't know her; she works in IS . . . What time's your
date?'

'I wouldn't call it that, but eight.'

'You better get ready,' he said briskly. 'If you think there might
be a connection with these murders, see if he knew Bobby,
Ashley, or that Carly girl. I'll let you know if I find out anything
from your boss . . . Have fun.'

Before she could say anything else, he'd crossed her living
room, retrieved his gun from the coffee table, and was out the
door.

'Crap,' she muttered, and listened as the door shut behind him.
It didn't slam, but she felt an accusation in it. She watched from
behind the linen curtains as he got into his Crown Vic and drove
off. She hated the way her relationship with Hobbs had turned
into a landmine of bad feelings, his . . . hers. She felt the impulse
to run after him, to call him. But what would she say? 'He's
seeing someone else. Let it go.'

But he had given her an idea. She booted up her laptop and
with her security clearance as a facility director had access into
the databases of all the state's social-service agencies, including
DFYS. Sitting cross-legged on her couch with the computer in
her lap, she logged onto their website and then into their client
files. She typed in 'Carly Sloan' and was confronted with
hundreds of electronic encounter records, essentially a history
of all services provided to the girl who'd left the agency's custody
less than a year ago. The information was limited, just what
service was provided and by whom. But one name snagged her
attention, Chase Strand, dozens and dozens of counseling sessions
that stretched back over two years. She then typed in 'Bobby
Dix' and scrolled through his history. No sign of Chase being
connected. Then she typed in Jerod's name, and because he'd
left the department a few years back, and the computer system
was relatively new, there was minimal information and no sign
of Chase. Again, the connection to Carly Sloan could just be
another coincidence, but there were too many.

She glanced at her watch, nearly seven. She pictured Chase

and wondered what she was stepping into. She caught her reflection in the TV screen, she was still in her clothes from the
morning minus her suit jacket, and between running down Jerod
and feeding Max she looked crumpled and filthy. She glanced
around her condo, and saw a bright orange stuffed duck on the
floor. It felt horribly empty. But now, without the baby around,
she had an odd thought. She was free tonight, and funky coincidences or not, she couldn't help but think of Chase. She closed
her laptop and went into the bedroom, opened her sliding closet
doors, and looked in. She tried to remember the last time she'd
been on an actual date, and was stunned to realize it had been
before she was married. Although there had been the ongoing
weirdness with Hobbs, and that horrible day he'd told her how
he felt about her, that he loved her. 'Stop it!' she told herself,
trying to figure out what she was supposed to wear, and wondering
if she had a single bra that fit.

Her eye caught on something silvery gray hanging in a dry-
cleaner's bag. 'Right,' and thinking of some of the outfits her
sister Justine might wear, she prepared for dinner with Chase,
and hoped he was the smart decent guy he appeared and not the
handsome sociopath that she suspected.

TWENTY

M arky found the envelope with the letter K, pulled it off
the bulletin board by the mailboxes, and slit it open. It
was eight and all he could think about was hooking up
with Chase at midnight. Seeing him at the Night Shade earlier
had made his heart race, and filled him with intense longing.
It was hard being around him, knowing that everyone in the
room was looking at him, wanting him.

Chase had told him that he wasn't mad about Jerod. He could
still feel Chase's hand on the side of his neck; he'd wanted him
to kiss him, but he hadn't. 'Later,' he'd said. 'Take care of this
and we can have the whole night.' He'd given him the bag of
house dope, said the regular stuff would come later in the week.
He'd said it wasn't as strong as usual and everyone would have
to double their doses.

He'd decided not to tell him about the raid on the 4th Street apartment. He hadn't been there, but Dan and Kat had given him the details. But shit like that happens, the six remaining members of the family – not counting him – were used to unexpected changes in venue. No need to bother Chase with day-to-day stuff that might upset him.

He followed Chase's instructions and walked past the elevator to the stairwell, climbed to the sixth floor, and got out. There was a small hallway and a single door. Whoever lived here had money; each floor in the narrow building had a single condo, it had to be worth millions.

From down the hall he heard high-pitched barks. Chase had said to ignore the dogs, that they were locked in the kitchen and wouldn't bother him. All he needed was to go to the big closet in the bedroom and take out all the gold coins and jewelry he could carry.

He turned the knob, unlocked just like Chase had said. He moved fast, barely taking in the surroundings, the fussy feminine living room, the bedroom with its massive canopy bed and silk pillows. He put on gloves . . . should have done it before . . . and went into the closet. As he went straight to the safe, he noted how all of the clothing was women's. Dozens of pairs of shoes, each in a clear plastic box. Handbags arranged in cubbies, and racks and racks of suits and dresses.

He peered into the large wall safe. 'Awesome!' he muttered, opening the first of the black coin boxes. It weighed a ton, each of the shiny coins sealed inside clear plastic. Chase had told him to grab as much as he could carry; he wasn't kidding. He'd said that gold was over $800 an ounce and that this was a major score that they'd split fifty–fifty. He loosened his black knapsack and tilted in the first box of coins. He wondered how much he'd be able to carry and maybe he could leave quick and come back a second time.

As he worked, hurriedly opening boxes and wondering which were worth more, things started to bug him. Something familiar, it was the smells, perfume, and the hint of something like burned hair and . . . orange, but maybe that was just left over from meeting Chase at the bar. He heard the dogs from the other room, and something else. Someone knocking at the door . . . the door he hadn't bothered to lock behind him.

'Dr. Fleet?' A man's deep voice came from the hallway. The buzzer sounded and the barks grew in pitch and frenzy.

Marky threw his knapsack over his back, the weight and the momentum made his knees almost buckle. He ran out of the closet and frantically looked around the bedroom, three windows, all facing 18th Street, two with bars. So no going back to the front door. He either had to hide, not a great option, or get the fuck out of there.

'Dr. Fleet, it's Detective Hobbs with the NYPD, please open the door, I'd like to speak with you.'

He heard the door open, and then the cop coming in. 'Dr. Fleet? Commissioner Fleet?'

He padded silently back to the bedroom door and closed it, hopefully buying him a few seconds. He heard the cop go to the kitchen and the barking dogs.

He ran to the fire-escape window. Scared shitless he opened the latch and using his legs for support pushed it open. It made a horrible screeching sound, as cool evening air rushed in. He heard the dogs race out of the kitchen and feared he had seconds before they came after him. No longer caring about any noise he made, he fumbled at the latch on the steel gate, got it open, and yanked it back. The coins weighed him down as he wiggled through the opening; he thought of abandoning them. They were worth a fortune, but more than that, Chase wanted him to do this and he wouldn't let him down. He hauled himself onto the fire escape and looked down at the street six floors below. He turned and banged his knee painfully against one of the iron railings. 'Shit!' He grabbed the banister and hobbled down, going as fast as he could, the iron slats rattling and squeaking with every step.

One flight from the bottom, he heard the cop shout out the window. 'Stop! Police! Stop, or I'll shoot.'

Yeah, he thought, *like that's going to do it. Don't turn around, just keep going.* He hit the bottom flight and looked down at the street; a twelve-foot drop and he was carrying eighty pounds on his back, not to mention the brick of house dope. He saw the hanging ladder, but how the hell did it work? There was a latch, but it was old, rusty, and his fingers couldn't get it to move.

'Marky!' the cop shouted.

He whipped his head around. *How the hell does he know my name?* He shucked off his knapsack and dropped it to the ground. It landed hard and he followed, dangling off the edge to lessen the fall. He let go, dropped, and rolled on the sidewalk. His knee shot red-hot pain where he'd scraped it. He got to his feet, and wondered if he'd broken anything, but his legs seemed to work. He spotted the pack; it would hold him back. But Chase would be so disappointed. He'd be angry. 'Fuck it!' He hoisted it into his arms and then over one shoulder. He heard the cop coming fast, the steps rattling overhead. Pushing as fast as he could, he hauled ass across the street, around the corner, and into the subway.

Hobbs rushed to catch the blond-haired kid before he dropped to the street. But he had too much of a head start. There was no clear shot at him, and even if there were, without knowing what was going on, Hobbs could never shoot a man in the back. More than that, and why he didn't give chase, was there was something very wrong in Janice Fleet's condo. The dogs locked in the kitchen, a burglary going on, and the front door open with no sign of its having been forced. Where was Janice Fleet? He'd called out Marky as a hunch, and while it was hard to see, the kid had turned around. 'Made you look,' he whispered.

He pulled out his cell and called in the burglary and the fleeing suspect. 'Caucasian male, blond, early twenties, about five eleven, dressed in jeans, leather jacket, red sweatshirt. Last seen heading south on Second.' He then added, 'His first name is possibly Marky.' Through the open window he heard the dogs; they weren't letting up, and it was more than barking, they sounded as if they were clawing at something.

He climbed back up and through the window. He thought of Barrett's comment – too many coincidences with Commissioner Janice Fleet. He followed the frantic yapping toward the front hall closet. The shih-tzus were in a frenzy, their black noses pressed in the crack of the door, their hard nails scraping off the white gloss paint and splintering the wood around the bottom.

He reached for the handle and one of the dogs stood up on its hind legs as he pulled it open. The little dog pushed its muzzle into the opening and let out a howl that sounded like a baby's cry. Hobbs couldn't quite tell what he was looking at – a closet in disarray, a stack of women's coats on the floor, some large cardboard boxes along the back. But then he saw a bit of light blue chiffon that seemed out of place, and something that looked a lot like skin with freckles.

All three dogs clamored inside. They pulled at the coats, and one had tunneled its way under the jumble, only its curved tail visible.

'Commissioner Fleet . . . Janice?' Hobbs said, his stomach in knots as he pulled off the coats. He lifted off a red-wool poncho and knew, even before he'd checked for a pulse, that the woman staring at him with a fresh exit wound on her forehead – the blood still shiny and moist – was dead.

He backed away from the closet and pulled the protesting dogs out. He heard a cruiser pull up outside. After nearly twenty years on the force, most of those working major crimes, his actions were automatic. Call in homicide and don't let anyone screw up the crime scene. He checked the time – just after eight – and let his senses drink in all of the ethereal bits of evidence that would soon be lost: the smells of Dr. Fleet's condo, the cast of the lights, the pitiful cries and whimpers from her dogs. He stood in her hall and tried to picture what could have happened, letting the images find him. The young man with the knapsack, presumably filled with stolen goods. Entered through the front door, no sign of force. Had Dr. Fleet known him? Did they have a relationship? He couldn't have been more than twenty-two or twenty-three. Was he someone she'd known from the DFYS, or from one of the drop-in centers . . . an old patient? His thoughts flew to Barrett, out on her date. Doctors weren't supposed to have relationships with their patients outside of the office, so why did she bring Jerod home? It was a chilling thought, what if the kid with his sad 'I'm a schizophrenic junkie' routine was just playing them? He'd be with Ruth . . . and the baby. Of course, he was pretty damn certain Ruth Conyors didn't have a wall safe filled with . . .

He walked back to the bedroom, and pulled out a pair of disposable gloves. He looked at the safe, and the closet floor littered with gold coins, but his thoughts kept going back to Barrett. She'd be sitting down with her hunky social worker, the one who'd been a patient of the now-dead Dr. Fleet. Hobbs had blown off her concerns about the guy's connections with Janice. Why'd he do that? Everything here felt connected, and if Blondie was Jerod's Marky . . .

He pulled out his cell. 'Barrett, can you talk?'

'Not really,' she said.

Hobbs heard sitar music and pictured Barrett and her date at one of those cozy Indian restaurants in the Village, fabric-draped walls and candles in red glass holders. 'Janice Fleet is dead. She's been murdered in her condo.'

'Oh my God, when?'

'Looks like a robbery. I came in in the middle; I think the perp was Marky; he fits the description. Where are you?'

'Bengali East,' she said.

'Your date?'

'Yeah.'

'Barrett, you were right; Fleet's somehow tied up in this mess with Jerod and the dead kids. I don't know how yet.' He glanced around the bedroom, trying to push down a sudden sense of panic. Nothing added up, the wall safe filled with God knows how much gold – pounds of it – and whatever else might have been taken, the dead commissioner with her legacy of drop-in centers, kids just out of foster care getting set up to sell dope to college kids, or getting overdosed when they decide to clean up their act . . . lots of organization. Not a one-person organization. 'Barrett, I'm coming to get you. I've got a bad feeling about your date.'

'You're not alone,' she whispered. 'Please hurry,' and the line went dead.

TWENTY-ONE

Barrett's date with Chase had started with promise. His cab pulled up to the red and gold restaurant facade just as she did. 'What a day,' he said, as he handed the driver a twenty, 'keep it,' striking a small but first wrong note of the evening.

She waited on the sidewalk. He was still dressed in the clothes he'd had on at the conference . . . only the shoes were different, not the Prada boots but equally nice, and far more practical, black leather walking shoes. 'You look like you just came from work,' she said, wondering why something about that seemed over-obvious, like why bring a briefcase to a date? And if he'd taken a cab, why the switch to comfortable shoes?

'Horrible day,' he said.

'That call you got?'

He let out a slow breath. 'Got to shake it off. It's no wonder why half the counselors are burned out and the other half just don't give a shit. You look really nice,' he said, letting his eyes do a thorough once-over. 'And I promise not to spend the whole time bitching about work.'

Unlike Chase, she had managed a quick, and necessary, change at home, ditching her navy suit for a pair of form-hugging black jeans, gray silk scoop-necked T-shirt with an empire waist that did wonders for her still-nursing breasts while concealing the barest hint of belly, a pair of low-heeled trendy black boots, and a mannish black sport coat worn open. She'd even put on makeup, and not just the usual dab of neutral-pink lipstick she wore for work, but smoky gray eye shadow, mascara, and lips painted a deep, almost fresh-blood red. 'Shop talk doesn't bother me,' she said, as she stepped down the few steps to the restaurant.

Chase swept an arm in front of her and opened the door, letting out the smells of a dozen spices.

The proprietor, an Indian man in his early seventies, greeted them. 'Dr. Conyors, how good to see you again.' He gave her a quick once-over, doing a small double-take at her outfit. 'You are most lovely tonight, the window is OK?'

'That would be nice, Sanjee,' she said, noting the covert glances of the diners checking them out.

As he led them to the dimly lit table, Chase whispered, 'Every man in this room wishes he were with you.'

'Please,' she said, enjoying the compliment and feeling a bit unnerved by his proximity, 'we're in the East Village, half of them are gay and wish they were with you.'

As they sat, he gazed at her. 'Do you have any idea how beautiful you are?'

She couldn't help but meet his stare, those amber eyes, the perfect symmetry of his features, the almost feline slant of his cheeks, and those lips . . . 'You ain't so bad yourself, kid.'

'It's not easy, is it?'

His response took her off guard. 'No, it's not,' she said, nervously pushing a hand through her bangs, wondering where he'd take this.

'I think we have a lot in common, and please don't think I spend my whole day in front of the mirror, but when you're very good-looking . . . or beautiful . . . it's not what other people think – kind of a double-edged sword.'

'Yes,' she said, finding the conversation odd and surprisingly easy, 'although I think the rules are different for men and women.'

'Don't be so certain,' he said. 'People think you're dumb and they like to do things for you . . .'

'They want to get you in the sack,' she said, wishing she'd kept that thought to herself.

'There is that,' he agreed, as their waiter came with menus. 'Kind of puts a sour spin on the whole thing. You know, somebody is nice to you, helps you out, and then you realize they'd like something in return . . . even if they don't say it. Anyway, enough of poor pretty us.' He reached under the table and retrieved his briefcase. 'I can't imagine how many rules this is breaking.' He pulled out a Manila folder that was a good five inches thick. 'Believe it or not I actually thinned this puppy down.'

'The stuff on Jerod,' she said, having forgotten Chase's earlier offer to go into his sealed records. And right there she knew that something was very wrong with Chase. Ever since she'd met him the evidence had trickled in, and part of her hated the way she couldn't just enjoy the attention of this stunning man. She'd spent ten years evaluating criminals, most of whom also had mental illnesses. And she'd met more than her share of sociopaths, men and women with no morality, no sense of empathy, driven only by their wants and desires. The smart ones, like this Chase, knew how to hide it, how to put on the trappings of normalcy, which in his case came with movie-star looks. She looked at the folder as he slid it toward her. 'You shouldn't have done that, you know that everything you download can be traced.'

'I thought you wanted it,' he said, his gleaming eyes on hers.

Her brain kicked into overdrive as competing thoughts burst forward. He'd set this date up with some underlying purpose, and she didn't yet know what it was. But now he was trying to turn her into an accomplice for a felony. He'd illegally removed sealed documents that belonged to the State of New York. And he'd broken federal regulations by copying privileged patient information, which he now intended to pass on to her. 'I can't take that, Chase. You shouldn't have done that, it's not what I wanted.'

The waiter returned with a steaming plate of assorted Indian breads, vegetable stuffed samosas, mango, chutney, and a cucumber and yogurt dip.

'I guess I misunderstood,' he said, a smile forming, as he pulled the folder off the table and dropped it back into his briefcase. 'Well, no big deal. You think anyone really knows how to trace what goes on with those state computers? I'll just shred it and end of story. You never saw it. Besides, by the time they do any kind of electronic audit, if they ever do, I'll be long gone.'

'Medical school,' she said, keeping her mounting panic under wraps. *He knows about computers, could he be the one who broke into my office?* Chase wanted something from her, and she sensed now it had little to do with getting her in the sack, at least not just that. 'You're not going to miss working with the kids?'

'Not really,' he said. 'But you know that's something else we'll have in common. You're a doctor, I'm going to be a doctor. Barrett,' his tone dropped, 'I don't know what it is . . . but ever since we met this morning I cannot get you out of my mind. This is not usual for me, and I'm sorry if copying Jerod's records freaked you out, but . . . Shit! I feel like an idiot.'

God, he's quick, she thought, noting how he'd deftly stepped away from the crimes he'd just committed, covering them up with a facade of what she could only describe as the 'love at first sight' defense. But the first rule in dealing with a sociopath is to never let them know you're on to them, so she played along. 'Forget it,' she said. 'And I've got to admit that you've popped into my brain a few dozen times today. So let's pretend none of this happened.'

'Sounds good to me,' he said, pulling off a piece of steaming pouri bread and dipping it into the golden-brown tamarind sauce.

'And seeing as you already know about Jerod,' she said, 'maybe you can help me with a few details. Not so much about him, but about some kids he was hanging out with.'

'If I can, what's this about?'

'It's a case I've been dealing with. A couple kids wound up dead in a shooting gallery and Jerod's the one who found them, and then there's this other girl, another sad case. What I can't figure out is how someone like Jerod, who can get pretty crazy, hooked up with kids who are basically normal. A couple of them were recent graduates of DYFS – Bobby Dix and Carly Sloan.' She looked across at him, trying to detect any hint of emotion or recognition.

He cocked his head slightly, and swallowed a bite of food. 'No, sorry, not ringing bells.'

The date's over, she thought, as her last thin thread of doubt about him vanished with his denial. He'd met with Carly Sloan on a weekly basis for over two years. He was the counselor who would have been responsible for helping her transition out of the department. *Date's over and time to go to work.* As she thought through strategies the waiter reappeared with a tray of shiny covered-brass dishes. He placed them on the table, raising the lid on each. 'Lamb kurma, chicken tandoori, vegetable curry.'

As the steam rose, she shifted her questioning into a style that was a blend of Hobbs's interrogation and a forensic approach she'd ordinarily take when dealing with a sociopath and his many layers of lies. 'The girl is particularly sad,' she said, taking the lid off the creamy kurma.

'Why's that?' he asked, putting a large spoonful of saffron rice in the middle of his plate.

'On so many levels,' she said, and thought of Jerod and his desperation to find his missing girlfriend, she couldn't screw this up. If anyone knew where Carly Sloan was, or what had happened to her, it was Chase. *Did he shoot that video, and if so, why?* 'I don't know how much you know about the kids living in the park tents in Brooklyn, a few left in the Lower East Side, and these last hold outs in the East Village, but apparently they're like little families. Many of them come from horrible backgrounds, either castoffs from DFYS or cast off for other reasons, a lot of runaways and some that just get kicked out of their houses.'

'We get a lot of those,' he commented, 'but the problem is most of them don't want what the department has to offer, so they run away . . . This restaurant is great. I'm glad you suggested it. It's been a long time since I've had Indian.'

She listened to the sound of the voice, and how he tried to redirect the conversation. It had the feel of sparring at Sifu Henry's dojo. *OK, Chase, let's see where we can spin this.* 'I do love Indian, and this is my favorite place. You've never been to this one?'

'No . . . I had a friend who'd insist we go to the ones in Jackson Heights. He said they were the best.'

'*Had* a friend?' she'd asked.

'He passed away.'

'A good friend?'

'Yes, very, someone who helped me out when I was leaving

my last group home, gave me a place to stay in exchange for looking after him.'

Interesting, she thought, from 'whatever happened to Carly Sloan', to Chase the do-gooder. 'He was ill?' she offered, wanting to let Chase feel he was controlling the conversation.

'AIDS. I took care of Dom for three years. I was with him at the very end.'

'That's commendable, what happened when he died? Were you suddenly out on the street?'

'No,' Chase said, and he motioned to the waiter. 'I'd like a glass of Bombay Beer.' He looked at her. 'You?'

'No, I'm good with tea,' she replied, noting he was again trying to shift topics. 'So, what happened after your friend Dom died?'

'He was generous. He'd known the end was coming and he'd had the deed to his condo put in my name.'

'Wow, generous is putting it mildly, where in the city?'

'TriBeCa . . . but he'd purchased it long before TriBeCa became . . . TriBeCa.'

A string of questions formed in her head, but she thought better of firing them at Chase, like, *Exactly how long after the change in the lease did your friend die?* And, *Was there an autopsy, or did people just assume, AIDS, dead, it was inevitable?* 'So you kind of lucked out.'

'If you call losing your best friend lucking out.'

'Sorry about that,' she said, 'I imagine he also left you enough to keep the place up, because God knows the condo fees and taxes in this city can be outrageous.'

'I'm sorry, Barrett, but this is kind of painful stuff to talk about, do you mind if we talk about something better . . . like you, and how the hell does someone wind up as a forensic psychiatrist?'

'That's easy,' she said, giving him her best smile, 'when I went through my rotations as a medical student, the one that was the most interesting was psychiatry; there's something about people and their stories and trying to understand how lives get played out in certain ways. A bad childhood can lead here, a quirk in genetics pushes someone there. A girl watches her father beat up on her mother and when she becomes a teenager she runs into the arms of the football jock who does the same to her. Call me twisted, but I find it fascinating. The forensic part came later, when I was a resident and started working in the emergency room. One case in particular actually turned into something relatively high profile. A woman had come into the emergency room; she was psychotic and hearing voices. She'd said the devil was coming to take her children and she needed to get them to safety . . . get them to heaven. When I heard that my first thought was, *Where are this woman's children?* Turned out she'd killed her one-year-old twins, smothered them with a pillow.'

'Post-partum psychosis?'

'This is where it got interesting, as I did her emergency-room evaluation I started to notice things. Like whenever I left the room and watched her on the closed-circuit monitor, she seemed less crazy. But the minute the nurse or I entered the room, suddenly she was in the presence of Jesus, and we caught it all on tape. End of the day it turned out she'd caught the babies' father with another woman and had decided that the best punishment would be to kill his children. She didn't have schizophrenia; she wasn't psychotic at all.' She made eye contact with Chase. 'It was cold, calculated murder, and she was trying to swing a "not guilty by reason of insanity" defense.'

'I take it that didn't work,' he said.

'No, but after that I became fascinated with the layers of deception and lies and trying to figure out how you cut through them and get to some semblance of truth . . . like with Carly Sloan, Chase.'

'What are you talking about?' he said, an annoyed expression flashing across his face.

Interesting, she thought, feeling a twinge of excitement and fear. 'You knew Carly Sloan, Chase.' She watched him intently, almost able to see his mind sort through the possible responses. Should he keep up the lie, or shift to a new one that incorporated some part of the truth? 'Maybe you just forgot the name, Carly Sloan.'

'I see a lot of kids. I don't understand what you're getting at.'

'But you do, Chase . . .' she said, 'you're just trying to figure how much I know.'

'What? You think I'm some kind of criminal, you think I had something to do with her disappearance?'

'Now that is interesting,' she said, pushing back from the table and wishing to hell Hobbs was there. At least she wasn't alone with him.

'What the fuck are you doing?' he said, realizing what he'd just let slip.

'Not me, Chase, you. I never said Carly Sloan was missing. Where is she?' And then her cell went off. It felt like the air had been sucked from the room. His beautiful face twisted into a rage-filled mask. She felt the tension, and had no doubt that he would attack her if they were not in a restaurant. She edged back and pulled her cell from the inside pocket of her blazer. The caller ID said, *Detective Edward Hobbs*.

'Janice Fleet is dead,' Hobbs said, 'she's been murdered in her condo.'

'Oh my God, when?' Barrett, asked, never taking her eyes off Chase.

'Looks like a robbery. I came in the middle; I think the perp was Marky; he fits the description. Where are you?'

'Bengali East,' she said, wondering what the fuck Chase was doing as he reached down to his briefcase.

'Your date?'

'Yeah.' She looked around the dimly lit restaurant, and wished she hadn't taken the window seat. She swatted down at a mosquito or spider that had chosen that moment to bite her leg. Her hand came away with something sticky, like she'd spilled something.

'Barrett, you were right; Janice Fleet is somehow tied up in this mess with Jerod and the dead kids. I don't know how yet. Barrett,' Hobbs said, 'I'm coming to get you. I've got a bad feeling about your date.'

'You're not alone,' she whispered, wondering why Chase was just sitting there and smiling. 'Please hurry.' The line went dead. She needed to get out of there, but something felt wrong when she tried to stand, her legs felt disconnected; it was hard to think. She was in a restaurant and there was a handsome man sitting across from her. He reached for her cell phone.

'Are you feeling OK?' he asked, dropping her cell onto the floor, and then kicking it under a radiator. 'You don't look so good, we should get you out of here.' He called for the check, and told the waiter, 'I think Dr. Conyors is coming down with something.' He threw a pile of twenties on the table, came around to her side, and put a strong arm around her back. 'Up we go,' he said, and practically carrying her, he got her out of the restaurant and onto 6th Street.

She needed to say something, but all she could think about

was the wonderful wave of peacefulness that pumped through her. The cool evening air scented like a delicious tea, the sounds of the street, the touch of the handsome man's silky hair against her cheek. Everything felt beautiful and good. All of her fears, her insecurities – they were gone. She was OK, everything was OK. Her world had never seemed so amazingly rich, so amazingly beautiful . . . so wonderfully safe.

TWENTY-TWO

Marky's nerves wouldn't let up and his knee was bleeding and hurt like a mother. He'd fucked up left and right and as he handed out plastic bags of dope to the eight trendily dressed members of the family his thoughts flitted from hooking up with Chase at midnight to the cop shouting his name and chasing after him to the gold coins in his knapsack hidden behind a stack of pillows. It was nearly ten and the family, which usually had around a dozen kids to cover the biggest dormitories in the city, needed new recruits. It was part of his job, and Chase was clear about which ones to pick, no families, homeless. Sometimes, like with Carly, Chase would give him a lead on a kid about to get kicked out of foster care or a group home. And they had to look right, they needed to blend. But as Marky got older – now twenty-two – it was getting harder for him to fit, and somebody needed to make sure the kids weren't screwing around with the dope or the money.

'You got clean needles?' the newest kid – Brad – asked.

'Bathroom,' Marky said, looking at the good-looking boy with killer blue eyes, who could have worked at a retail store if he didn't have a criminal record and no high-school diploma. Recruiting him had been simple, Chase had directed him down to the drop-in center, given Marky his description. It wasn't hard, *'You need money? A place to stay? You want to try some good dope? Come with me, you'll have fun. We're like a family and not the shitty kind, either.'*

He looked around the dimly lit room that he'd decorated with tiny Christmas lights. He looked at the family members – Jen, Dan, Kat, Oscar, Yvette, Blake, and Jason – as they paired off and settled on the purple-draped mattresses arranged around the periphery like a three-sided bed. He thought of Bobby – nice kid – and how his girlfriend used to bring down curtains and shit like that to the places on 4th Street – it had looked nice. He remembered other kids who'd come and gone, some ran away, some got in trouble like Bobby, some Chase took away in the middle of the night . . . like Carly. He'd never asked Chase where they went; not his business and it scared the shit out of him.

He flopped back on the mattress, the one he always took, right in the center. He felt behind for the knapsack. He needed to chill and one little bag wouldn't hurt anything, might take the edge off the pain. He'd be in good shape for Chase. He'd said he wasn't mad, and maybe the big bag of gold – he'd said they'd split it – would make everything good again. He carefully dumped the brownish heroin onto a silver tablespoon, and lit a candle. He watched as it bubbled up and then melted down into a clear liquid. He pictured Chase, and couldn't wait to be with him . . . just a couple more hours. He pulled up his baggy pant leg and tied a rubber tourniquet around his calf. In the dim light he spotted the tiny vein he liked best, nestled in the crook made by his big toe and the one next to it. He drew the dope up into a plastic syringe, felt with his finger for the vein, and pierced the flesh with a tiny pinch. He pressed down, and like taking an elevator to the moon, felt the first giant rush of bliss. *Chase was wrong,* he thought, *this is fucking fantastic dope!* He fumbled for the tourniquet, just barely able to get it off before it rolled over him. He looked around, his vision bleary as the family shot up, and a real bad thought pressed through. This wasn't crap dope at all . . . it was killer.

TWENTY-THREE

Barrett smiled, she wondered if she'd ever been happier, so completely at peace. *It must be a dream*, as the beautiful man holding her up signaled for a cab. 'Chase,' she whispered.

'Yes, Barrett.'

'I love you,' she said, 'I want to always feel like this.'

'I love you too,' he said, as the sparkling headlights of a cab stopped before them.

They glittered and cast rainbows and Barrett knew that this was love, true, beautiful, and perfect. She barely felt his arm on her back; they were like dancers, he would lead and she would follow. She looked down at her clothes, and wished she'd worn something frilly. She giggled.

'What are you laughing at?' he asked, moving her toward the cab, opening the door.

'I want a tutu,' she said.

'I'll get you one,' and he gallantly helped her inside.

'Dr. Conyors.' An Indian man's voice entered her dream. 'Dr. Conyors. Dr. Conyors!'

Sitting in the back of the cab with her legs still on the sidewalk she looked past Chase and saw Sanjee – what was he doing in her dream? – running up from the restaurant wearing his traditional white outfit. She supposed he'd always worn it, but how did it stay so white; it glowed. *Is he an angel?* As she stared at Sanjee, feeling Chase try to scoop up her legs and get her into the cab, she saw a circle of light around the restaurant owner's head; he had a halo. She stared.

'Dr. Conyors,' he ran up to them, 'you dropped your phone. It's ringing.'

'Thank you,' she said, wishing that Chase weren't pushing so hard, and not liking the harsh metal sound her phone made.

'We need to go now,' Chase hissed.

'But Sanjee is an angel,' she said, willing her legs to stay on the ground. She didn't want to get into the cab yet. She wanted to see Sanjee. How could she have missed how beautiful and glowing he was?

'Barrett, now!'

Sanjee Singh was now just a foot away, holding out her cell. She stared into his face, he was looking at her and then at Chase, who kept trying to get her into the cab. Why was he in such a hurry and why did Sanjee look so concerned? 'Are you OK, Dr. Conyors? You do not look well.' He looked at Chase, and the expression on his face shifted, as though he could see inside the younger man. 'Are you taking her to a hospital?'

'Yes,' Chase answered, 'I think she's having some kind of allergic reaction, can you help me get her into the cab?'

'That's not true,' Barrett said, not liking these dark, scary undertones the dream was taking on. 'We were going for my tutu, but that was a lie.' She looked up at Sanjee. 'Be careful,' she said, 'he lies, I don't want to go with him.' She tried to stand, but now Chase was pushing her back, handling her too rough. He didn't love her. 'Let go!' She kicked out, her legs strong from years of martial-arts training.

Chase stumbled back and Barrett pulled herself out of the cab. Her ankles caught on the curb and she fell forward. She knew there was something very wrong, this wasn't a dream at all. Sanjee tried to catch her, and he too fell backwards, landing on the dirty sidewalk. The cell kept ringing. Chase was pulling at her back, but Sanjee held tight around her middle. She hung fast to the Indian, not daring to let go.

'Bitch!' Chase swore. 'Cunt! Let go!'

'Get off me!' she screamed, her voice weak in her head. She tried to look up, but even that was too much of an effort, her arms were weakening.

'Leave her alone!' Sanjee shouted, holding tight to Barrett. 'Leave! Help! Help! Help!'

Suddenly Chase let go, and she collapsed against Sanjee, who held her fast.

The cab pulled away, and Chase was gone. It was almost funny, chasing Chase, him chasing her, but the beautiful floaty feeling had left. There was something heavy in her chest, and darkness pressing on her vision. 'I can't breathe,' she gasped, as Sanjee released his grip. 'I've been drugged.'

'You will be OK, Dr. Conyors.' He sounded frightened. 'The ambulance will be here. I will not leave you.'

She wanted to answer him, to keep his light-filled face in her vision, but she couldn't keep her eyes open, and each breath took such effort. She drifted off to the sound of the cell, and fell into a dream. She was running down a back stage dressed in a pink tutu. She was supposed to give a performance, but she had to tell someone she couldn't dance, she played piano. There had been a horrible mistake, somewhere in the distance an orchestra was tuning, all the instruments playing out of pitch, somewhere a violin gave an 'A', it droned on. They couldn't be serious about having her dance. A loudspeaker boomed, 'The show must go on.' Right, if she had to fake it she'd do her best. Sifu Henry appeared from a dressing room, he was in a tux. 'Just remember your form,' he instructed, as he gave her his hand

and led her onto the stage. There was applause; a curtain went up, the lights in her eyes were too bright, she couldn't see who was in the audience, but in the center of the stage was a curtained bassinet, and next to it Jerod in a tuxedo singing in a beautiful tenor – *I didn't know he could do that.* 'Max!' She ran forward, but the more she tried to reach her baby and Jerod the further away they became. 'Max! Jerod! Wait for me. I'm sorry. I'm sorry.' She tried to run faster, her body wouldn't respond; she looked down and saw her feet getting swallowed in a rising tide of blood. It was hard to breathe, and with each step she sank deeper, the blood was up to her thighs, her chest, her chin. In desperation she looked over the sea of blood to see Max's blue bassinet, like a boat bobbing on the rolling waves – Jerod beside him, singing, but the sound not carrying. He's going to be OK, she thought, and she wasn't; she was going to drown. 'I'm sorry, Max. I love you. Your mother loves you.'

Then, like water leaving a tub, the blood receded. It was still hard to breathe, and her arms and legs felt stiff and unresponsive. There was a sharp pain in her left arm, and noises, people talking but too low to understand what they were saying. Max was gone and she was lying on a dinner table. I'm not a turkey, she thought, as she looked around at her mother, Justine, Hobbs, Houssman, and Sanjee. 'Why am I on the table?' she asked.

'Because we're out of oatmeal,' her mother replied.

She heard a whoosh, and felt something deep in her throat. 'Is that why it's hard to breathe?'

Sanjee's heavily accented voice broke through. 'Is she going to be OK?'

'Why does she do this?' her sister asked, pushing away the last wisps of the dream.

There was another whoosh and tightness in her chest as it expanded. Her throat ached and she tried to swallow only something hard had been rammed down her windpipe. She gagged, and her eyes cracked open. It was hard to focus, the lights were so bright. She tried to speak, but couldn't get out the words, her brain scrambled to figure out what had happened. She was in a hospital, and that whooshing was a ventilator. She managed to turn her head a few centimeters and saw Hobbs in his leather jacket and Justine in scrubs and a white coat with the University Hospital logo and her name embroidered below that – Justine Conyors, MD, Department of Surgery. With effort she rolled her head slightly to the other side – *Why is it so hard to move?* – and saw her mother with Max strapped across her chest in his blue sling. Jerod was next to her, and he looked like hell, sweat beading his forehead and dribbling down his cheeks, his dreads tied back with a red handkerchief making his face incredibly gaunt. And finally there was Sanjee Singh, his lips mouthing a string of words she couldn't hear. She spotted an IV in her arm and panic flooded her; she couldn't move her arms, and not just because they'd been taped down to boards at her side.

'Barrett, no,' Justine said, putting a hand on her forehead. 'Don't fight the ventilator, relax or you'll hurt yourself. You're in the hospital, you nearly died, but you're going to be fine.'

The whoosh came again, expanding her lungs like a pair of balloons. She needed to get out of there, to have them take her off that horrible machine. She looked at Hobbs, and hated the way they were all standing around . . . like in that weird dream. *I'm not a turkey.*

'Barrett,' Justine said, her voice pitched low, 'I'm going to try and get you off the machine; get you extubated, please be patient.'

She felt her sister's fingers find hers.

'Squeeze my fingers.'

Barrett focused on the task, freaked by how hard it was for her muscles to obey her brain. She thought of the horrible things that could land a person in an intensive-care unit on a ventilator. *Did I have a stroke, a brain hemorrhage, a tumor? Maybe a horrible spine-crushing fall.* She tried to remember.

'Squeeze my fingers,' Justine repeated. 'We can't take you off the ventilator until you have adequate muscle control. Just try.'

She felt a warm hand on her forehead. Her mother's voice. 'It's OK, baby. You're going to be fine.' She tried to see Max, but could only catch a bit of his gold hair, his face nestled against her mom's chest.

Barrett focused on her fingers, the feel of Justine's hand. Slowly she got them to grip, and then she pressed further.

'Good,' Justine said. 'I'll get the respiratory therapist and get you off this thing. I'll be right back, just stay calm, I know this is weirding you out, but you're going to be OK. They had to give you Pavulon so you wouldn't buck the ventilator. It's wearing off and you'll be fine. You're not paralyzed, it's just the drug.'

Justine disappeared and Barrett tried to relax. Her eyes met Hobbs's. He smiled, but she could see how upset he was, his expression hard, somewhere between cold anger and concern. She had so many questions, and why was Sanjee there? She saw Jerod, looking sick and worried, and a slew of connections raced through her mind, hurtling her back in time. Hobbs's question about why she cared so much about Jerod suddenly made sense. It was all in the dream – she was a turkey. Her mind flitted over a long-ago series of wonderful hours with Madeline Flemming, one of her supervisors when she was in her psychiatric training. An intense time in her life, with oppressive on-call duties, too little sleep, and endless stress in emergency rooms and psych wards. Madeline Flemming was a Jungian analyst to whom Barrett had been assigned for supervision; she was a throwback from all the biologically minded researchers, even her looks, with flowing almost Gypsy outfits, her long gray-streaked hair loose, and bright high-heeled sandals – once she'd even glimpsed a silver ankle bracelet with bells. Every week she'd meet in Madeline's cozy office, be offered a cup of herb tea and an hour's respite from a life that was running far too fast. It was Madeline who'd taught her about the near-lost art of dream interpretation. 'It's our subconscious wanting to chat with us,' she'd explain, 'just like your piano playing it's theoretically straight forward, but if you don't practice you'll never get good at it.'

As Barrett drifted, trying to stay calm, waiting for Justine to return, she remembered those long-ago instructions, how to pull apart a dream and find its inner meanings. Over the years she'd practiced quite a bit, amazed at just how much could be discerned from the seemingly nonsensical and random. Now, she thought back through the dream and let her mind softly focus on what it found most interesting or important. Like, she was supposed to give a performance and now that she thought of it, the stage was a lot like the one at the high school for performing arts. And why was Jerod there . . . and that's when it hit; it was Jerod and it wasn't. Tears came to her eyes; she tried not to choke on the ventilator as she remembered her freshman year at Performing Arts. Accepted a year early, at thirteen, tall and gawky, she'd hide in the basement practice rooms, just her and a piano with a soundproof door against all the high energy and glamour of the other kids. Then, early in the year, a knock at the door, he'd not waited for her to answer just came in, tall and beautiful, an infectious smile, blue eyes, and an easy grace. He'd told her to keep playing – Mozart, not her favorite but the fussy turns and trills helped push her fingers to be fast and precise. 'I'm Kyle,' he'd said, but she'd already known he was Kyle Matthews, seventeen, a junior, a beautiful tenor voice, featured in the big musicals and in the jazz quartet. Her first crush . . . and her first heartache. He'd asked if she could play anything modern, and soon they were jamming, he scatting jazz riffs, she following along. She'd go to bed hugging her pillow, imagining it was him, wondering what it would be like to have her first kiss with him. Daily, she'd go down to the practice rooms and wonder if he'd show – more often than not he would. Now, as she lay in the ICU, hearing and feeling the push and pull of the ventilator, something throbbed deep inside – how long since she'd thought about Kyle. How they'd made plans to do street music during the summer, she'd bring a keyboard and he'd sing, they'd go into the subways, or just on the streets or even to Washington Square Park. But then summer came and he never called. Each day, she'd think maybe today, but it never came. Had he just been making fun of her? Finally she pulled together her courage, found his number and dialed. It was his mother. 'No, Kyle can't come to the phone.' Barrett pressed, 'Is he OK?' Then an uncomfortable silence; his mother asked who she was. 'A friend from school,' Barrett said, and added, 'We play music together.' His mother told her that Kyle was in the hospital. 'What's wrong with him? Can I see him?' she pleaded, and finally the woman told her – a hospital she'd never heard of on the Upper West Side. Without telling anyone, she went to visit. Kyle, as she'd later come to understand, had had a psychotic break and become delusional – the details she'd never know. But that day, seeing him in pajamas and a bathrobe in the middle of the day, surrounded by other patients, all the light and excitement gone from his eyes, she never forgot. He'd tried to act normal, 'They told me I have schizophrenia,' but he could barely form whole sentences – now of course she knew it was the meds. The ones that Jerod – whom she could barely see huddled back in the corner of her room – didn't want to take, the ones he said made him feel dull and not real. It was a weird moment of clarity – Kyle Matthews, her first crush, and she'd cried for nights after. He never returned his senior year, and she never went back to visit. Jerod, with his warmth, humor, quirky free spirit . . . and craziness, reminded her so much of him.

'It's OK,' her mother said, misinterpreting the tears that spilled from her eyes. 'Justine said she'd be right back.'

Slowly, the dream retreated and other thoughts intruded, the dinner with Chase. He'd drugged her, but what with? Hobbs's phone call: someone had shot Janice Fleet – a robbery. Images from the last couple days, from finding the dead kids, to chasing Jerod on the roof. But the face that haunted her was Chase's. She'd caught him in a big lie, he'd known the girl on the video, been her counselor for years. He had to be tied in with the dead kids and Hobbs thought it was Marky who had robbed and killed Janice, so she too was connected. Janice was Chase's therapist; he said she'd saved his life. It was a circle . . . only someone wanted to break it apart, to destroy it.

Justine returned with a balding man in a short white coat over green scrubs. He looked at Barrett.

'Yup, she's awake.' He said, 'Let's get her off this thing. OK, Barrett, I need you to wink your right eye and then your left . . . good. Now squeeze my fingers . . . excellent. I'm going to disconnect the ventilator and I want you to try and breathe on your own with the tube still in your throat, OK? It's going to feel funny, so just try and move some air through the tube. One, two, three.'

Barrett felt the last mechanical breath go in, and then nothing, just that awful tube down her throat. She pushed her diaphragm in and out, feeling the air move out her lungs, through the tube and across her lips, which felt dry and cracked.

'I want you to keep this up, for thirty seconds,' the man said.

Seconds ticked as she focused on her breath, and on trying not to gag.

'OK, we're good,' he said, 'out it comes.' With a single practiced sweep he pulled the white-plastic tube out of her throat.

She coughed and gasped. 'What happened?' she croaked.

'Don't try to speak,' Justine said, 'we'll tell you what we know. Mr. Singh brought you here in an ambulance a little before nine. You'd stopped breathing and were going into cardiac arrest; the paramedics intubated you on the way in. He told us that the man you were with tried to take you away in a cab and that you didn't want to go with him. Mr. Singh thought you'd been drugged, and yes, your toxicology came up positive for some kind of opiate. You've been poisoned. We sent for further testing to find out exactly what, whatever it was had to be strong.'

Justine's voice cracked, and she turned her face away. 'You nearly died, Barrett. If it hadn't been for Mr. Singh . . .'

'Who was it, Barrett?' Hobbs asked.

'Chase,' she croaked, struggling to remember his last name. 'He works for DFYS. He knew Janice Strand. He was Carly Sloan's counselor.'

'That's Marky's boyfriend,' Jerod said, filling the last gap in Barrett's circle. 'I heard him talking on the phone to someone named Chase when he thought I was nodded out.'

'Help me up,' Barrett said, feeling aimlessly for the metal bars of her hospital bed. Her fingers felt clumsy and numb, but now at least she knew why, that on top of whatever drug Chase had used, the hospital had given her a paralytic agent to keep her calm on the ventilator. *It's wearing off*, she reminded herself, feeling new fear. She looked at the IV bag hanging by the bed, and squinted. 'Narcan,' she said.

'Yes,' Justine replied, 'it reversed the effects of whatever he gave you. Who is this Chase? Why would he do this?'

Hobbs turned to Justine. 'He was her date.'

'Figures.'

'Comedy,' Barrett said, each word an effort through her sore throat and tender vocal cords, her mouth was bone dry. 'Sanjee, did you see where he went?'

'No, the street is one-way, he went east, but then I cannot say.'

She struggled to put the information together; it was too much. Chase had tried to kill her, but the toxicology screen said it was an opiate. 'I felt something like an insect bite. I need water.'

'When?' Hobbs asked, pouring her a glass of ice water from a pink plastic pitcher.

She sipped the cool liquid, having to go slow, and feeling it burn as it hit the back of her bruised throat. 'At the restaurant, everything started to go funny. But if he'd given me heroin . . . I've never had heroin, but still it would take a fair amount and a decent-sized needle.'

'Plus, he'd have to cook it up,' Jerod said, his arms wrapped around his sides, his teeth chattered. 'You'd have seen that, and it wouldn't have been like a bug bite. You need a vein; if you just stab it into muscle, it takes forever to work.'

'Good,' she said, feeling like a thick layer of cotton was clouding her brain. 'So it wasn't heroin. It was something stronger.'

'Fentanyl,' Justine offered, 'or God forbid, Sufentanil.'

'Translation, please?' Hobbs asked.

'Synthetic opiates,' Justine said, motioning for Barrett to save her voice. 'Fentanyl is strong; it's used for severe pain and it can be given through the skin, but the most potent is Sufentanil; it's mostly used by surgeons for almost immediate and complete pain control. But when we use it, the patient has to go on a ventilator because it's so powerful it depresses the respiratory drive.'

'Can it be given through the muscle?' Barrett asked, having forgotten this archaic factoid from medical school.

'We don't,' Justine said, 'but it could. That might account for why it took a few minutes for you to pass out. It would be slower than a vein . . . and all it would take is a tiny amount.'

'Like an insect bite,' Barrett said. She pictured Chase. 'He wanted me dead, not just to drug me . . . and Janice Fleet is dead.' She looked at Hobbs. 'He's pulling up stakes, some kind of end-game, and it's not going right. I don't think he came to that restaurant intending to kill me. I forced his hand.'

'And he just happened to have a loaded syringe of super dope . . .' Hobbs added.

'A contingency. He keeps lots of backups. Before I caught him in the lie about Carly Sloan, he kept trying to show how much we had in common. I think he wanted to . . . date me.'

Ruth, who'd been staying in the back of the crowded ICU room, holding the baby, and keeping a watchful eye on Jerod, couldn't contain herself. 'Sweet Jesus, why is it that you can't find a normal man, Barrett?' She looked meaningfully at Hobbs. 'Someone who doesn't take you out for a lovely dinner and then try to kill you.'

Barrett caught the connection between Hobbs and her mother. *Has he said something to her? But that ship sailed, he's seeing someone else. I am a turkey, one big fucking Thanksgiving turkey.*

'Justine,' Hobbs said, 'it looks like I've got my work cut out, I'm going after this Chase guy. If you could have them run what-ever tests they need to confirm this Sufentanil, or whatever other drugs she might have been given. Tell the lab to keep chain of custody . . . in fact I'll have someone from forensics do a confirmatory.'

'Where are you going?' Barrett asked, finally getting the bed positioned so that she was sitting up.

'There's every chance that he thinks you're dead, of course

now he's got the problem of Mr. Singh to worry about. So Mr. Chase's Plan A has gone down the crapper. It's time for him to get out of town, which is what I expect he's doing this very minute.'

A thought played at the back of Barrett's mind, something so evil . . . 'No! It wasn't just that he wanted a date with me . . . I was supposed to be part of his alibi.'

'I already figured that,' Hobbs said, 'the timing of Janice's murder, your dinner . . . too convenient.'

'That's not all,' she said, and looked at Jerod. 'All those other kids . . . Marky. If the plan was to eliminate anyone who could tie him to the dope, the dead kids . . . Carly Sloan. He's going to kill them all, if he hasn't already.'

'Bet he'll do it with the house dope,' Jerod said. 'Every week Marky gives out enough to get everyone through the week. It's different from what they sell. It's kind of a ritual and everyone shoots up together.'

'Where?' Hobbs asked. 'We've locked up the two apartments on 4th and C.'

'There's another place,' Jerod said. 'I don't know the address, but I could show you.'

'We need to hurry,' Barrett said, inching her legs toward the bed's edge. Before Justine could stop her she yanked the IV needle out of her vein, and bent her arm to stop the bleeding.

'Are you out of your fucking mind?' Hobbs swore.

'Where are my clothes?' she asked, not caring that her flimsy hospital gown was giving them a scenic view of her backside.

'Get back in bed,' Hobbs said.

'Where are my clothes?' she repeated, trying to appear steady on her feet, when it felt like her knees and ankles wanted to drop her to the floor.

'The EMTs cut them off you,' Justine said, 'in case you forgot you just had a near-death experience.'

'Got it!' Barrett shouted back, her sudden anger surprising everyone. 'I'm fine now, and I've got work to do . . . like finding the bastard who just tried to kill me and do it before he wipes out a group of kids.'

'That's it!' Hobbs said. 'I'm out of here. Jerod, come with me.'

'Hobbs—' Barrett tripped on the ventilator cord, nearly fell, and managed to hang on by grabbing the side of the machine.

'Look, Barrett, stop this. I'll check in with you later . . .'

He looked at Jerod. 'Come on, you have to show me where they are.'

'Sorry,' Jerod said to Barrett, 'you got to take care of yourself, Dr. Conyors. You got a baby. You can't do shit like this if you got a kid. Don't be a shit mother.'

And he was out of the room, following Hobbs back toward the nursing station and the exit.

Barrett looked around at her mother, Max, Sanjee, and her sister. 'I should go with them,' she said, but felt powerless, weak and stung by Jerod's parting words.

'Dear,' her mother said, gently pushing Barrett back toward the bed, 'I think that Ed put it best, "You're out of your fucking mind." Now back to bed. I hate to say this, sweetie, and you know I love you more than you'll ever know, but there is something wrong with you. You're not a cop, and even if you were, just look at you . . . You have to sit this one out, Detective Hobbs will do the right thing . . . so let it go.'

Looking a bit embarrassed, Sanjee said his goodbyes, 'I hope to see you back soon,' and left the three Conyors women and Max.

A half-hour and then forty-five minutes passed with little conversation. Ruth unstrapped Max from the baby sling and put him on the bed beside Barrett; he was fast asleep, occasionally making a little chirping noise, or moving a chubby arm as though swatting at something in his dream. Barrett sat up, wondering where Hobbs and Jerod were, if they'd gotten to the kids in time; it was agony. *There really is something wrong with you.* She ran a hand through Max's silk-fine hair and tears flowed. She sank down into the bed, holding him close. He woke and turned his head into her chest, looking for her breast. 'Mom,' Barrett said, 'do you have a bottle with you? I don't want to nurse with God knows what still in my system.'

'Hold on.' Ruth fumbled through the diaper bag. 'Here.'

Cuddling Max, feeling his warmth against her body, his heartbeat fast and regular, his hair smelling of shampoo, she gave him his bottle, positioning it as if it were a breast. Outside her curtained room, she heard the dings and beeps of the intensive-care unit. She thought of Hobbs and of how much he cared for her, she looked at her mother, who in the midst of all this mayhem had managed to bring along needles and yarn and was working on a red-and-blue-striped baby beanie, having already completed the matching sweater.

Justine came to the side of the bed. 'He is so beautiful,' she said.

'I know,' Barrett said, 'he's a good boy.'

'He is,' Justine said, meeting her gaze. 'And he needs his mother.'

'I know,' she said, holding him tight, feeling his lips suckle the bottle while his chubby fingers kneaded at her breast.

Just past midnight, Justine's pager went off. She picked up. 'How many?' she asked. 'I'll be right down.'

'What is it?' Barrett asked.

'They're bringing in a group of young adults from a shooting gallery. They'd all overdosed . . . they need all the cardiac code teams in the ER.'

At which point the overhead pager system sounded. 'Code red, emergency room areas B, C, and D . . . Code red, emergency room.'

'Got to run, sweets,' and leaning over she kissed Max on the top of his head and Barrett on her forehead.

TWENTY-FOUR

Feeling sick at heart and desperate, Chase ignored the stench of rotting alley garbage; he needed information and needed it fast. Dinner with Barrett had gone terribly wrong. She'd treated him like scum, her transparent word-games had revealed her true colors – a first-class bitch, no, not for him. He smiled in the dark. *And if not for me, for no one.* Too bad things hadn't gone better; he had liked her and could have seen her as his partner and wife. Doctors Strand and Conyors, or maybe she would have taken his name, or they could have hyphenated. They looked so good together, and their children would have been gorgeous. Too bad, the bitch got what she deserved – a lethal dose. Pity that stupid Indian had got in the way. But she was gone, and New York was a big place, that restaurant host didn't know his name, and probably was an illegal immigrant anyway who wouldn't get involved. 'It's going to be OK,' he told himself as he cowered in the shadows of an alley on the north side of 13th between C and D. He looked up to the top floor of the decrepit tenement in front of him. One by one these six- and seven-floor roach hotels had been eaten up by developers, harassing the rent-stabilized tenants, getting them to leave and then overhaul and hike up the rent. He desperately wanted to get inside and pictured the scene unfolding in Marky's sixth-floor walk-up. While the date with Barrett had gone south, if this went well . . . 'Almost home,' he whispered. There'd be no one left to trace him back to the dope or the silly girls they'd auctioned off. He had a moment of near nostalgia; he thought of Janice. They'd had some fun, although lately not so much, and her constant reminders of how she'd helped him, how if it hadn't been for her . . .

Is it done? The uncertainty was killing him. He emerged from the alley, waited for a taxi to zip past, and darted across the street. Keeping his head down, he took the half flight to the double front doors and keyed in. Four years ago he'd helped Marky find this place. The other tenants – mostly illegal sublets and mono-lingual Latinos – kept to themselves. The flights of worn marble stairs were a bit of a pain, but it was cheap, and like all the locations he selected, it had roof access. Being here was risky, but he pushed that aside; too much had gone wrong. He needed to know that this final ploy had worked, that they were all dead.

He cleared the final flight and turned to the right. He'd pulled out his keys when a loud crash came from six floors below. He froze, someone had just busted in the security door. He heard a shout, 'It's all the way up,' then pounding footsteps.

Without pause, and moving silently, he raced back to the building's only staircase and flew up the last flight. He pressed on the wood door to the roof. Someone had tried to put a lock on, but at least here Marky hadn't screwed up. The lock was broken and Chase pushed through. He ran across the roof and looked down at the street. A single dark sedan parked in front, but then a cruiser with lights and sirens appeared at the end of the block, followed by a second. They honed in on the building, the flashing lights sending swirls of red and blue around the dingy brick buildings. He wanted to scream; there was no getting away from it, everything was coming undone. Medical school, life as a top Manhattan plastic surgeon, a beautiful wife and children . . . it was gone.

He started to shake, there was no one he could go to; he was entirely alone. He looked back at the door and heard movement from the floor below. He needed to get out, but a part of him still wanted to see. Maybe things weren't so bad. Maybe one of the kids had called 911 on a cell phone, or maybe a neighbor had heard something. He had to see, but every minute he stayed here was a horrible risk.

He padded back to the roof door and pressed his face against the wood. He opened it a crack and could see the top of the stairwell. A tall man with a scarred face appeared with a young guy in baggy jeans and a hoodie – Jerod. 'This one,' Jerod said and Chase heard the man pound on the door to Marky's.

'Police, open up, now!'

Chase heard the rattle of a doorknob. He swore under his breath when he heard the creak of hinges. Marky, the fucking moron. He didn't even lock his door!

'Jerod, stay back,' the man said.

Chase felt his breath pass slow through his nostrils, his face pressed to the crack in the door. He saw Jerod's back – the crazy kid must have been here before. He'd led the cops. Chase had to get out of there, but he also had to know. Marky was the only one left who could identify him. If he was dead, maybe he could salvage things . . . still go to medical school. Then more footsteps on the stairs, fresh sirens screaming up the avenue. Over the clamor he heard the man's voice from inside Marky's apartment. 'Jerod, get in here. I need help now.'

Jerod had known where Marky would bring the family. He'd never been inside, but Carly had pointed it out one day. 'That's Marky's place, sometimes we go there to pick up shit and drop off money.' She'd even tried to talk Marky into bringing Jerod into the family; but he'd said no, and Jerod didn't need to ask why. He knew he didn't fit, Marky knew that, and only Carly . . . who'd seen past his sickness and weird behavior had thought he was just fine.

Detective Hobbs had told him to stand outside, and he heard other cops on the way up. As he stood there, struggling to catch his breath from the run up six flights, he felt gooseflesh on his arms and waves of nausea. He tried to think of something that could make him feel better, and Carly's face, her wavy brown hair, her soft eyes formed before him. '*Lots of people hear voices.*'

It calmed him a little, and then the detective's urgent voice from inside; he needed help. Jerod entered.

'Oh no,' he said, as he walked past the linoleum-covered entry and into the living room. 'No,' his feet like lead on the floor, his mind screaming, just like Bobby and Ashley. He recognized them all. He looked to Detective Hobbs, who was bent over one of the girls. He was counting and then breathing into her mouth.

'Do you know CPR?' Hobbs asked, while he placed his face against the girl – Kat's – chest and listened.

'Yeah,' Jerod said, looking around at Marky's living room arranged in a semicircle of mattresses.

'Pick one and get started.'

Jerod couldn't figure why, but he went to Marky, who less than twenty-four hours ago had tried to kill him. He was slumped against the wall, eyes partly open. 'Marky, wake up!' Jerod tried to remember the CPR instructions from the times he'd taken the course. The last time by volunteers who did the needle-exchange program at the drop-in center. 'Marky!' He rubbed his knuckles over the center of the blond man's chest; he did it hard knowing that it was supposed to hurt and get him to wake up. Nothing happened; he reached up to Marky's neck; it was still warm and he felt a faint pulse.

He thought about the other kids, maybe they deserved help more than Marky, but someone had to answer for this. And if Marky wasn't the one responsible, he was the only one who'd know who was. He grabbed Marky by the arms, awkwardly pulled him forward off the mattress and onto the hard wood floor. He turned him flat on his back. He breathed in deep, put his mouth over Marky's, and put in two long breaths. He felt the pulse again, just barely there. Counted the same way Detective Hobbs was and gave another two. The footsteps on the stairs were close, and then cops were coming through. He didn't look up as other officers attended to the kids. He tried not to cry as he listened to their counting, and the comments in the crowded space with its funky Christmas lights and pillows like the ones Ashley used to sew. 'This one's got no pulse.' 'Mine neither.' 'One and two and three and four and . . .' 'What's taking the paramedics?'

A woman officer who was working on a brown-haired boy next to Jerod looked at him between breaths. 'You shouldn't be doing that without a face mask,' she said.

Jerod's finger was on Marky's pulse, and the parts of CPR he'd forgotten came back fast by watching Hobbs and the others. His cheek was turned against Marky's lips, he could almost feel a breath, but didn't want to take the chance by stopping. 'I don't have one,' he said, 'it's OK. I don't need it.'

'Here,' she pulled a plastic mask from out of her belt, 'use this.'

He took the clear plastic circle, looked at how she was using hers, and placed it around Marky's lips. 'Thanks.' Tears streamed as he counted breaths, felt for a pulse, and listened for breath. He wasn't crying for Marky, and he wondered why he hadn't told Dr. Conyors or Detective Hobbs that he'd tried to give CPR to both Bobby and Ashley. Only they'd been dead too long, or he hadn't done it right. Maybe if he'd had Narcan like they'd handed out at the drop-in center. It killed him that he'd waited those minutes to call the crisis center, and that he should have just called 911. When he'd finally had the sense to look for a phone, and had found the two on Bobby, the first number that came to him was the crisis center and Dr. Conyors.

'What did you do to her?' Jerod whispered to the unconscious man, feeling Marky's pulse, and this time certain there was breath leaving his mouth. 'Where's Carly? What did you do to her?' He had the impulse to hit Marky, to get him to wake up, to force him to tell. Instead, he put his lips against the plastic and gave another two breaths, not sure if that was right, when Marky might have started breathing on his own. Someone had found the overhead light as paramedics with stretchers, oxygen tanks, and orange kit boxes piled in.

'It's OK, kid,' a medic in a navy uniform said, as he snapped a mask onto Marky's face. 'We got it from here. You wait outside and give us some room to work.'

'It's an overdose,' Jerod said, 'you got Narcan?'

The medic looked at him. 'You undercover or something?'

'No,' Jerod said, shaking his head and trying to stand. He felt his pulse racing and sweat dripped under his shirt and down his pants. He looked around, each of the kids now either had a cop and medic or pair of medics attending to them. The lady officer who'd given him the face mask was standing on top of a mattress, her back pressed against the wall. The brown-haired boy she'd been working on, who couldn't have been more than eighteen, had an oxygen mask strapped to his face and a paramedic had just ripped open his shirt and put on paddles. 'Clear.'

The kid's chest surged up and then back. Jerod looked at the little LED screen on the medic's defibrillator. No heartbeat; the kid was flatlining. The paddles were rapidly recharged, the voltage increased. 'Clear.'

'Give me an amp of epi,' the medic called, as his partner grabbed a syringe and handed it over.

Jerod turned to the lady officer; he could tell she was trying not to cry. He squeezed past a stretcher and went over to her. 'His name's Brad,' he said. 'He was new.'

They watched as the paddles were applied for a third time.

'He's too young,' the cop said, her eyes intent on the monitor.

'I've got a pulse,' the medic said, 'let's get him out of here.'

'What's your name?' the lady cop, who couldn't have been much older than he, asked.

'Jerod,' he said. He could tell she was trying to push past the horror of the scene. It was hard not to compare this with what happened before – Bobby and Ashley should have had paramedics. He should have done something different. He should have been able to save them. He sank to the floor and sobbed.

'It's OK, Jerod,' she said, sitting next to him. 'I'm Officer Stanton . . . Kate.' Her gaze fixed on the boy and his tenuous heartbeat. She glanced across at Jerod. 'You use, don't you?'

'Yeah.'

'Why?' she asked. 'Why do people do this to themselves?'

He watched as Marky was hoisted onto a stretcher, a mask hooked to oxygen over his mouth and nose. 'It numbs everything,' he said, 'nothing hurts . . . but it doesn't last. I'm never doing it again,' he said, realizing that this was the truth. 'I'd rather be dead than go though this again.'

'That's good,' she said. 'You knew these kids?'

Jerod looked up as Detective Hobbs pushed through a pair of empty stretchers and came toward them. His shoulders sagged and he was shaking his head. He tried to speak, and his voice choked.

'Damn,' Hobbs finally managed, batting something from his eye. He turned and surveyed the scene, as one by one the kids were strapped onto stretchers and carried down the six flights. 'I'm going back to the hospital, Jerod. You want to come with me?'

'Yeah,' Jerod said, pushing back against the wall. His whole body ached, as though he'd been beaten.

The lady officer also stood and looked at Hobbs. 'What happened here?'

'Somebody just tried to exterminate their work force. If not for Jerod these kids would all be dead. As it is, we have no clue how many will make it.'

As Hobbs spoke, Jerod watched them carry out Marky, the blond man's eyes blinked. 'You need to have somebody watch him,' Jerod said, 'that's Marky. If anyone knows what happened; it's him. You can't let him get away.'

'I'll go with him,' Officer Stanton said, getting to her feet. 'My partner's over there,' she said, indicating an older heavyset cop who'd made it up after the medics. She looked at Hobbs. 'I think he'll be happy doing some babysitting at the hospital.' She turned to Jerod. 'You just saved a bunch of lives,' she said, looking him in the eye. 'I hope you get off the dope, because I don't know you, but I think you're somebody pretty great.'

Her words hit him hard. How to respond? She'd called him a hero, sort of, not a fuck-up, not a junkie, not the crazy piece of shit his parents couldn't deal with. 'Thanks, Officer Stanton.'

'Kate,' she said, and headed toward her partner.

'Let's get out of here,' Hobbs said. 'They're transporting them all to University Hospital. It'll be easier having them in one place.'

'Will he try again?' Jerod asked, struggling to keep up with Hobbs as they squeezed past a stretcher and started down.

'If he knows he didn't succeed; he might.'

'You think he's watching?'

'If it were me,' Hobbs said, 'and you always have to think like that if you want to be a cop, I'd want to know what was happening.'

'Makes sense. Course I'm not exactly cop material, but maybe . . . Fuck!'

'What?' Hobbs asked, stopping.

'Rooftops. Bobby told me that the reason they had the apartment on the top floor was that if they ever needed to bolt, they could go over the roof. That's why Marky's apartment is up here. If he's anywhere, that's where he's . . .' Before he could finish the sentence, Hobbs reversed direction and raced up the steps.

Jerod watched him as the last of the stretchers started down. The girl they carried – Yvette – had ghost-white skin and dyed black hair. She'd hung out with them a few times; she'd always been nice. *How could someone do this?* He suddenly didn't care that his body felt like he'd been beaten or that waves of knife-sharp cramps kept rolling through his gut, he had to help, to somehow make this better, and pushing through the pain, he ran after Hobbs.

TWENTY-FIVE

For the second time that day Hobbs struggled to force a rooftop door. Jerod was right. The perp – Barrett's date – had been watching, checking if he'd succeeded in killing off Marky and his family of dealers. And now he'd barricaded the door.

He rammed his shoulder into the solid oak, the lock had been smashed but something on the other side was holding it shut and with the bulb out overhead and only filtered light from below he couldn't see a damn thing. He hurled himself at the door for a third and fourth time. His shoulder ached. He stepped back and kicked at it with his steel-toed shoe – the sound of wood cracking. He didn't stop. He kicked hard and again. On his eighth or ninth try something snapped and the door banged open.

He drew his revolver and stepped into the night. It was lighter outside, the moon and the background glow of the city. Sirens wailed as he surveyed the roofscape. The building was wedged between others like it to his right and left. He saw ladders that ran over the side, but couldn't see anyone. So either this Chase made his escape, or he was hiding. He turned slowly taking in the scene; pulled out his phone and called the sergeant at the 9th for more backup, even though he knew it was getting more futile by the second.

Jerod came up behind him. He shivered and Hobbs knew the kid was trying to appear normal even though he was clearly jonesing. 'You should get back to the hospital,' he told him.

'I want to help,' he said, his teeth chattering despite the warm air.

'OK, go tell Barrett – Dr. Conyors – what happened, she might have some ideas. If this was the guy who just drugged her; she could have remembered something else. You need to get out of here.'

A pair of uniformed officers came through the doorway. 'It's
a fifty-fifty shot,' Hobbs said. 'You take that way, I'll go this
way.' He looked back at Jerod – he really was trying to hold it
together – and began to understand what Barrett saw in him.
'Kid, go back to her. Stay with her.'

'You think he'll go after her again?'

Hobbs started to jog to the ladder on the east side of the
building. 'Don't know, but she's the only one we've got who
can tell us who he is . . . and Jerod, you did real good back there.
Real good.' He looked over the edge, and then toward the distance.
How much of a lead did this guy have? He pushed back a
dangerous sense of futility, and grabbed the ladder, knowing that
if there were fingerprints he'd just destroyed them. He lowered
his legs over the side, and looked down at the roof next door –
a small drop, three or four feet. He let go of the ladder and
landed on the tar-paper surface. He ran to the rooftop door, locked
from the inside. He unclipped a Maglite from his belt and ran
its beam over the surface of the roof from the ladder to the door.
They'd been so close . . . He looked for disturbances on the black-
gray roof. Playing the light around the threshold, he saw no sign
of scuffing, the hinges looked undisturbed. It meant little. The
thing could have been wide open; this Chase went through it
and then just locked it from inside. Or . . . each second that
passed gave away the advantage.

Hobbs ran to the ladder on the east side. He grabbed hold
and felt a small give; one of the bolts was loose – could be an
old problem, or a new one. He ran his flashlight over the roof
of the adjoining building. No footprints, but the door to the
roof had a crack of light showing through. He climbed over
and down, and was hit by the sweet smell of marijuana. He
headed toward its source and found a man and woman in lawn
chairs facing uptown, glasses of wine in hand, a joint being
passed. As he approached, Hobbs caught a bit of their conversation. 'Spending three thousand dollars on rent is for chumps.
You got to buy something, Monique, 'cause you're just throwing
that . . .'

'Police,' Hobbs said.

'Oh shit!' The man dropped the smoldering joint.

'I don't care about that,' Hobbs said. 'Did anyone come through
here in the last couple minutes?'

The woman, a tall freckled blonde with a riotous mass of

curls, turned back to look at Hobbs. 'There was,' she said, 'but more like ten minutes ago.'

'Damn! Did you see him?'

'Just a little.' Her gaze fixed on his scarred face. 'But I don't think he saw us. I thought maybe he was one of the neighbors; I didn't recognize him.'

'What did he look like?'

'Like a movie star . . . dark hair kind of falling over one eye, and a face like out of a magazine – perfect profile. I heard him go down into our building. I just assumed he lived there, that maybe he'd just moved in. Should we be worried?'

'No,' Hobbs said, heading toward the rooftop entry. 'But I'd ditch the joint; there'll be cops swarming all over this place.'

'Thanks.'

He stopped at the door, ten minutes was a long time. He looked around; the man was sucking down the last of the joint, clearly not wanting to waste any. This was the easternmost building on the block. Hobbs jogged to the edge that faced the avenue, and sure enough there was an entryway both there and on the north side. Chase could easily have exited without being noticed by the squad cars and ambulances parked in front. From there he could hop a cab to wherever . . . or he could be holed up in an apartment right here . . . or the stoned lady could be wrong altogether. But it was unlikely Chase would hang around.

He pulled out his cell and called Barrett. No one answered. He felt a pang of anxiety. Well, it could mean any number of things, and he dialed University Hospital and got put through. She picked up before the second ring. 'Glad to see you're still there.'

'Thanks to you,' she said. 'Did you find him? Did you find—'

'We found a bunch of late teens and early twenties all OD'd.'

'Dear God. Dead?'

'Not all, don't know the score yet. You come up with the last name of your dream date?'

'It's Strand, Chase Strand, and he works for DYFS as a counselor.'

'Any chance you got a home address for lover boy.'

'Knock it off. And no, I don't have an address. Although he said he went home during the lunch break of the conference. Wait a minute, he told me . . . God, my brain is scrambled. It's TriBeCa, he had a friend give him a loft in TriBeCa.'

'Nice friend.'

'Apparently he'd taken care of this guy who had AIDS.'

'A real prince. What about a phone number?'

'He gave me his card . . . Oh shit, I don't have my purse or any of my things – not even my cell. They must have locked them up when I came in . . . Mom, could you go out to the nurses' desk and get my bag? Thanks . . . OK, now give me the details.'

'Let me call this in first so we can get an address. He's on the run, but he might need to pick up a thing or two. If you get his number or an address, call me.'

'Hobbs, I could meet you. I recognize him, no one else does.'

Hobbs paused. He thought of her in intensive care, of how close she'd just come to dying. 'You need to stay there.'

'I'm fine. The drugs have all worn off; I could help you.'

'Stay there, Barrett, and call me if you find anything, like an address.'

'Hobbs!'

He hung up. He looked down at the street; at least now he had a name and something of a description. He headed back toward the stoned couple, who still reeked. 'You two are going to need to give statements. Don't worry about the pot; just tell the officer everything you can remember. The guy we're looking for just tried to kill a bunch of kids, so take it serious.'

The woman looked back at him, again studying his face, as though she were trying to remember every line, the way the scars and skin grafts created unnatural layers of interwoven flesh. 'I hope you find him,' and then added, 'It's odd how some people can be so beautiful on the outside and absolute monsters on the inside.'

'It is,' he said, backing away, *but the pretty monsters get dates with Barrett and I get 'can't we just be friends'*. As he ran down the stairs and toward his car, he reminded himself that his infatuation with Barrett was in the past, but that was a whopping lie. He hated feeling this way, scared to death that she'd been hurt . . . or killed, hating that she'd been interested in a man she'd just met at a conference. It didn't help that he was attractive . . . like she was and he wasn't. *Who you kidding? Barrett is not attractive . . . she's a goddamn knockout; no way you'd ever fit – beauty and the freak.*

He yanked open the Crown Vic and booted up the computer. He accessed the department's database and put in Chase Strand – no priors, no outstanding warrants, not even a traffic violation.

Next, into the DFYS website and again put in his name. He came up as a Counselor II with an office on 14th Street, an email address, and a phone number. No way he'd be at work, but at least he'd get his home information by tearing up his office, a thought that gave him a glimmer of pleasure. It was five past midnight when he called in for an emergency search warrant. He hoped that the building had on-site security, as he drove and fantasized about meeting up with Mr. Strand and rearranging various features of his pretty face.

TWENTY-SIX

T he clock in Barrett's ICU cubicle hit 1 A.M. A tentative knock came at the sliding Plexiglas door. The lights had been dimmed, but she caught the outline of Jerod's dreads. 'Come in,' she said, wondering why he was dressed in blue maintenance scrubs and whether Hobbs was with him.

'They wouldn't let me back,' Jerod said in a low voice, his arms wrapped around his chest, 'I'm in disguise. Where did your mom go?' he asked, sliding the door closed behind him.

'I told her to take Max home,' Barrett said, impressed by his ingenuity and wondering if there were maintenance people with shoulder-length dirty-blond dreadlocks and bright red sneakers. 'Turn around while I get dressed,' and she pulled a blue scrub top over her head, the silk blouse she'd worn on her date having been cut open by the medics. At least they hadn't destroyed her jacket, having pulled it off prior to getting her on the stretcher. 'Tell me everything,' she instructed, while stepping into her jeans.

'Are you supposed to be out of bed?' he whispered.

'I'm fine, tell me what happened.'

As Jerod went through the events at Marky's, Barrett struggled to recall anything Chase might have said that would tell her where he'd gone. The card he'd given her was standard state issue, name, job title, office number and email at DFYS. She stared at it, while listening to Jerod. The horror of what Chase had done, had tried to do to her, felt unreal, incomprehensible. He had no soul, no empathy for any of these people, including Janice Fleet, all just means to his becoming a doctor. She flipped the card over. 'Oh shit!' Something she hadn't seen before.

'What?' Jerod said, his face drenched with sweat, his pupils almost obliterating the irises.

She pulled her cell out of a blue plastic patient-belongings bag, and dialed Hobbs. Her voice low, 'Ed, I think I got something, a cell number for him.'

'Let me have it; if he's still got it on him and the battery's good we'll be able to triangulate his location.'

'Where are you?'

'In his office on 14th Street. It's been scrubbed. No personal mail, no address book, nothing. There's two freaky things, though.'

'What?'

'It's a new one on me, orange peels in his bottom drawer all stitched together, and another drawer full of what I think is surgical thread and funky needles.'

'Of course. He wants to be a surgeon, it's something gung-ho medical students do who want to be surgeons. That's his big goal. Does he know that I'm alive? And the kids in that apartment, does he think any of them survived, especially anyone connected to him?'

'My gut says yes, but I'm not a hundred percent. The creep was watching us and probably bolted when the medics showed up. Let me call in this number, and if you find anything else, call.'

'Wait,' she said. 'Hobbs, you said there were two things, what was the other?'

He paused. 'A photo-montage of you and Max; it was in his desk drawer.'

'He took it from my office,' she said, totally creeped out.

'Like I said,' Hobbs added, 'you know how to pick 'em,' and he hung up.

'What are you doing?' Jerod asked.

Barrett looked at him: from the tips of his dreadlocks to the soles of his red sneakers he was miserable, bobbing from foot to foot, in obvious pain, his nose and eyes running. 'You sure you don't want some help with that? I can get you medication.'

'Please stop offering. I need to do this, but let me stay with you . . . I don't care what you're doing. I can't be alone right now and I want to help. Where do you think Chase is?'

'Running,' she said, looking down at her feet in blue rubber-soled hospital slipper socks. She poured out everything from the patient-belongings bag; her boots were missing. 'I want to go to the emergency room and see those kids, can you do me a favor?'

'Name it.'

'See if you can swipe a lab coat, one of the long ones. I bet there's some behind the nurses' station.'

'Right back,' he said, sliding open the door.

She watched as he wheeled a bucket-and-mop cart away from her cubicle to the center of the ICU. He never looked up as he passed the long counter where a night-duty nurse was entering her notes into the computer. A couple minutes passed and he was back. He pulled back her door and handed her a white coat he'd concealed in the trash bag. 'This OK?'

'I think I'm renaming you Slick.'

He smiled. 'How many times have I been picked up for boosting?'

'I don't know,' she said warily, taking off her jacket and putting on the lab coat, 'two that I'm aware of.' She quickly looked through her wallet, her faculty ID wasn't in there.

'I've only been *caught* twice.'

'Great, we'll stick that on your college application under extracurricular activities – accomplished shoplifter . . . Stick close,' she said, pulling back the door. And taking a lead from Jerod, she didn't even glance at the nurse on duty and headed toward the door. Many of Barrett's rotations in medical school and residency had been done here at University. She knew her way around and headed to the busy emergency department on the ground floor. She was torn, part of her wanted to call Justine to get the lowdown, but if she told her sister she'd left her room, chances were good she'd rat her out.

'You really think I could go to college?' Jerod asked, following behind with his metal bucket and mop.

'Why not,' she said, 'you got your GED last year, and clearly you got some skills. You could do it if you wanted to.'

In front of them now was the door to the emergency department that connected it to the main hospital. Without her ID and its electric bar code, it wouldn't open. 'Look busy, and follow my lead,' she said, as the door opened and an aide wheeled out a patient on a stretcher. Barrett smiled at the old woman hooked to an intravenous and a cardiac monitor and walked past her into the ED with Jerod close behind.

University's emergency department was unique; two concentric circles at the center of six broad corridors for the patients. A bird's eye view would be like a child's drawing of the sun. Its core was a glass-fronted station where dozens of doctors, nurses, and technicians could work simultaneously on computers without being barraged by the noise outside; around that was an open staff area that led down the corridors of patient cubicles. It had been redesigned over the past few years to accommodate a growing need, as financially distressed area hospitals were forced to close their doors, and more of the city's uninsured looked here for care. But even with a renovation that cost eight figures, tonight looked bad, patients on stretchers spilling out of the rooms and up and down the broad hallways.

'Stay close,' Barrett said, glad that the controlled chaos would hopefully keep anyone from noticing she was wearing patient slipper socks. Of the six corridors, three would be possibilities for the overdoses – trauma, general medicine, or telemetry. 'Keep your eyes open and tell me if you recognize anyone,' she whispered.

'That girl over there,' Jerod said, pointing to a dark-haired young woman on a stretcher that was hooked to a portable ventilator. 'That's Kat.'

They walked over and looked down. The girl was out, and probably, like Barrett, she'd been given additional drugs to keep her calm while she was on the breathing machine. Barrett looked across at the IV bag; a steady drip of Narcan to try to ride out the overdose. On the cardiac monitor the girl's heart was going good, so unless she'd had a period of prolonged respiratory arrest, her chances were good. If not, she'd live, but with brain damage. As Barrett stared at her, a shiver ran through her, this was her just a few hours back. 'Do you recognize anyone else?'

'Let's keep walking,' he said, peering into rooms and pulling back curtains.

Barrett watched how Jerod moved: sick as he was, he blended, keeping his head down, doing little cleaning tasks as he went, emptying bedside garbage pails into the black bag. She followed suit, going quickly from room to room; it would have been so much easier to find Justine, who was probably working on one of these kids right now. As she had that thought, she heard her sister's voice from the next room.

'Just give him a few minutes; I think he's through the worst, and if we don't have to tie up another vent so much the better.'

Barrett caught Jerod's eye and motioned for him to keep hidden, while she took cover behind the curtain of an obese asthmatic woman having a breathing treatment inside a plastic tent.

Jerod shook his head violently back and forth. 'You are crazy,' he hissed, 'worse than me,' and instead of following her direction he walked out and to the next cubicle.

Before he got far, Barrett heard a strange woman's voice stop him. 'What are *you* doing here?'

Followed by Justine's voice. 'Jerod? Why are you dressed like . . . Oh, right, where are you, Barrett? Come out, come out.'

'Sorry.' Barrett stepped out to meet her sister. She was with a tall athletic-looking female officer who'd been stationed outside the room. Inside was a young blond man on a stretcher, who appeared unconscious but not on a vent.

'You shouldn't be here, Jerod,' the officer said, 'and who's that?' she asked, eyeing Barrett's outfit from her lab coat to her patient slippers.

'I'm Dr. Conyors,' Barrett said, extending her hand. 'I work with Detective Ed Hobbs . . .'

'You awake, Marky?' Jerod asked, having pushed his way into the room. 'You asleep or you faking it? 'Cause if you're pretending I can get through that real quick, you piece of shit!'

'You need to get out of here,' the officer said. 'Jerod . . . what are you doing?'

Jerod looked across at the young policewoman, with her shiny brown hair tied back in a ponytail. 'Kate,' his voice pleading, 'Marky is the only one who can help us find the guy who did all this. He tried to kill me and Dr. Conyors.' He swallowed hard. 'He murdered two of my friends and he's done things to girls . . . If we don't stop him . . .'

Officer Kate Stanton looked behind her, as though expecting her partner to suddenly reappear from the all-night cafeteria. 'Be quick,' she said looking at Jerod and then at Barrett, 'I'll wait outside.'

'So this is Marky,' Barrett said, looking at the seemingly unconscious man with his short platinum hair caked with sweat and matted to his head. 'Marky, I'm Dr. Conyors. I need to talk to you.' She watched his chest rise and fall, his eyelids quivered faintly.

'He's awake,' Jerod said, 'you can tell.'

Justine pulled the curtain around them. 'You really shouldn't be here,' she said. And then more to herself, 'Not like that's going to stop you.'

'Marky,' Barrett said more forcefully, 'open your eyes.' She looked at his intravenous, and then at her sister. 'Throw in another amp of Narcan.'

Justine was about to argue, that this wasn't Barrett's patient, that she could get into mountains of trouble . . . 'I'll be right back.'

Barrett looked at Jerod and then back at Marky. 'You really think he's faking?'

Without waiting for a response Jerod reached under the sheet and pressed down hard on Marky big toenail.

'Ow!' The blond man's eyes opened. He glared up at Barrett and then saw Jerod by his feet. 'What the fuck are you doing here?' he slurred.

'Fuck you!' Jerod replied. 'Look what your boyfriend did.'

Marky's head rolled from side to side. 'Is he here? Is he here?'

'What do you think, ass-wipe. You think he's going to try and kill you and then hang around . . . although,' he looked across at Barrett, 'he could be here.'

'I know,' she said, and gently put a hand across Jerod's chest, moving him away from Marky. The Narcan had pulled Marky from death's door, but his pupils were still tiny; he was still high; she needed him to be less numb, and she wouldn't have minded if he were in a bit of pain. 'Look, Marky, you nearly died; some of your friends aren't going to make it. It's clear you're implicated; if I were you I'd start by telling me where we can find Chase Strand.'

'Implicated, my ass,' Jerod spat out, 'he dosed those kids just the way he tried to do me. You're going to fry, Marky. You think your boyfriend's going to hang around for that? He wants you dead, so you can't rat him out. That's what he wanted. Ain't love a fucking kick in the pants?'

Barrett shot Jerod a look. Was he for real or was he doing his impersonation – and a pretty decent one – of good cop, bad cop? 'Marky, focus, give us an address for Chase.'

'It's not true,' Marky said, thick white spittle caking his mouth in the corners. 'He loves me.'

Barrett could almost have felt sympathy, but every second that passed increased the chances that Chase would vanish; the man was a chameleon, fooling her, Janice . . . Marky, God knows how many others. She startled at the sound of the drape pulled back.

Justine had returned with two amps of Narcan. 'You got him awake,' she commented. 'We won't need this.'

'Oh yes we will,' Barrett said, grabbing one of the glass vials from her sister's hand. 'Give me the needle.'

'What are you doing?' Justine asked. 'He's awake, if you give him more you're going to throw him into withdrawal.'

Barrett's hand shot out with lightning speed, snatching the plastic-wrapped syringe. 'Exactly.' She tore open the package, broke the tip off the vial, drew it up, and then pierced Marky's IV tubing, just inches from where it went into his vein.

'Barrett!' Justine stared at her sister. 'I can't be part of this.'

'You're right,' Barrett said, depressing the syringe, not wanting to look at Justine's worried face. 'You shouldn't be here.'

'This isn't you,' Justine said, her eyes fixed on the syringe, and in a whisper, 'this is torture.'

Marky twitched, his face turned to a grimace, and in the course of a few seconds he went from barely rousable to moaning and curled up in a ball. 'What's wrong with me?' he gasped.

'No more bullshit,' Barrett said. 'Give us Chase's address and we'll give you medication to make you feel better.'

'Give it up, Marky,' Jerod said, 'Chase just tried to kill you. He's been playing you all along, getting you to do his shit work. She can help you feel better,' he said. 'She gave me something when I was bad sick and it made it all go away.'

'You got to give me something. Give me a shot, anything,' Marky pleaded. He grabbed for a pink plastic bedpan, missed, and vomited on the floor.

'An address,' Barrett persisted. 'Where does he live?'

'TriBeCa,' Marky said, as sweat beaded on his forehead. He held the bedpan and looked back at Jerod and then at Barrett. 'You got to help me. Please don't leave me like this.'

'TriBeCa isn't an address,' Barrett said.

'I don't know the fucking number!' Marky spat back. 'Just give me something!'

'Can't do that without an address,' Jerod said, pushing his face close to Marky's. 'Look, you piece of shit, you're dope sick, big fucking deal. It ain't going to kill you, and until you tell us what we need to know, it'll feel like your guts are on fire, like something inside is going to explode. Nice, ain't it?'

'Give me a shot,' Marky pleaded, as tears flowed. 'You can't do this to me.'

'Yeah, we can,' Jerod said. 'Where in TriBeCa? What's the street?'

'He's got a loft off Church,' Marky gasped. 'Top floor.'

'What street?' Jerod persisted. 'You don't owe him a thing.'

'We're in love,' Marky said. 'I'm going to move in with him.'

Jerod shook his head. 'The street.'

'Duane, off the corner.'

Barrett had her cell out and was dialing Hobbs. 'Describe the building, and north or south side of the street?'

'North,' Marky gasped. 'It's got a store on the first floor that sells hair stuff, like wigs and shit.'

Barrett stared at the sweaty blond man. She'd pushed him into a full-blown opiate withdrawal, and Jerod was right, it wouldn't kill him, just make him wish he were dead. She'd seen no choice, but as Hobbs picked up, she knew that she'd crossed an ethical line. 'Hobbs,' she said, 'Chase has a loft on Duane, off of Church, north side of the street and the building has a store front on the first floor with some kind of wig store.'

'I take it you're out of bed,' he answered wryly.

'I'm in the ED with Jerod,' she said. 'We've found Marky, he's up and talking.'

'They got a cop there? 'Cause if he's awake, he'll try to bolt.'

'Yeah, she's outside the door. Any luck with the cell?' Barrett asked.

'He ditched it in a trash can on Avenue A. I got to go. And please don't do anything . . . foolish.'

He left her no time to respond, and she didn't like his parting comment, mostly because it struck true.

Suddenly Justine shouted from behind the curtain, 'You need to stay in bed!'

'Fuck you!' Marky responded, as the blue and gray plastic curtain shot out, followed by the thrashing of limbs, and then Marky. His arm dripped blood from the ripped-out IV; he gripped his stomach and his dilated eyes shot around, looking for an escape. 'Get off me!' he shrieked, as Officer Stanton tackled him from behind the other side of the curtain. He thrashed violently, sending the policewoman off balance, her head landing hard against the metal edge of the door. There was a sick cracking noise as she crumpled over, and Marky made a barefooted sprint past her fallen body toward the door.

Justine appeared from behind the curtain. 'Security! Security!'

Barrett didn't hesitate, and while her body still felt disconnected and sluggish, she chased after him.

Marky, for someone in obvious pain, moved fast. He looked back once, and saw Barrett, not twenty feet behind. He bolted to the right, past the central nurses' station, and headed toward the ambulance bays.

Barrett's hospital slippers made good traction, but she wasn't able to push fast enough to keep up. He was getting away. She looked for the security guards, but they were nowhere to be seen. She felt helpless as Marky sprinted for the exit. He rammed his shoulder into the electronic door and was outside.

She didn't let up, just wished her legs felt more normal, like each step was slogging through sand.

Jerod appeared on her right, matching her pace. 'What's the plan . . . I say follow him, 'cause you know he's going to Chase.'

'Smart,' she puffed, as they cleared the ambulance exit, spotting Marky in the streetlight. He had a fifty-foot lead, but dressed in jeans and a billowing pale blue hospital shirt he was easy to spot. His head whipped around as he got his bearings, and then sprinted east toward Washington Square Park.

Barrett and Jerod followed, sticking to the dark side of the street, wanting to stay hidden, to let Marky think he'd gotten away free and clear. She fumbled with the pockets of her white coat, got her cell phone, clipped it to her jeans, and stripped the coat off, letting it fall in a heap on the sidewalk. They nearly lost him in the park, much of it fenced off due to construction, but then she caught sight of him heading south.

At Houston and Wooster, Barrett grabbed Jerod and yanked him back behind a kiosk, as Marky's head whipped around. Through the glass of the electronic poster that covered the wall they got a clear look; he seemed crazed, barefooted, dripping with sweat, his face contorted in pain. Late-night pedestrians swerved to avoid him, as he turned around, shifting his weight from foot to foot, looking in all directions. With a small hop he started to run, sprinting across Houston.

Barrett and Jerod emerged from the kiosk, and raced across one of the busiest thoroughfares in Manhattan. They lost the light and cabs sped toward them as they dodged their way across. Jerod stuck close to Barrett. 'You have got to be the craziest shrink in the world,' he commented, as they bolted across the final two lanes.

She wasn't about to argue as her eye caught on something blue crumpled on the ground ahead – Marky's hospital gown. 'Damn! Where are you?' She scanned Wooster, with its ancient cobblestones and minimal street lighting.

'There!' Jerod pointed toward a bare-shirted man half walking and half jogging two blocks ahead.

'Good eyes,' Barrett said, picking up the pace while sticking to the shadows. Her feet ached, and her eyes struggled to follow Marky, while keeping a watch for broken bottles and shards of glass that would shred the thin soles of her slippers . . . and her feet.

'Something's wrong,' Jerod whispered, as they watched Marky put on a burst of speed and run across Canal Street.

'What?' Barrett asked, as they followed.

'Asshole!' Jerod hissed as Marky, instead of turning right onto Church, kept east. 'He gave you the wrong address.'

'Figures,' Barrett said, glad that Marky's pace had slowed to a half jog, 'but when people lie, they usually give you some of the truth. So he'll be close.'

'You feel bad for him, don't you?'

'Some, not much,' she said.

'He's scum,' Jerod said, matching his pace to hers.

'It's not so simple,' she said.

'He's killed people. He had something to do with Carly; I can't even think about that,' his voice cracked, 'is she even alive? He's evil, and this Chase guy has got to be like Satan . . . He's going down Broadway, close like you said.'

When they turned the corner of Broadway and Canal, Marky was gone. 'He's got to be close,' she said.

They jogged down Broadway, checking each building as they passed. They crossed Walker and then she stopped as they came to the corner of White. 'You hear that?' There was a banging coming from inside a doorway two buildings in. They padded toward the source, the noise got louder and then Marky's voice: 'Come on, man, open up. Let me in.'

Barrett pulled out her cell, her heart skipped when the battery showed it was nearly dead. She dialed Hobbs, and before he could say anything gave him the address on White Street.

'I told you to stay put,' he said.

'Ed, just get here.'

'Don't go after him,' Hobbs warned, and with that she lost the signal.

Jerod looked at her. 'You're going to ignore him, aren't you?'

'Don't come with me,' she said, advancing on the doorway.

Jerod said nothing and followed.

They heard Marky pound on the door, and bang his fist on the buzzer. 'Chase, don't do this, man. You got to let me in.'

Barrett positioned herself on the sidewalk, straight in front of the doorway. Marky was probably the only one still breathing who had a clue as to where Chase might run, and while Hobbs was only a few blocks away every second could make the difference. She also knew that she'd get only one shot. 'He's gone, Marky.' Her voice was loud and she made certain that each syllable landed. 'He left without you.'

Marky pivoted. His face twisted, tears poured both from the heroin withdrawal and from the realization of just how deeply he'd been betrayed, set up, and nearly killed. His skinny torso was streaked with sweat while gooseflesh made his naked arms look like sandpaper.

She moved closer, her eyes bored into his. 'He didn't love you . . . obviously. He wants you dead because you know too much, because you could turn him in. Where is he, Marky?' She was in the doorway; if he tried to run, he'd have to go through her.

'Get away from me. I don't know,' he said as he looked up and to the left.

She glanced once at the names on the door buzzer, one for each floor. The bottom three were commercial spaces and the top two just last names . . . the top being Strand. He was making, or had made, his getaway through the roof.

She backed out.

'He'll get away,' Jerod said.

'Not so important.' Standing in the middle of the street she surveyed the building, and then darted toward a narrow alley on the right that was walled off by an eight-foot padlocked chain-link fence, which had three strands of razor wire across the top. She heard the clang of metal from high up on the fire escape. 'Son of a bitch!' and she dug the soft toe of the hospital slipper into the chain link and climbed. Her mind, trained by nearly two decades with Sifu Henry, willed the muscles of her arms and

legs to function like machines as she breathed through the pain
in her hands and feet, making it dissolve, her strength centered in
her belly. When she reached the top, she gripped one of the
rounded fencepost caps and used it to support her weight as she
got her feet to the top crossbar. The strands of razor wire, spaced
inches apart, tore at her arm and snagged her jeans. Holding
tight to the post cap with both hands and using it like a fulcrum,
she forcefully kicked her left leg up and back, followed by her
right and swung them onto the other side of the wire. She felt
something slice through her left leg below the knee, but no time
to assess the damage as she stood doubled over the sharp razors.
She grabbed at the top wire, the fingers of her right hand clutching
a three-inch span between the jagged and rusted blades; she
gripped hard, and then did the same with her left. She again
heard noise from high above on the fire escape.

He's going to get away. She heard Marky shout for Jerod to
let him go, and caught the sound of car engines coming to a
stop in front of the building. *You don't have to do this*, she
thought, and then pictured Chase's beautiful face, the way he
drew her in, how he'd tried to shape himself into what she wanted
in a man. She thought of him with the picture of her and Max.
She felt a surge of revulsion and her feet pushed back from the
fence, as her fingers let go. The eight-foot drop felt like an eter-
nity; she landed in a roll, not letting her ankles and knees get
damaged by the impact. Unfortunately the rest of her was less
lucky as the alley was a favorite spot for people to toss bottles
and cans. Her bare arms and the side of her face started to bleed,
how bad she couldn't know.

She sprang to her feet and ran toward the fire escape. The
ladder was in the up position, and the trapdoor to the bottom
was shut. There was a good ten feet between the landing and
the ground. Her one break was a metal trash container just off
to the right. She climbed on top, focused on a paint-chipped
metal bar on the outside edge of the fire escape, and leapt. Her
fingers grasped the cold iron. Bits of rust dug into her palms as
she held tight and swung up. Her feet in the supple slippers
grabbed onto cross bars in the floor. With her body clinging tight
she edged her way up the side and over the railing. She strained
to hear any motion up above, but instead heard Hobbs or someone
else working away at the padlock on the alley gate with a pair
of bolt cutters.

Moving fast and silent on the creaky stairs, she raced up. She fought against a mounting desperation that she was too late, that Chase would be far away, never to be found, setting up some new life, destroying innocent people wherever he went. When she got to the roof her heart sank. He was gone; she could see how he could have retrieved whatever he'd needed, and made his escape. But then she heard something. She ran toward the east. This building was two in from Broadway. Was that his destination? She glanced at the distance between the two buildings, too far to jump and no bridge between the two.

She ran to the western edge – a long haul to Church Street, and not at all feasible, with buildings of all heights, and a parking lot halfway down, like a missing tooth . . . like . . . and that's when she saw him, two rooftops away, moving fast; she knew where he was headed.

She ached to follow, but instead ran toward the front of the building, and shouted down, 'Hobbs!'

'Barrett, what the hell are you doing . . .'

'He's headed toward the parking lot,' she yelled, her throat still burning from the ventilator. 'He's got a car.' And not wanting to hear a Hobbsian tirade as to why she shouldn't chase Chase, she went after him. As she ran over the first two rooftops, she realized that Chase had worked this exit route in advance. Where there should have been locked gates between roofs, or other barriers, they'd been removed or tampered with. On the third building she found a padlock to an iron door that had been carefully cut and put back in place. She pushed it apart and stepped through.

It was a crazy obstacle course, with ladders hooked and bolted over the sides of buildings or small gaps separating them, one misstep could end in a six- or seven-story drop. As she cleared the edge of her sixth building she caught sight of Chase's black-clad figure; he had something strapped to his back and another bag slung over his right shoulder. He was on the far end of the building preparing to climb an aluminum extension ladder that was angled to get him across a tight alley and up about ten feet to the roof of the next and last building before the garage.

She hesitated. What if she were wrong about the parking garage? What if he vanished inside the next building with some other carefully worked-out exit route? She padded quickly across the roof and waited for him to get two-thirds up the ladder.

Keeping her distance, and assuming he was armed, she shouted after him, 'Is it too soon to call?'

He froze.

She could tell that whatever he was carrying was heavy. He maneuvered awkwardly, but managed to slip his right hand into his coat pocket. *He's got a gun*, she thought. *Don't do this, Barrett.* Keeping to the shadows of an air-conditioner compressor unit, she tried to hold him. 'I mean after a first date, how much time should a girl give?' *Where the hell is Hobbs?*

He didn't turn. 'Let me go, Barrett, I didn't mean to hurt you. I'm so relieved you're OK. I was worried they wouldn't know what to do.'

She marveled at how calm he sounded, how reasonable, even now laying on the charm. She had to hold him, give Hobbs a chance to block any escape routes. 'I know you didn't mean to hurt me,' she said, keeping any irony from her voice. 'Accidents happen. I pressed too hard. I shouldn't have done that. I'm sorry, Chase. I'm not good with men.'

With his body pressed against the ladder, he turned slightly, his perfect profile caught in a silver silhouette. 'I really liked you,' he said, his voice smooth and resonant. 'Even more than that . . . I was hoping we could be together,' and then added, 'I'm surprised you're not armed.'

'Why would I need to be armed?' she said, wondering when Hobbs and a herd of officers would swarm the roof.

He looked past her. 'You came here alone?'

She had a moment's hesitation. 'Of course,' she said, making rapid diagnoses of Chase's personality structure, knowing that with intense sociopathy frequently came a level of narcissism that could blind him to certain things . . . like flattery. 'I had to see you,' she said, gambling that his belief in his own powers of seduction and of holding others in thrall would make him bite.

'I'm glad,' he said, 'but I can't stay.'

'Please, I have to be with you,' she said, wondering if Janice Fleet or Marky had said similar things. Had he made them beg? She laid it on, each second that he didn't move increasing the chances the bastard would get caught. 'Take me with you. I know detectives and judges; the whole thing can be fixed. You could blame it on one of those kids . . . They're all dead, anyway.' She realized her mistake the minute it slipped from her lips.

'How would you know that?'

She didn't skip a beat. 'They took them to the same hospital they took me.'

It was too late; he looked into the distance and saw movement three buildings back. 'Fucking bitch! All the same.' He pulled his hand from his pocket and aimed.

She dove behind the metal compressor as the gun went off. A second shot hit the steel and ricocheted into the night; a third tore a rut in the tar paper inches from her foot. She braced and waited for a fourth. Seconds passed as shouts came from the direction of the next roof.

She peered around the edge of the compressor. Chase was on the move; shouldering his bag and pack, he started up the last few rungs.

Hell, no! She broke cover and ran. She dove for the base of the ladder and pulled hard. It sprung forcefully from her hands, throwing her back.

He had just reached the top rung as the ladder shot out from under his feet. He clutched for the roof edge, missed, and fell forward. He screamed and grabbed frantically, managing to catch the iron railing where the fire escape was bolted to the brick. He hung on, as the flimsy ladder fell hard next to Barrett. It balanced like a teeter-totter on the edge of the roof and then slid over the edge; it bounced off the side of the building, shattered a window, and crashed to the ground.

She stared in horror as Chase held fast to the railing, a few short inches from the rooftop. He was also close to safety, just needed to pull himself over the railing and onto the fire escape. She could tell that the weight of whatever he had in those bags wouldn't give him much time. She imagined the frantic thoughts running through his head – *Safety and the fire escape . . . but certain capture, or back to the roof and a last stab at escape.*

'Drop the bags, Chase! Just pull up onto the fire escape. You can make it,' she shouted. 'It's not worth dying for.'

He said nothing, but his answer was obvious as he tried to dead-lift his weight. He balanced on the fire-escape railing, pressing his body tight against the brick wall, his chin cleared the rooftop. His right arm swung up and gripped the roof edge.

Behind her she heard the pounding of footsteps as she watched Chase cling to the building's edge. He was actually going to make it. His left arm found a grip, but the bag he'd slung over his shoulder slipped back. He tried to correct the shift in weight, but his right hand faltered and lost its hold. He tried to hang on with his left, but the weight was too much. For a moment he seemed to hang, defying gravity, pressed to the side of the building, like a giant spider . . . and then he fell.

She stood frozen to the spot and listened. The sound his body made hitting the asphalt six stories below was complex, like a chord with a heavy thud in the bass, something hard and metallic in the middle, and the cracking of bones in the upper register. It made her feel sick as she realized that no one could survive that; he was dead.

Across the alley she saw uniformed officers swarm the roof, as Hobbs approached from behind. 'You OK?' he asked.

'Not really,' she said, feeling awful that she was responsible for Chase's death. Yes, he'd shot at her, but when she'd grabbed that ladder, his back was turned. *Why didn't you just leave him for the cops?*

'I'm getting you back to the hospital,' he said. 'We can take your statement later.'

She looked down at her torn jeans, and at an oozing four-inch gash on her upper arm – *might need stitches*. She thought to argue. What she really wanted was a bath and her bed, to fall asleep and not have to picture Chase clinging to the wall, or looking into her eyes over dinner like a man in love.

'Where's Jerod?' she asked, hoping that Hobbs wouldn't notice the tears.

'He's OK.'

As is if on cue he appeared, his mass of dreads tucked under a navy NYPD cap. 'You look like shit, Dr. Conyors. Did he get away?'

'No,' she answered dully.

'You shouldn't be up here,' Hobbs commented to Jerod.

'I know, I just can't help it. I've got this role model who keeps breaking rules, what's a guy to do?'

Barrett felt drained, her heart pounded in her ears. 'I want to get out of here . . . Hobbs, could you please just get me home or to my mom's. I need to see Max.'

'No hospital?'

She looked at the gash on her arm. 'It's just a little ooze. They'll keep me for hours and what I need is sleep.'

'Your call.'

She looked at Jerod, the blacks of his eyes like saucers, patches of sweat drenching his clothes – but somehow marshalling strength and humor. 'How are you doing?' she asked, amazed at how little she knew this young man who she'd evaluated on multiple occasions.

'Been better,' he admitted, taking a deep breath and letting it out, 'been worse. Keep thinking about dope.'

'My offer stands,' she said, 'you could do this much more easily with drugs.'

'Thanks . . . but I want to feel this . . . remember it.' He looked at Hobbs. 'You're not going to let them forget Carly, are you? I know she's out there. I don't want to think about where, or what they've done to her. Marky's gotta know something.'

'I won't forget. And we'll need a statement from you, as well. But it can wait till tomorrow. So let's get you both out of here.'

TWENTY-SEVEN

Barrett woke in the tiny bedroom she'd grown up in. Justine's matching twin bed was gone, replaced by Max in his crib. Light streamed through the sheer green curtains of the single window that faced the Bowery and the high-rise condo building on the other side. Sensing somehow she was awake, Max let out a soft cry. Feeling aches deep in her bones and joints she moved slowly, pulling her pajama-clad legs to the edge of the bed, dangling them off. She glanced at the lit numbers on the alarm clock; after ten. She tried to think through the events of last night, and of how she and Jerod had finally made it to her mother's just before 4 A.M. All she'd been able to manage was a quick shower; slapped some gauze and tape around her arm and thigh and fallen into bed.

'Ow.' Blisters throbbed on the soles of both feet. She stood slowly, and peered over Max's crib; she reached down. He felt soft and warm and she held him close, then settled back on her bed and unbuttoned her thin cotton top. She led his mouth to her nipple, his little hands kneading the flesh of her breasts as he suckled. It was peace, her thoughts quiet, as she batted away the realities of the day ahead. But in that moment, she realized little of that

mattered, not really. Max was all; he was everything. He was beautiful and he was a part of her. His blue eyes, the color of the
morning sky, looked up as he fed. She remembered the mockingbird song her mother used to sing, and quietly hummed, and then
sang, '*Hush, little baby, don't you cry. Momma's gonna buy you
a mockingbird . . .*'

A gentle knock, and her mother's voice. 'Barrett . . . honey,
can I come in?'

'Sure.'

The door opened and Ruth, in jeans, a black T-shirt from
the bar, and her hair in a red kerchief, came in and settled next
to her.

'Where's Jerod?' Barrett asked.

'Out like a light. How much longer till he feels better?'

'He should be through the worst of it, but it's different with
everyone.'

'I like him,' Ruth said, 'there's something sweet about
him . . .'

'I know,' Barrett said, again thinking of how much he reminded
her of that long-ago crush on Kyle Matthews, 'but he's got no
one. No place to go, no money, nothing.'

'He's got you, sweetheart.'

'Not really,' Barrett said, feeling her bubble of calm begin to
pop, harsh realities pressing in. 'I'm his doctor; that's about it.'

'He can stay here,' Ruth said, as she stood and walked over
to the dresser and got a fresh towel. 'I wasn't sure about that
before, especially with the baby, but I have a feeling about him.
He's got a good heart.'

Barrett took the towel from her mother and draped it over her
left shoulder. She hefted up Max, every day a bit heavier, and
laid him gently down, rubbing his back in circles and then gently
patted him. She looked around the room, thinking about how
her mother had packed Justine and her into a car in rural Georgia
when they were small and driven through the night to escape a
husband who got drunk and beat her. Barrett barely remembered
her father, tall and angry with a shock of black hair. But the
couple who'd taken them in – Sophie and Max – two Holocaust
survivors who'd adopted the three of them as though they were
blood relatives still crisp in her mind and heart. 'You know he
has problems,' she finally said.

'Is he dangerous?'

'No.'

'Then it doesn't matter. We all have problems . . .' She let out a long sigh, 'It's been a long time since we've talked, Barrett, I mean really talked.'

'I know . . . it's just . . .'

'I'm not pushing. Whatever it is you feel you can't tell me can wait. Just don't shut me out. I need my girls.'

'I need you too,' Barrett said, and wished the moment could last, as Ruth carefully reached over and hugged her daughter, and her grandson.

Finally, she pulled back. 'I hope it's OK, but I called your secretary to let her know you'd be late . . . or maybe not in at all.'

'Thanks,' Barrett said, as she realized that Janice was dead and there were a ton of questions to be answered. And then an avalanche of other things that needed to be done, including giving a statement. Well, at least she'd see Hobbs. She owed him a huge apology, and just like she'd underestimated Jerod, she needed to find a way to repair their friendship, and maybe there was something more there. 'Mom?'

'Yes.'

'You like Ed, don't you?'

'Of course, he's kind of a vanishing breed.'

'I know . . . he's solid, and funny and smart and . . . I really messed things up with him.'

'Do you love him?'

Ruth's bluntness stunned her, but the answer that came fast and clear shocked her. 'I do. I really do, but he's seeing someone else and . . . I . . .'

A knock at the door. 'Can I come in?' Jerod asked.

'Hold on,' Barrett said, buttoning her pajama top. 'OK.'

The tip of his head poked through, his dreads concealed beneath a red kerchief identical to the one her mother wore. 'You want coffee?' he asked, pushing the door with his foot while carrying three steaming mugs. He was wearing a pair of blue scrubs and his feet were bare.

'That would be great, and who are you?' Barrett asked. 'What happened to Jerod?'

'It's me. I didn't know what either of you took, so it's the junkie special for everyone.'

'What's that?' Ruth asked.

'Four sugars and half of it's milk.'

'How does that make it a junkie special?'

'Sugar, something about dope, you always want sweets. Plus where you don't think too much about food, and all your money goes for dope, it turns a cup of coffee into a meal. Sugar has calories and you can take as much as you want for free, same thing with milk,' he explained.

Barrett put Max back in his crib and sipped the hot sweet coffee. 'It's not bad.' She usually took it black, but found something comforting in it, like a child's first taste of coffee, all the bitterness buried under sugar. 'Are you hurting?' she asked, looking at Jerod. The circles under his eyes were less extreme, but his pupils had still not returned to normal.

'Craving like a mother,' he said, settling down on the rocker beside the crib, 'but I think the worst is past. The voice is there,' he said, 'keeps telling me to use, that I'm not going to be able to stay clean. I figure I'll stay in as much as possible, maybe vacuum or something. I have to stay busy.'

'Vacuum?' Barrett asked.

'I don't know why,' he said, 'it's soothing, the noise and the feeling like you're getting something done.'

'You can vacuum all you want,' Ruth said, 'not my favorite thing.'

'Good, because if you're going to let me stay here, you've got to let me do stuff. I'll do all the cleaning, and if you need me to look after Max, it's no problem.'

Ruth shot Barrett a look.

'I saw that,' he said. 'If you don't want me looking after Max I understand.'

'It's not—' Barrett began.

He interrupted her. 'Dr. Conyors, you don't have to explain. You've done too much already. And letting some junkie schizophrenic look after your kid . . . probably get DFYS knocking at your door.'

'You know,' Barrett said, 'I've got other fish to fry and if DFYS want to complain about my child-rearing, they've got plenty of their own problems to answer for.'

'No kidding,' Jerod said, taking a gulp of the super-sweet coffee. 'I hope you don't get mad . . . but I kind of heard what you were talking about . . . You know he's into you?'

Barrett felt blood rush to her cheeks, 'I think you're wrong,' she said, wanting to avoid a coffee-klatch over her non-romantic life.

'I'm not,' he affirmed, 'he's always looking at you, and you can just tell. I think if you gave him half a chance.'

'Can we please talk about something . . . anything else,' Barrett said, but wondering if Jerod was right, and then relieved by the sudden ringing of the phone. 'I'll get it,' she said. It was Marla.

'Dr. Conyors, I hate to bother you, but I just got off the phone with the Lieutenant Governor, there's a meeting in two hours and he insisted that you be there. He said it has to do with the department and Dr. Fleet. I told him you hadn't come in and weren't feeling well. He got kind of rude, said this wasn't optional, and that you were expected.'

'OK, Marla, just tell me where and when. Also, what are people saying about what happened?'

'It's wild. She was murdered in her apartment, they're saying it was a failed robbery.'

'Anything else?' Barrett asked.

'No, why?'

'I can't say, but keep your ears open, let me know about any gossip and who's doing it.'

'Does this have something to do with whoever broke into your office?'

'Among other things.'

'I do have one tidbit,' Marla offered.

'Yes?'

'It seems Hugh Osborn reported his key card as being stolen.'

'When?'

'Yesterday.'

'Interesting, but it shouldn't give him access to my office anyway.'

'Well . . . that's what I thought,' Marla said, 'and then I asked a few questions down at security, it turns out that when he was trying to take over your office during your leave, he'd told them to give him access . . . and they had. When you returned they never deactivated it.'

'Excellent work, Marla,' she felt a sense of satisfaction as one of the missing pieces slid into place, 'but don't let Hugh know what you just told me. I've got to figure out just how much of this mess he's involved with.'

'It wasn't a robbery, was it?' Marla asked.

'The break-in?'

'No, I meant Dr. Fleet. It was something else, wasn't it?'

'Yes, but why would you think that?'

'Something the Lieutenant Governor said about the meeting, called it damage control . . . that and I've had half a dozen reporters try to get through to you.'

'Anything else?'

'That's about it. Just please be careful. I've seen how these higher-ups use everyone below them as target practice.'

'I'll do my best.' Barrett hung up and looked at the clock. She hated the feeling of being ordered around, but her curiosity was blazing. Janice had been a darling of this administration; depending on what came out in the press, 'damage control' was going to be tough.

Now eleven and she'd need to be downtown in less than two hours . . . at least they hadn't insisted on meeting in Albany. 'Mom, do you still have that gray suit I got you?'

'Just wore it the once,' she admitted. 'Not really my style – I think it's still in a dry-cleaning bag.'

'Could you find it, and some kind of neutral blouse. You wear nines, right?'

'Yes, dear, you inherited your mother's big feet.'

'Please get me your most boring black pumps, preferably something with a low heel . . . although it doesn't matter.'

'Where are you going?' Ruth asked. 'You're telling me after all you went through last night, you have to go to work?'

'No choice.'

'You have court today?'

'No, apparently I'm about to meet the Lieutenant Governor, and Lord knows who else. I have a feeling heads are about to roll. My boss had wanted me fired and until they appoint someone as acting commissioner I guess I report all the way to the top. Wonder if I'll have a job at the end of the day.'

'Serious?' Jerod asked.

'This could blow up in the press,' she said, wondering just how involved Janice had been with the drugs and whatever creepy dealings Chase had had.

'You want me to go with you?' Jerod asked, clearly alarmed. 'I can vouch for you. You're the only doctor who's ever really cared. I mean look at all you've done for me. People don't do that.'

'Jerod,' Barrett said, wondering what he would look like without all that hair, 'that's sweet. But caring and competence have nothing to do with politics . . . there's going to be all kinds of investigations.'

'You're serious,' her mom said. 'You think they'd try to blame what happened on you?'

'Don't know,' Barrett said, feeling a surge of determination, 'but I've a feeling this is going to be one hell of a day.'

On the cab ride down, Barrett called Houssman. Her long-time mentor had earlier called. 'It made the papers,' he reported, 'not a lot of particulars and still entirely separate stories.'

'How did you even know about it?'

'Spies in low places,' he said.

'Whatever,' suspecting he'd gone through Marla, who was still devoted to George – her former boss. 'Give me the details. I literally just rolled out of bed and was commanded to this high-echelon meeting, tell me what they wrote.'

'OK,' he said, papers crinkling. 'Page two, Metro section, we've got a police manhunt in TriBeCa, gunshots fired . . . one seriously injured suspect, another in custody.'

'Stop there. Seriously injured, not dead?'

'Not dead and names not released either, which unless they were minors, why keep the names out? Right there, you know something's up.'

'What else?' she asked, feeling a burden of relief that she'd not killed Chase, followed by a severely queasy feeling that he was still alive.

'The big news . . . front page, *Commissioner of DFYS murdered in her Chelsea home . . . apparent robbery . . . undisclosed amount of jewelry and cash . . . police looking for suspects*, and then quite a lovely bio of Janice . . . *creator and founder of the Mother's Milk drop-in centers . . . a force for at-risk youth*, and on and on. Hmm.'

'What?'

'Well, usually when a top-ranking official dies the reporters throw in some accolades from politicos. Not today.'

'This all happened in the early a.m., George, I doubt they had the time to—'

'Of course they did,' he interrupted, 'look at how quickly they rallied the forces for whatever inquisition you're about to step into. I know I don't need to tell you this, Barrett, but keep your ears open and shift into day-at-court mode, answer truthfully but don't elaborate. Yes and no are two very good words.'

'Got it,' she said, as the cab pulled up to the state's downtown administration building. Middle of the lunch hour and a gorgeous day, which any New Yorker who'd survived 9/11 could tell you is not always a good thing; sometimes nightmares happen on beautiful days.

She caught her reflection in the plate-glass doors, and then in the admiring glances of the two security guards – one young and thin, the other close to retirement – who had her remove all metal objects and step through the detector.

'Barrett, wait up.'

She turned and saw Hobbs, dressed in a navy suit, starched white shirt, and striped tie, as he pushed through the doors, and stripped off his sidearm, cell phone, detective shield, and all other metal. 'You look nice,' he said.

'Thanks,' and quickly added, 'you too.'

'Right,' he said passing through and setting off the detector. He raised his arms and stood still as the younger guard passed the wand over him.

'It's your belt,' he commented. 'You can go on in.'

'So what's this all about?' Barrett asked, as they waited for the elevator.

'Wish I knew, Schmitt told me to put on a suit and get my butt downtown. Apparently our shenanigans last night have got some of the big boys worried.'

'I hate this part . . . so Chase isn't dead?'

'Nope, pretty banged up, though. Should I ask him if he wants another date?'

'Bastard.'

The doors opened and a dark-suited aide met them. 'Dr. Conyors, Detective Hobbs, please come this way.'

Barrett shot Hobbs a look. The aide led them to a corner conference room, and opened the door on to a sun-filled space with two middle-aged men, one with gray hair and glasses, the other with a large center bald spot, both in shirtsleeves and ties, their jackets on the back of their chairs.

The balding man, who had a gut, looked at Hobbs. 'Ed, good to see you.'

'Same,' Hobbs said, going to shake hands, and then turned

to Barrett, 'Dr. Conyors, this is Daryl Fisk, Deputy Chief of Detectives.'

The other man was Reginald Compton, the Lieutenant Governor. Introductions were made, hands shaken, and first names agreed upon before they took seats at one end of the large burnished mahogany table.

'Let me come straight to the point,' the Lieutenant Governor began. 'We've been made aware that Dr. Fleet has been implicated in illegal activities, and that she used her position and influence to carry these out. We need to know the extent of her involvement and that of any other state employees. Where there's a criminal investigation,' and he looked toward Hobbs and the Deputy Chief, 'we'll need close coordination between the NYPD and our own internal investigation, as well as considerable . . . sensitivity. My understanding is that the two of you have the greatest sense of what we're dealing with, and to be blunt, I need to know just how bad this is.' He looked at Hobbs and then Barrett. Neither spoke. 'Well?'

'Go ahead,' Daryl Fisk instructed Hobbs.

And Ed dispassionately laid out the facts of the case, from the peddling of dope in the city's college dormitories to a high degree of suspicion that young girls were being sold into the sex trade. He described how he came to discover Janice Fleet's body and how she was likely connected to her one-time patient Chase Strand – a DFYS counselor.

The Lieutenant Governor said nothing as Ed went on to recount the events of the past week. His elbows rested on the table, the tips of his fingers in front of his mouth. He waited for Hobbs to finish and looked at Barrett. 'This Chase Strand who . . . fell from the roof, how well did you know him?'

'I met him yesterday.'

'No prior contact whatsoever?' he asked.

'No.'

'And yet you went out to dinner with him last night.'

'Yes,' she said, feeling defensive, 'and he tried to kill me.'

'What will he say when he's interrogated?' the Lieutenant Governor asked.

The question defied George's counsel of sticking to yes and no. 'It depends on what offers are made,' she said, imagining the clockwork ticking behind the Lieutenant Governor's wire-framed glasses. 'Chase is a sociopath with a high IQ, he feels no remorse for his many killings, and will do anything possible to receive the lightest punishment. Problem is, he's directly implicated in several murders, and if he didn't pull the trigger himself, they would have been under his direction. He'll try to shift the blame to Janice Fleet. The likely problem is his lieutenant, Marky, and if he's not under close supervision I'd be concerned that something bad will happen to him.'

'How so?'

And for the next three and a half hours Barrett and Hobbs were grilled on the facts and asked to posit different scenarios – how many state employees did they think would be implicated? How many kids had been recruited to sell drugs? What did they think happened to the naked girl in the video? And how many people outside Marky and Chase and of course Ed and Barrett knew?

As the meeting finally wound down, oblique statements and directives were lobbed at both of them. To Barrett, the Lieutenant Governor remarked, 'How and how much of this finds its way into the press can make or break careers. I am aware of your past achievements, and can see that you're clearly someone who goes above and beyond . . . Not always a good thing, and still . . . there will be new opportunities, Barrett, both in the Department of Mental Health and in Family and Youth Services. The Governor is watching this closely. He'll need to appoint an acting commissioner and that person will need to be above reproach. Barrett,' he leveled his gaze at her, 'you have impressive credentials . . . you should think about it.'

Her knee-jerk reaction was to say, *Hell, no*, but he'd already shifted his attention to Hobbs. 'Ed,' he said, as though they were all good friends, 'I've asked Daryl to have you oversee this case and to report to him directly.'

Hobbs started to speak, but wasn't given the chance.

'I know this is going over your usual chain of command, and I am not asking for a cover-up,' the Lieutenant Governor continued. 'God knows that only makes things worse. What I am asking for is a careful and prudent investigation. I know without doubt that the Governor's office knew nothing of Janice Fleet's criminal activities. We'll handle that side of things, and I'd request that both of you be circumspect with the press. But after talking with the two of you I have some sense of what we're dealing with, and I am sickened by it.' His voice cracked, and he swallowed hard. 'I want to assure you that I'm giving you the juice to get full cooperation from all involved agencies. If you require anything from the Governor's office I'd ask that you contact me directly, and I will make certain you get what you need.'

Then another round of hand-shaking accompanied by the exchange of cards. Hobbs and Barrett left. In the elevator down, Barrett looked over at Hobbs. 'What was that?'

'Fear,' he said. 'So, you want to be a commissioner?'

'What are my choices? And could I just opt for a sharp stick in the eye?'

He laughed, but then stopped as he caught her gaze. 'What?'

Barrett felt his closeness and the downward movement of the elevator. She couldn't pull herself from his eyes, how they twinkled and made something inside of her feel happy and safe. Her gaze floated over the scars, the thought that ran over and over through her head, *I love you . . . am in love with you.* While other thoughts screamed not to say it, not to ruin a friendship that meant so much to her.

'What?' he repeated, as the elevator lurched to a stop and the doors opened.

Her hand shot out and she randomly pressed the button for the top floor.

He looked at her, and waited.

'OK,' she swallowed hard, and broke from his gaze. *Don't do this, Barrett, don't, don't, don't.* 'I was wrong, Ed,' she blurted, not wanting to stop herself, 'I made a mistake. I do have feelings for you, you told me once that you . . .'

'Sshh.' He closed the small gap that separated them.

She felt the heat of his body, and smelled something musky and masculine. She looked up, and felt as though she'd launched into the air, like a high-wire acrobat with no net. One of his hands landed on the side of her cheek.

'I'm so sorry,' she said.

'No need,' he whispered. He pulled her in, his lips finding hers, the kiss soft at first.

She felt something deep inside burst and she grabbed hard. Her hands around his neck, their bodies tight, joined, the kiss like a fire sparked to a flame. Neither caring that the doors had opened, closed, and then opened again back in the lobby.

'Excuse me,' the older security guard's voice intruded.

They broke apart. Barrett felt winded and weak-kneed – Ed was grinning.

'Hate to break this up,' the guard said. 'You do know it's all on camera?'

Hobbs burst out laughing as Barrett glanced at the security booth and the younger guard, standing in front of the monitor, smiling back at them. 'Come on, Barrett,' Hobbs said, 'let's get out of here,' and he did something that made any resistance vanish, he took her hand. 'Come on.' He squeezed her fingers.

'OK . . .' she said, not able to focus. As soon as they were out the door, she was inundated with sensation, the smell of flowers, the sun, her hand in his. 'Ed,' she stopped, not wanting the moment to pass. Not caring who saw them, she pulled him close, and they kissed again, slower, as they both savored the sweetness of it.

'So what do we do?' she finally said.

'Anything we want, but right now, I'm really hungry . . . so how about something to eat?'

Her internal warning bells tried to ring out as the most imprudent of all thoughts popped into her head. 'I love you, Ed,' she said. 'I can't believe how I almost screwed this up.'

He kissed the tip of her nose, and then again found her mouth. 'So it's a date?'

'Yes,' she said, loving the way he smiled at her.

'OK, but this will take some planning. I mean if we're talking about you, should I bring roofies and duct tape?'

She butted her forehead into his shoulder. 'No. I've had enough of that.'

He growled in the back of his throat, 'Glad to hear it,' and then they kissed again.